Praise for *Drawing Conclusions* by Donna Leon

"This fine novel is Leon's twentieth mystery featuring Commissario Guido Brunetti, the unparalleled Venetian police investigator who enlivens this intelligent series. . . . As always, Brunetti's investigative acumen, his patience, and most of all, his profound comprehension of the human psyche enable him to bring the case to a closure of sorts. Yet the powerful conclusion does not, in fact, directly divulge the solution, and it is this haunting ambiguity that renders *Drawing Conclusions* Leon's most provocative novel to date. . . . Aficionados of literary mysteries such as those written by P. D. James and Michael Dibdin will revel in this stellar book."

—Lynne F. Maxwell, *Library Journal* (starred review)

"Leon's twentieth novel starring Venetian police Commissario Guido Brunetti is one of her best. . . . When [Brunetti] muses, the reader listens almost hypnotically, transfixed by the somehow ennobling ordinariness of this remarkable man's humanity but also by the subtlety of his mind and his absolute refusal to succumb to the tyranny of bureaucrats and moralists. . . . Leon's popularity among mystery fans has grown steadily, but over the last several years, she has become a must-read for all those who favor character-driven crime stories."

—Bill Ott, *Booklist* (starred review)

"There is always doubt mixed with anticipation before diving into the latest in a favorite mystery series. The uncertainty is always there—will it deliver the same fascination as previous books? Or will it disappoint? . . . The compelling characters and complex plot in Leon's *Drawing Conclusions* place it among her best. The atmosphere of the city, along with Leon's sharp insights and powerful narrative, validate her often-recognized status as a master of literary crime fiction."

—Merle Minda, *Minneapolis Star-Tribune*

"Leon's fine twentieth Commissario Guido Brunetti mystery explores violence against women and the treatment of the elderly. . . . Leon provides a vivid view of Venice, balancing the city's 'glory days' with the reality of 'the flaking dandruff of sun-blasted paint peeling from shutters.' Compassionate yet incorruptible, Brunetti knows that true justice doesn't always end in an arrest or a trial." —*Publishers Weekly*

"As languid in its movement as a gondola ride. Yet none of Brunetti's earlier cases is as remorselessly clear in connecting the delicately comic anti-authoritarian gestures Brunetti winks at to the miasma of corruption that hangs over his beloved Venice." —*Kirkus Reviews*

"Donna Leon does for Venice what Tony Hillerman did for Navajo country and Ed McBain did for New York City."
—Jim Higgins, *Milwaukee Journal Sentinel*

"Leon brings so much to her work in addition to her subtle and entertaining plots. With her elegance of prose, the sympathy she invests in her characters, and the vibrant portrait she paints of Venice, she creates literary fiction at its best. But the main attraction, as always, is Brunetti himself, humane and intuitive, sensitive and determined, who revels in his family life and does his best to bring justice to a lovely but corrupt city."
—Jay Stafford, *Richmond Times-Dispatch*

"From the very first page, you are drawn into the story with no desire to leave it until the final line." —LJ Roberts, I Love a Mystery bookstore

"A great tale . . . Readers will relish sailing the watery streets of Venice with the caring commissario who understands justice and the law are not always in sync."
—Harriet Klausner, *The Midwest Book Review*

"Brilliant writing."
—Joe Hartlaub, BookReporter.com

"Donna Leon's vivid, atmospheric writing brings the city of Venice and its sights, sounds, and smells to life, and her charming cast of characters and sense of social justice make her novels a delight to read. In *Drawing Conclusions*, Commissario Brunetti investigates the death of an elderly woman, whose suspicious bruises and missing artworks suggest that a simple heart attack was not the only cause of her death. Suspenseful and satisfying."
—Carol Schneck, Schuler Books and Music, Okemos, MI

"It could have been a natural death. Costanza Altavilla died of a heart attack. Yes, there's some traces of bruising around the neck. It could be natural causes . . . or not. Inspector Brunetti suspects that there is more to the story, perhaps traced to Altavilla's work helping abused women. In the end, the story doesn't go where you think it will. Letter-of-the-law investigations and traditional moral solutions are not hallmarks of a Guido Brunetti case. The experience of reading *Drawing Conclusions*, however, goes well beyond the plotting. Every so often there's a turn of phrase that is positively breathtaking. It blows my mind how consistently good Donna Leon is, but her newest is particularly wonderful."
—Anne McMahon, Boswell Book Company, Milwaukee, WI

"Remarkably, for a long-running series, Leon's characters are more interesting now than they were eighteen years ago. Even more remarkably, Leon's own skills, honed over so many books, have grown and matured, and that makes this most recent novel her best book so far."
—Margaret Cannon, *The Globe and Mail* (Toronto)

A PENGUIN MYSTERY

DRAWING CONCLUSIONS

Donna Leon, who was born in New Jersey, has lived in Venice for many years and previously lived in Switzerland, Saudi Arabia, Iran, and China, where she worked as a teacher. Her mysteries featuring Commissario Guido Brunetti include (in order of publication) *Death in a Strange Country*; *Dressed for Death*; *Death and Judgment*; *Acqua Alta*; *Quietly in Their Sleep*; *A Noble Radiance*; *Fatal Remedies*; *Friends in High Places*; *A Sea of Troubles*; *Willful Behavior*; *Uniform Justice*; *Doctored Evidence*; *Blood from a Stone*; *Through a Glass, Darkly*; *Suffer the Little Children*; *The Girl of His Dreams*; *About Face*; and *A Question of Belief.*

Donna Leon

Drawing Conclusions

PENGUIN BOOKS

PENGUIN BOOKS

Published by the Penguin Group

Penguin Group (USA) Inc., 375 Hudson Street, New York, New York 10014, U.S.A.

Penguin Group (Canada), 90 Eglinton Avenue East, Suite 700, Toronto,
Ontario, Canada M4P 2Y3 (a division of Pearson Penguin Canada Inc.)

Penguin Books Ltd, 80 Strand, London WC2R 0RL, England

Penguin Ireland, 25 St Stephen's Green, Dublin 2, Ireland
(a division of Penguin Books Ltd)

Penguin Group (Australia), 250 Camberwell Road, Camberwell,
Victoria 3124, Australia (a division of Pearson Australia Group Pty Ltd)

Penguin Books India Pvt Ltd, 11 Community Centre,
Panchsheel Park, New Delhi – 110 017, India

Penguin Group (NZ), 67 Apollo Drive, Rosedale, Auckland 0632,
New Zealand (a division of Pearson New Zealand Ltd)

Penguin Books (South Africa) (Pty) Ltd, 24 Sturdee Avenue,
Rosebank, Johannesburg 2196, South Africa

Penguin Books Ltd, Registered Offices:
80 Strand, London WC2R 0RL, England

First published in Great Britain by William Heinemann 2011
Published in Penguin Books 2012

1 3 5 7 9 10 8 6 4 2

Map printed by permission of Martin Lubikowski

ISBN 978-0-14-312064-3
CIP data available

Printed in the United States of America

For Jenny Liosatou and Giulio D'Alessio

In the name of God Amen. I George Frederick Handel considering the uncertainties of human life doe make this my will in manner following . . .

Last testament of George Frederick Handel

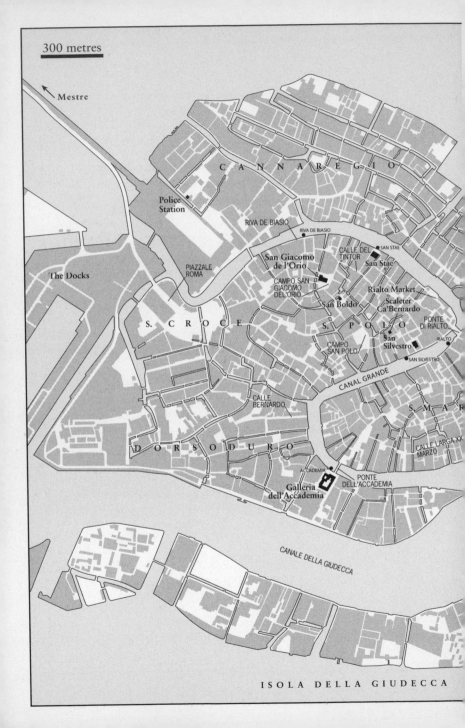

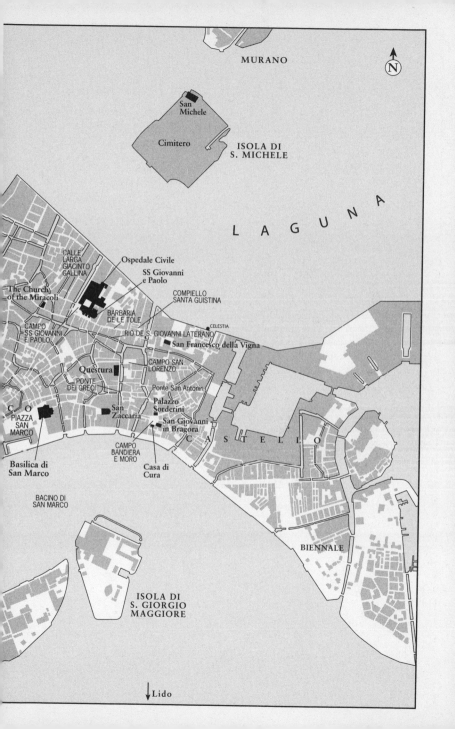

1

Because she had worked for decades as a translator of fiction and non-fiction from English and German to Italian, Anna Maria Giusti was familiar with a wide range of subjects. Her most recent translation had been an American self-help book about how to deal with conflicting emotions. Though the superficial idiocies she had encountered – which had always sounded sillier when she put them into Italian – had occasionally reduced her to giggles, some of the text returned to her now, as she climbed the stairs to her apartment.

'It is possible to feel two conflicting emotions about the same person at the same time.' So it had proven with her feelings towards her lover, whose family she had just returned from visiting in Palermo. 'Even people we know well can surprise us when they are placed in different surroundings.' 'Different' seemed an inadequate word to describe Palermo and what she had found there. 'Alien', 'exotic', 'foreign': not even these words did justice to what she had experienced, yet how explain it? Did they not all carry *telefonini*? Was not everyone she met exquisitely well dressed and equally well mannered? Nor was it a question of language, for they all spoke an Italian more elegant than anything she heard from her Veneto-cadenced family and friends. Nor financial, for the wealth of Nico's family was on view at every turn.

She had gone to Palermo in order to meet his family, believing he would take her to stay with them, yet she had spent her five nights in a hotel, one with more stars awarded it than her own translator's earnings would have permitted her, had the hotel accepted her insistence that she be allowed to pay the bill.

'No, Dottoressa,' the smiling hotel director had told her, 'L'Avvocato has seen to it.' Nico's father. 'L'Avvocato.' She had started by calling him 'Dottore', which honorific he had dismissed with a wave of his hand, as though her attempt at deference had been a fly. 'Avvocato' had refused to fall from her lips, and so she had settled on 'Lei' and had used the formal pronoun, after that, for everyone in his family.

Nico had warned her that it would not be easy, but he had not prepared her for what she was to experience during the week. He was deferential to his parents: had she seen this behaviour in anyone other than the man she thought she loved, she would have described it as fawning. He kissed his mother's hand when she came into the room and got to his feet when his father entered.

One night, she had refused to attend the family dinner; he had taken her back to the hotel after their own nervous meal together, kissed her in the lobby, and waited while she got into the elevator before going meekly back to sleep in his parents' *palazzo*. When she demanded the next day to know what was going on, he had replied that he was the product of where he lived, and this was the way people behaved. That afternoon, when he drove her back to the hotel and said he'd pick her up at eight for dinner, she had smiled and said goodbye to him at the hotel entrance, gone inside and told the young man at the desk that she was checking out. She went to her room, packed, called for a taxi, and left a note for Nico with the concierge. The only seat on the evening plane to Venice was in business class, but she was happy to pay it, thinking it took the place of at least part of the hotel bill she had not been allowed to pay.

Her bag was heavy and made a loud noise when she set it down on the first landing. Giorgio Bruscutti, the older son of her neighbours, had left his sports shoes on the landing, but tonight she was almost happy to see them: proof that she was home. She lifted the bag and carried it up to the second landing, where she found, as she had expected, neatly tied bundles of *Famiglia cristiana* and *Il Giornale*. Signor Volpe, who had become an ardent ecologist in his old age, always left their paper for recycling outside the door on Sunday evening, even though there was no need to take it out until Tuesday morning. So pleased was she to see this sign of normal life that she forgot to pass her automatic judgement that the garbage was the best place for both of those publications.

The third landing was empty, as was the table to the left of the door. This was a disappointment to Anna Maria: it meant either that nothing had arrived in the mail for her during the last week – which she could not believe – or that Signora Altavilla had forgotten to leave Anna Maria's post for her to find when she got back.

She looked at her watch and saw that it was almost ten. She knew the older woman stayed up late: they had once each confessed to the other that the greatest joy of living alone was the freedom to stay up reading in bed for as long as they pleased. She stepped back from the door to Signora Altavilla's apartment and looked to see if light filtered from beneath the door, but the landing light made it impossible to detect. She approached the door and placed her ear against it, hoping to hear some sound from within: even the television would indicate that Signora Altavilla was still awake.

Disappointed at the silence, she picked up her bag and set it down loudly on the tiles. She listened, but no sound from inside followed it. She picked it up again and started up the steps, careful to let the edge of the bag bang against the back of the first step, louder this time. Up the stairs she went, making so much noise with the bag that, had she heard someone else do it, she would have made some passing reflection on human thoughtlessness or stuck her head out of the door to see what was wrong.

At the top of the steps she set the bag down again. She found her key and opened the door to her own apartment, and as it opened, she felt herself flooded with peace and certainty. Everything inside was hers, and in these rooms she decided what she would do and when and how. She had no one's rules to obey and no one's hand to kiss, and at that thought all doubt ended, and she was certain she had done the right thing in leaving Palermo, leaving Nico, and ending the affair.

She switched on the light, looked automatically across the room at the sofa, where the military precision of the cushions assured her that her cleaning lady had been there in her absence. She brought her suitcase inside, closed the door, and let the silence drift across and into her. Home.

Anna Maria walked across the room and opened the window and the shutters. Across the *campo* stood the church of San Giacomo dell'Orio: if its rounded apse had been the prow of a sailing ship, it would have been aimed at her windows, and would soon have been upon her.

She moved through the apartment, opening all the windows and pushing back and latching the shutters. She carried her suitcase into the guest room and hoisted it on to the bed, then moved back through the apartment, closing the windows against the chill of the October night.

On the dining room table, Anna Maria found a piece of paper with one of Luba's curiously worded notes and, beside it, the distinctive buff notice that indicated the attempted delivery of a registered letter. 'For you came,' the note read. She studied the receipt: it had been left four days before. She had no idea who could have sent her a registered letter: the address given for '*mittente*' was illegible. Her first thought was a vague fear that some government agency had discovered an irregularity and was informing her that she was under investigation for having done, or failed to do, something or other.

The second notice, she knew, would have come two days after this one. Its absence meant that Signora Altavilla, who over the years had become the custodian of her post and deliveries, had signed for the letter and had it downstairs. Curiosity overcame her. She set the receipt on the table and went to her study. From memory, she dialled Signora Altavilla's number. Better to disturb her this way than to fret until morning about the letter that would turn out, she told herself, to be something innocuous.

The phone rang four times without being picked up. She stepped aside and opened the window, leaned out and heard the ringing below. Where could she be at this hour? A film? Occasionally she went with friends, and sometimes she went to babysit her grandchildren, though sometimes the oldest spent the night with her.

Anna Maria hung up the phone and returned to the living room. Over the years and even though separated in age by almost two generations, she and the woman downstairs had become good neighbours. Perhaps not good friends: they had never had a meal together, but now and then they met on the street and had a coffee, and there had been many conversations on the stairs. Anna Maria was sometimes called to work as a simultaneous translator at conferences and thus would be away for days, sometimes weeks, at a time. And because Signora Altavilla went to the mountains with her son and his family each July, Anna Maria had her keys, in order to water the plants and, as Signora Altavilla had said when she gave her them, 'just in case'. There was a clear understanding that Anna Maria could – indeed, should – go in to get her post whenever she returned from a trip and Signora Altavilla was not at home.

She took the keys from the second drawer in the kitchen and, propping her own door open with her handbag, switched on the light and went down the stairs.

Though she was certain no one was home, Anna Maria rang the bell. Taboo? Respect for privacy? When there was no answer, she put the key in the lock, but, as often happened with this door, it would not easily turn. She tried again, pulling the door towards her as she turned the key. The pressure of her hand moved the handle down, and when she gave the sudden pull and push the recalcitrant door proved to be unlocked and opened without resistance, pulling her a step forward into the room.

Her first thought was to try to recall Costanza's age: why was she forgetting to lock her door? Why had she never changed it and got *una porta blindata* that locked automatically when it closed? 'Costanza?' she called. '*Ci sei?*' She stood and listened, but there was no answering call. Without thinking, Anna Maria approached the table opposite the doorway, drawn by the small pile of letters, no more than four or five, and that week's *Espresso*. Reading the title of the magazine, it struck her that the light in the hallway was on and that more light was coming down the corridor from the half-open door to the living room, as well as, closer to her, from the open door of the larger bedroom.

Signora Altavilla had grown up in post-war Italy, and though marriage had made her both happy and prosperous, she had never unlearned the habits of frugality. Anna Maria, who had grown up in a wealthy family in booming, prosperous Italy, had never learned them. Thus the younger woman had always found quaint the older's habit of turning off lights whenever she left a room, of wearing two sweaters in the winter, and of expressing real satisfaction when she found a bargain at Billa.

'Costanza?' she called again, more to stop her own thoughts than because she believed there would be an answer. In an unconscious attempt to free her hands, she set the keys on top of the letters and stood silent, eyes drawn to the light coming from the open door at the end of the corridor.

She took a breath, and then she took a step, and then another and another. She stopped then, and found she could go no farther. Telling herself not to be foolish, she forced herself to lean forward and take a look around the half-open door. 'Costan . . .' she began but slapped her mouth closed with one of her hands when she saw another hand on the floor. And then the arm, and the shoulder, and then the head, or at least the back of the head. And the short white hair. Anna Maria had for years wanted to ask the older woman whether her refusal to have her hair dyed the obligatory red of women her age was another manifestation of her learned frugality or simply acceptance of how her white hair softened the lines of her face, adding to their dignity.

She looked down at the motionless woman, at the hand, the arm, the head. And she realized she would never get to ask her now.

2

Guido Brunetti, Commissario di Polizia of the city of Venice, sat at dinner across from his immediate superior, Vice-Questore Giuseppe Patta, and prayed for the end of the world. He would have settled for being abducted by aliens or perhaps for the violent irruption of bearded terrorists, shooting their way into the restaurant, bloodlust in their eyes. The resulting chaos would have permitted Brunetti, who was, as usual, not wearing his own gun, to wrest one from a passing terrorist and use it to shoot and kill both the Vice-Questore and his assistant, Lieutenant Scarpa, who, seated to the left of the Vice-Questore, was at this very moment passing his measured – negative – judgement on the grappa that had been offered at the end of the meal.

'You people in the North,' the Lieutenant said with a condescending nod in Brunetti's direction, 'don't understand what it is to make wine, so why should you know about making anything else?' He drank the rest of his grappa, made a small moue of distaste – the gesture so carefully manufactured as to allow Brunetti to distinguish easily between distaste and disgust – and set his glass on the table. He gave Brunetti an open-faced glance, as if inviting him to make a contribution to oenological frankness, but Brunetti refused to play and contented himself with finishing his own grappa. However much this dinner with Patta and Scarpa might have driven Brunetti to long for a second grappa – or the second coming – the realization that acceptance would prolong the meal led him to resist the waiter's offer, just as good sense led him to resist the bait offered to him by Scarpa.

Brunetti's refusal to engage spurred the Lieutenant, or perhaps it was the grappa – his second – for he began, 'I don't understand why Friuli wines are . . .' but Brunetti's attention was called away from whatever deficiency the Lieutenant was about to reveal by the sound of his *telefonino*. Whenever he was forced into social occasions he could not avoid – as with Patta's invitation to dinner to discuss candidates for promotion – Brunetti was careful to carry his *telefonino* and was often saved by a generous Paola, calling with an invented urgent reason for him to leave immediately.

'*Sì*,' he answered, disappointed at having seen it was the central number of the Questura.

'Good evening, Commissario,' said a voice he thought must be Ruffolo's. 'We just had a call from a woman in Santa Croce. She's found a dead woman in her apartment. There was blood, so she called us.'

'Whose apartment?' Brunetti asked, not that it mattered that he know this now, but because he disliked lack of clarity.

'She said she was in her own apartment. The dead woman, that is. It's downstairs from hers.'

'Where in Santa Croce?'

'Giacomo dell'Orio, sir. She lives just opposite the church. One seven two six.'

'Who's gone?' Brunetti asked.

'No one, sir. I called you first.'

Brunetti looked at his watch. It was almost eleven, long

after he had thought and hoped this dinner would end. 'See if you can find Rizzardi and have him go. And call Vianello – he should be at home. Send a boat to pick him up and take him there. And get a crime scene team together.'

'What about you, sir?'

Brunetti had already consulted the map of the city imprinted in his genes. 'It's faster for me to walk. I'll meet them there.' Then, as an afterthought, 'If there's a patrol anywhere near, call them and tell them to go over. And call the woman and tell her not to touch anything in the apartment.'

'She went back to her own, sir, to make the call. I told her to stay there.'

'Good. What's her name?'

'Giusti, sir.'

'If you speak to the patrol, tell them I'll be there in ten minutes.'

'Yes, sir,' the officer said and hung up.

Vice-Questore Patta looked across at Brunetti with open curiosity. 'Trouble, Commissario?' he asked in a tone that made Brunetti aware of how different curiosity was from interest.

'Yes, sir. A woman's been found dead in Santa Croce.'

'And they called you?' interrupted Scarpa, placing just the least hint of polite suspicion on the last word.

'Griffoni's not back from vacation yet, and I live closest,' Brunetti answered with practised blandness.

'Of course,' Scarpa said, turning aside to say something to the waiter.

To Patta, Brunetti said, 'I'll go and have a look, Vice-Questore.' He put on his face the look of a beleaguered bureaucrat, reluctantly pulled away from what he wanted to do by what he had to do; he pushed back his chair and got to his feet. He gave Patta the chance to make a comment, but the moment passed in silence.

Outside the restaurant, Brunetti left the business of getting there to memory and pulled out his *telefonino*. He dialled his home number.

'Are you calling for moral support?' Paola asked when she picked up the phone.

'Scarpa has just told me we northerners don't know anything about making wine,' he said.

There was a pause before she said, 'That's what your words say, but it sounds as if something else is wrong.'

'I've been called in. There's a dead woman in Santa Croce, over by San Giacomo.'

'Why did they call you?'

'They probably didn't want to call Patta or Scarpa.'

'So they called you when you were with them? Wonderful.'

'They didn't know where I was. Besides, it was a way for me to get away from them. I'll go over to see what happened. I live the closest, anyway.'

'Do you want me to wait up?'

'No. I have no idea how long it will take.'

'I'll wake up when you come in,' she said. 'If I don't, just give me a shove.'

Brunetti smiled at the thought but confined himself to a noise of agreement.

'I have been known not to sleep through the night,' she said with false indignation, her aural radar having caught the precise nuance of his noise.

The last time, Brunetti recalled, was the night the Fenice burned down, when the sound of the helicopter repeatedly passing overhead had finally summoned her from the deep abyss to which she repaired each evening.

In a more conciliatory tone, she said, 'I hope it's not awful.'

He thanked her, then said goodbye and put the phone in his pocket. He called his attention back to where he was walking. The streets were brightly lit: more largesse from the profligate bureaucrats in Brussels. If he had chosen to do so, Brunetti could have read a newspaper in the light from the street lamps. Light still poured from many shop windows: he thought of the satellite photos he had seen of the glowing night-time planet as measured from above. Only Darkest Africa remained so.

At the end of Scaleter Ca' Bernardo, he turned left and passed the tower of San Boldo, then walked down from the bridge and into Calle del Tintor and went past the pizzeria. Next to it a shop selling cheap purses was still open; behind the counter sat a young Chinese girl, reading a Chinese newspaper. He had no idea what the current laws were about how late a shop could stay open, but some atavistic voice whispered to him about the unseemliness of engaging in commercial activity at this hour.

A few weeks ago he had had dinner with a commander of the Frontier Police, who had told him, among other things, that their own best estimate of the number of Chinese currently living in Italy was between 500,000 and five million. After saying this, he sat back, the better to enjoy Brunetti's astonishment. In the face of it, he had added, 'If the Chinese in Europe were all wearing uniforms, we'd be forced to see it as the invasion it is.' He had then returned his attention to his grilled calamari.

Two doors down he found another shop, with still another young Chinese girl behind the cash register. More light spilled into the street from a bar; in front of it four or five young people stood, smoking and drinking. He noticed that three of them drank Coca-Cola: so much for the nightlife of Venice.

He came out into the *campo*; it too was flooded with light. Years ago, just when he had been transferred back from Naples, this *campo* had been infamous as a place to buy drugs. He remembered the stories he'd heard about the abandoned needles that had to be swept up every morning, had a vague memory of some young person who had been found dead, overdosed, on one of the benches. But gentrification had swept it clean; that or the shift to designer drugs that had rendered needles obsolete.

He glanced at the buildings on his right, just opposite the apse. The shadowy form of a woman stood outlined in the light from a window on the fourth floor of one of them. Resisting the impulse to raise his hand to her, Brunetti went over to the building. The number was nowhere evident on the façade, but her name was on the top bell.

He rang it and the door snapped open almost immediately, suggesting that she had gone to the door at the sight of a man walking into the *campo*. Brunetti had been the solitary walker at this hour, tourists apparently evaporated, everyone else at home and in bed, so the odd man out had to be the policeman.

He walked up the steps, past the shoes and the papers: to a Venetian, this amoeba-like tendency to expand one's territory beyond the confines of the walls of an apartment seemed so entirely natural as barely to merit notice.

As he turned into the last ramp of stairs, he heard a woman's voice ask from above him, 'Are you the police?'

'*Sì*, Signora,' he said, reaching for his warrant card and stifling the impulse to tell her she should be more prudent about whom she let into the building. When he reached the landing, she took a half-step forward and put out her hand.

'Anna Maria Giusti,' she said.

'Brunetti,' he answered, taking her hand. He showed her the card, but she gave it the barest glance. He estimated she was in her early thirties, tall and lanky, with an aristocratic nose and dark brown eyes. Her face was stiff with tension or tiredness; he guessed that, in repose, it would soften into something approaching beauty. She drew him towards her and into the apartment, then dropped his hand and took a step back from him. 'Thank you for coming,' she said. She looked around and behind him to verify that no one else had come.

'My assistant and the others are on their way, Signora,' Brunetti said, making no attempt to advance farther into the apartment. 'While we wait for them, could you tell me what happened?'

'I don't know,' she said, bringing her hands together just at her waist in a visual cliché of confusion, the sort of gesture women made in the movies of the fifties to show their distress. 'I got home from vacation about an hour ago, and when I went down to Signora Altavilla's apartment, I found her there. She was dead.'

'You're sure?' Brunetti asking, thinking it might upset her less if he asked it that way rather than asking her to describe what she had seen.

'I touched the back of her hand. It was cold,' she said. She pressed her lips together. Looking at the floor, she went on. 'I put my fingers under her wrist. To feel her pulse. But there was nothing.'

'Signora, when you called, you said there was blood.'

'On the floor near her head. When I saw it, I came up here to call you.'

'Anything else, Signora?'

She raised a hand and waved it towards the staircase behind him, as if pointing to things in the one below. 'The front door was open.' Seeing his surprise, she quickly clarified this by saying, 'Unlocked, that is. Closed, but unlocked.'

'I see,' Brunetti said. He was silent for some time and then asked, 'Could you tell me how long you've been away, Signora?'

'Five days. I went to Palermo on Wednesday, last week, and just got home tonight.'

'Thank you,' Brunetti said, then asked solicitously, 'Were you with friends, Signora?'

The look she shot him showed just how bright she was and how much the question offended her.

'I want to exclude things, Signora,' he said in his normal voice.

Her own voice was a bit louder, her pronunciation clearer, when she said, 'I stayed in a hotel, the Villa Igiea. You can check their records.' She looked away from him in what Brunetti thought might be embarrassment. 'Someone else paid the bill, but I was registered there.'

Brunetti knew this could be easily checked and so asked only, 'You went into Signora Altavilla's apartment to . . .?'

'To get my post.' She turned and walked into the room behind her, a large open space with a peaked ceiling that indicated the room had – how many centuries before? – originally been an attic. Brunetti, following her in, glanced up at the twin skylights, hoping to see the stars beyond them, but all he saw was the light reflected from below.

At a table she picked up a piece of paper. Brunetti took it from her outstretched hand: he recognized the beige receipt for a registered letter. 'I had no idea what it could be and thought it might be something important,' she said. 'I didn't want to wait until tomorrow to find out, so I went down to see if the letter was there.'

In response to Brunetti's inquisitive glance, she continued. 'If I'm away, she gets my post, and then leaves it out when I come home, or I go down and get it from her.'

'And if she's not there when you get home?' Brunetti asked.

'She gave me the keys, and I go in to get it.' She turned to face the windows, beyond which Brunetti saw the illuminated apse of the church. 'So I went down and let myself in. And the letters were where she always put them: on a table in the entrance.' She ran out of things to say, but Brunetti waited.

'And then I went and looked in the front room. No reason, really – but there was a light on – she always turns them out when she leaves a room – and I thought maybe she hadn't heard me. Though that doesn't make any sense, does it? And I saw her. And touched her hand. And saw the blood. And then I came back up here and called you.'

'Would you like to sit down, Signora?' Brunetti asked, indicating a wooden chair that stood against the nearest wall.

She shook her head, but at the same time took a step towards it. She sat down heavily, then gave in to weakness and leaned against the back. 'It's terrible. How could anyone . . .'

Before she could finish her question, the doorbell rang. He went to the speaker phone and heard Vianello announce himself, saying he was with Dottor Rizzardi. Brunetti pushed the button to release the downstairs door and replaced the phone. To the seated woman he said, 'The others are here, Signora.' Then, because he had to ask, he said, 'Is the door locked?'

She looked up at him, confusion spread across her face. 'What?'

'The door downstairs. To the apartment. Is it locked?'

She shook her head two, three times and seemed so unconscious of the gesture that he was relieved when she stopped it. 'I don't know. I had the keys.' She searched the pockets of her jacket but found no keys. She looked at him, confused. 'I must have left them downstairs, on top of the post.' She closed her eyes, then, after a moment, said, 'But you can go in. The door doesn't lock on its own.' Then she raised a hand to catch his attention. 'She was a good neighbour,' she said.

Brunetti thanked her and went downstairs to find the others.

3

Brunetti found Vianello and Rizzardi waiting in front of the door to the apartment. Vianello and he exchanged nods, having seen one another only that afternoon, and Brunetti shook hands with the pathologist. As always, the doctor was turned out like an English gentleman emerging from his club. He wore a dark blue pinstripe suit with the conspicuously invisible signs of hand tailoring. His shirt looked as though he had put it on while starting up the stairs to the apartment, and his tie was what Brunetti vaguely classified as 'regimental', though he had no certain idea of what that meant.

Though he knew the doctor had recently returned from a vacation in Sardinia, Brunetti thought Rizzardi looked tired, which he found unsettling. But how to ask a doctor about his health?

'Good to see you, Ettore,' he said. 'How . . .' Brunetti started to ask, quickly changing his question to the less intrusive, '. . . was your vacation?'

'Busy. Giovanna and I had planned to spend our time on the beach, under an umbrella, reading and looking at the sea.

But at the last minute Riccardo asked if we'd like to take the grandkids with us, and we couldn't say no, so we had an eight-year-old and a six-year-old.' Brunetti saw pass across his face the look common to people who had suffered violent assault. 'I'd forgotten what it's like to have children around.'

'And there went sitting under the umbrella and reading and looking at the sea, I assume,' Brunetti said.

Rizzardi smiled and shrugged it away. 'We both loved it, but I feel better if I pretend we didn't.' Then, idle chat over, the doctor adjusted his tone and asked, 'What is it?'

'The woman upstairs came home from vacation, didn't find her post left out for her, so she came down and let herself in to look for it and found the woman in the apartment dead.'

'And she called the police and not the hospital?' Vianello interrupted.

'She said she saw blood: that's what made her call,' Brunetti explained.

The door, Brunetti noticed, was an old-fashioned wooden one with a horizontal metal handle, the type of door seldom seen any more in this theft-beleaguered city. Though Signora Giusti's entry would certainly have damaged or destroyed any fingerprints on the handle, Brunetti was still careful to open it by pressing his open palm against the end of the handle to push it down.

Entering, he saw a table against the wall to his left, with a set of keys lying on top of some envelopes. Light came in from an open door on his right and from another at the end of the corridor, at the front of the apartment. He walked to the first of them and leaned into the room, but all he saw was a simple bedroom with a single bed and a chest of drawers.

Habit made him open the door on the opposite side of the corridor, careful again to touch only the end of the handle. Enough light filtered past him for Brunetti to see a smaller room with another single bed, a bedside table next to it, and a low chest of drawers. The door to a bathroom stood ajar.

He turned and continued towards the room at the end of the corridor, vaguely conscious that the other men were glancing into the rooms as he had. Inside, the woman lay on her right side, back to him, blocking the door with the side of her foot, one arm outstretched, the other trapped beneath her. She looked no bigger than a child; surely she couldn't weigh fifty kilos. There was a patch of blood a bit smaller than a compact disc, dry and dark now, on the floor beside her and partially covered by her head. Brunetti stood and took in the short white hair, the dark blue cardigan made of thick cashmere, the collar of a yellow shirt, and the thin sliver of gold on her ring finger.

Brunetti considered himself the least superstitious of men and took pride in his intense respect for reason and good sense and all the virtues he associated with the proper functioning of the mind. This, however, in no way prevented him from accepting the possibility of less tangible phenomena – he had never been able to find a clearer way to express it. Something that, though unseen, left traces. He felt those traces here: this was a troubled death. Not necessarily violent or criminal: only troubled. He sensed it, though vaguely and fleetingly, and as soon as the sensation rose to the level of conscious thought, it vanished, to be dismissed as nothing more than a stronger than usual response to the sight of sudden death.

He quickly scanned the room and registered furniture, two floor lamps, a row of windows, but his intense awareness of the woman at his feet made it difficult for him to concentrate on anything else.

He returned to the corridor. There was no sign of Vianello, but the pathologist waited a few steps away. 'She's in here, Ettore,' Brunetti said. As the doctor approached, Brunetti was distracted by the sound of footsteps from below. He heard men's voices, a deep one followed by a lighter tone, and then a door closed.

The footsteps continued towards the apartment, and then Marillo, the assistant lab technician, appeared at the open door, two men close behind him carrying the cases of their trade. Marillo, a tall, thin Lombard who seemed incapable of understanding anything save the simple, literal truth of any statement or situation, greeted Brunetti then came into the apartment, moving forward to allow his own men to enter behind him. The last man closed the door and Marillo said, 'Man downstairs wanted to know what all the noise was about.'

Brunetti greeted the men, but when he turned back to where Rizzardi had been, he realized the pathologist had gone into the other room. He told the men Vianello would tell them where to begin photographing and dusting for prints. He found Rizzardi bent over the woman's body, his hands carefully stuffed into the pockets of his trousers. He stood upright as Brunetti approached and said, 'It could have been a heart attack. Perhaps a stroke.'

Brunetti pointed silently to the small circle of blood, and Rizzardi, who had been in the room long enough to take a careful look around, pointed in his turn to a radiator that stood below a window not far from where the woman lay.

'She could have fallen against it,' Rizzardi said. 'I'll have a better idea when I can turn her over.' He took a step back from the woman's body. 'So let's get them to take the photos, all right?' he asked.

With any other doctor, Brunetti might have lost patience at his refusal to read the bloodstain as a sign of violence, but he was familiar with Rizzardi's insistence that he concern himself only with the immediately evident physical cause of death and only when he saw it or could prove it for himself. On occasion, Brunetti had managed to get the doctor to speculate, but it was no easy task.

Brunetti allowed his attention to drift away from the doctor and the woman at his feet. The room seemed to be in order save for two sofa cushions on the floor and a leather-bound book lying face down beside them. There was a wardrobe, but both doors were closed.

The photographer entered, saying, 'Marillo and Bobbio are dusting for prints, so I came down here to do her first.' He walked past Brunetti, towards the body, right hand fiddling with a knob on his camera.

Brunetti left him to it. He heard the low murmur of Rizzardi's voice behind him but ignored it as he walked back along the corridor.

In the larger bedroom, Vianello, wearing thin plastic gloves, stood in front of the open drawers of the chest. He was leaning forward to examine some papers that lay on the top of the chest. As Brunetti watched, Vianello slid the top sheet to the side with the tip of his finger, then read the one below before shifting it aside to read the last one.

Reacting to Brunetti's silent presence, Vianello said, 'It's a letter from a girl in India. "To Mamma Costanza." Must be one of those organizations that let you sponsor a child.'

'What does she say?' Brunetti asked.

'It's in English,' Vianello answered, waving at the papers. 'And it's handwritten. From what I can make out, she's thanking her for the birthday gift and telling her that she'll give it to her father so that he can buy rice for the spring planting.' Nodding to the papers, Vianello added, 'She's included her school report and a photo.'

Carefully, Vianello patted the sheets of paper back into place. 'You think they're legitimate, all these charities?' he asked.

'I hope so,' Brunetti said. 'Or else a lot of money has been going to the wrong places for a long time.'

'Do you do it?' Vianello asked.

'Yes.'

'India?'

'Yes,' Brunetti said, feeling something close to embarrassment. 'Paola takes care of it.'

'Nadia does, too,' Vianello said hastily. 'But why we're giving money to places like India and China is something I don't understand. Can't pick up a newspaper without reading how powerful they are economically, how the world is going to belong to them in a decade. Or two. So what are we doing, supporting their children?' Then Vianello added, 'At least that's what I ask myself.'

'If Fazio is to be believed,' Brunetti said, naming his friend who worked for the Frontier Police, 'what we shouldn't be doing is buying their clothing and toys and electronic equipment. Doesn't hurt to give a couple of hundred euros to send a kid to school, though.'

Vianello nodded. 'Kids there still have to eat, I suppose. And buy books.' He stripped off the gloves and put them into the pocket of his jacket.

Just then the photographer came to the door and told Brunetti that Rizzardi wanted to see him. The dead woman had been turned on to her back, both arms at her sides: looking at her, Brunetti could not recapture the feeling conveyed to him by the first sight of the body. Her eyes were closed, her mouth open, her spirit fled. There could be no hope that a spirit still lingered near this body. One might choose to debate where it had gone, or even if it had ever existed, but there could be no question about the absence of life here.

Above the corner of her right eye, just above the eyebrow, Brunetti saw a cut, the flesh around it swollen and discoloured. The cut had leaked a dark paste, similar in consistency to sealing wax, into her hair and was obviously the source of the blood on the floor. Her cardigan was unbuttoned, and her yellow shirt had been pulled to one side when she was turned on to her back, exposing an oblong smudge on the outer left-hand side of her collarbone.

Unconsciously, Brunetti moved his hands close together in front of his thighs, fingers bent, to measure the distance between his thumbs. When he glanced at Rizzardi, he saw that the doctor was staring at his hands.

'Her eyes would be bloodshot,' Rizzardi said, reading the message of violence in his hands.

From behind him, Brunetti heard someone let out a long stream of breath. He turned to see Vianello, whom he had not heard arrive. The Inspector's face wore a look of practised neutrality.

Brunetti looked back at the dead woman. One of her hands was clenched tight, as if frozen in the act of trying to keep her spirit from leaving: the other lay open, the fingers loose, encouraging the spirit to depart.

'Can you do it tomorrow morning?' Brunetti asked.

'Yes.'

'Will you take a look at everything?'

Rizzardi's response was a sigh, followed by 'Guido,' said in a low voice, in which could be heard an effort at patience.

Rizzardi looked at his watch: Brunetti knew the doctor had to put the time she was declared dead on the death certificate, but the pathologist seemed to be taking an inordinate amount of time deciding. He finally looked at Brunetti. 'There's nothing more for me here, Guido. I'll send you the report as soon as I can.'

Brunetti nodded his thanks, saw that it was already almost 1 a.m., and thanked the doctor for coming, even though he knew Rizzardi had no choice in the matter. The doctor turned to leave, but Brunetti moved closer to him, placed his hand briefly on his upper arm, saying nothing.

'I'll call you when I'm finished,' Rizzardi said. He moved away from Brunetti's hand, and left the apartment.

4

Brunetti closed the door, dissatisfied with his exchange with Rizzardi and disappointed by his own need to make the doctor see things as he wanted him to see them. Before he could speak to Vianello, they heard noise from below: again, a door opening, then an exchange of male voices. Marillo came to the door of the bedroom where he was working with his men and said, 'The doctor called a while ago for them to come and get her: I guess that's them.'

Neither Brunetti nor Vianello answered, and the noises of the technicians working in the other room ended. The men in the apartment awaited the arrival of their colleagues who dealt with the dead, their voices and bodies stilled by the magic spell that approached. Brunetti opened the door. The two men who appeared on the landing , however, looked quite ordinary and wore the long blue coats of hospital orderlies. One of them carried a rolled-up stretcher under his arm: all of the men in the apartment knew that a third member of the squad waited downstairs with the black plastic casket into which the body would be placed before they took it outside to the waiting boat.

There were nods and muttered salutations; most of them had met in similar circumstances in the past. Brunetti, who knew their faces but not their names, pointed them down the corridor. After the two men went into the room, Brunetti, Vianello, and Marillo, and behind him the two members of his crew, waited, pretending not to hear, trying not to interpret, the noises from the other room. A short time later, the men emerged with the stretcher, the form on it covered by a dark blue blanket. Brunetti was glad to see that the blanket was clean and freshly ironed, though he knew it made no difference.

With a nod to Brunetti, the two men left the apartment; Vianello closed the door behind them. No one in the room said anything as they listened to the men's descent. When all sound ended, they took it to mean the dead woman had been taken from the house, but still no one moved. Marillo finally broke the spell by turning away, herding his technicians into the bedroom and back to work.

Vianello went into the smaller guest room, and Brunetti joined him. The bed was neatly made, the white sheet pulled back over a simple grey woollen blanket. They saw no sign of disturbance in the room. It was military – or monastic – in its simplicity. Even the signs that the technicians had checked the room for prints seemed sparse.

Brunetti walked across the room and pushed open the door to the bathroom. Whoever had made the bed must also have ordered things on the shelves here: there were miniature sample bottles of shampoo and a small paper-wrapped bar of soap, the sort one found in hotel rooms; a comb in a plastic wrapper; a similarly wrapped toothbrush. Fresh towels and a washcloth hung on a rack beside the enclosed shower.

A man's voice called Brunetti's name. He and Vianello followed the sound into the larger bedroom, where Marillo was standing beside one of the windows. 'We're finished here, Commissario,' he said. As he spoke, one of his men collapsed his tripod, hefted it on to his shoulder, and slipped past Vianello and Brunetti into the corridor.

'You find anything?' Brunetti asked, looking around at powder-covered surfaces in the room, almost as if he wanted Marillo to follow his glance and find, just *there*, whatever it was that would make his search worthwhile and important.

The residue on so many surfaces reminded Brunetti of how hard he found it to believe that any reliable physical evidence could be drawn from the overlying mess of finger and palm prints that covered every surface in every room he had ever searched. Some of the powder had dropped into the bottom drawer, which was open. Faint traces of it could be seen on the silk scarves and sweaters that lay intermingled there.

'You know I don't like to talk about that sort of thing, sir,' Marillo finally answered, speaking with noticeable reluctance. 'Before I write the report, that is.'

'I know that, Marillo,' Brunetti said. 'And I think it's the best policy. But I wondered if you could give us some sort of idea about how thorough Vianello and I should be when we . . .' he began, then waved his hand around the room, as if asking the handles of the drawers to speak to Marillo about what was to be revealed inside.

The remaining technician, still on his knees beside the bed, looked up from the light he was shining into the space underneath, first at Brunetti and then at his superior. Aware of his glance, Marillo shook his head and turned to walk away.

'Come on, Stefano,' the technician said, making no attempt to disguise his exasperation. 'They're on our side. And it'll save them time.' Brunetti wondered if the technician was simply using a cliché, or if it were now necessary for one policeman to vouch for the integrity of others.

Marillo stiffened, either at being spoken to like this by one of his men in front of his superior or at the thought of having to venture an opinion rather than simply report on what was observed and recorded. 'All we do is dust the place and take the photos, Dottore. People like you and Vianello have to figure out what the results mean.' This might have been construed as opposition or obstructionism; in Marillo, it was meant to be simply a declaration of what he took his duties, and theirs, to be.

'Oh for the love of God,' the other technician snapped, still on his knees beside the bed. 'We've been in a hundred places, Stefano, and we both know there's nothing suspicious here.' He looked as if he was about to continue, but Marillo silenced him with a glare. Some time had passed since Brunetti had been troubled by the sight of the body, and the man's remark added to his desire to see and interpret facts, not feelings. No thief – at least not the sort that broke into houses in Venice – had been at work here. Anyone in search of gold or jewellery or cash would have pulled out the drawers and dumped their contents on the floor, then kicked them around, the better to separate and see everything. But the bottom drawer, Brunetti realized, looked no worse than his daughter's after she had hunted for a particular sweater. Or his son's.

The technician near the bed broke the silence by scuttling across the floorboards to unplug his lamp. Slowly, he got to his feet and wrapped the electric cord noisily around the handle, then slipped the plug under the last loop of cord to anchor it in place. 'I'm done here, Stefano,' he said abruptly.

'That's it, then,' Marillo said with audible relief. 'I'll give Bocchese the photos and he can check the prints. There's a lot of them, some of them perfectly clear. He'll give you a report, sir.'

'Thanks, Marillo,' Brunetti said.

Marillo glanced at Brunetti and bobbed his head in an expression that acknowledged his superior's thanks and his own embarrassment at not having been willing to provide more. The other technician followed him to the door, where the third man stood ready, slipping camera and flash into their case. Together, the three men made quick work of assembling their equipment. When they were finished, Marillo said nothing more than goodnight, and his team, silent, followed him from the apartment.

'I'll finish in there,' Brunetti said, deciding to return to the smaller bedroom. He had noticed when he glanced in before just how simple the room was, but now that he had time to look around, he saw that it was even more modest than he had first observed. There was no covering of any sort on the wooden floor. It was not parquet but the narrow wooden boards of a restoration – and not an expensive one – that must have been done about fifty years before. A low, thick-legged chest stood next to the bed, on it a short lamp with a yellow cloth lampshade from the bottom of which hung a circle of aged yellow tassels. This could have been a room in his grandmother's house, had he been taken back in a time machine.

In the half-open top drawer of the chest lay a number of plastic-wrapped packets of women's underclothing: three in each, simple white cotton pants, and in three different sizes. He had never seen Paola wear the like. These were functional pants he assumed a woman would buy at a supermarket, not a lingerie shop, fashioned for utility, not style, and certainly not meant to attract attention. Mixed in with them were unopened packets of white cotton T-shirts, also in three sizes. The packets lay neatly in the drawer in their separate piles, separated by a stack of ironed white cotton handkerchiefs.

He slid the drawer shut, no longer having to be careful about what he touched. The next drawer contained a few unopened packets of women's tights and six or seven pairs of socks, also unopened, all grey or black, again in different sizes and arranged with military precision. The bottom drawer held sweaters, cotton on one side, wool on the other, though here the two piles had mingled. At least with these the colours were a bit brighter: one red, one orange, another light green, and though all had at one time been worn, they had the look of garments that had been washed and ironed before being placed in the drawer. A pair of freshly laundered and ironed blue flannel pyjamas lay to the right of the sweaters, a packet of lavender-scented sachets behind it.

Brunetti closed the last drawer. He moved closer to the bed and got down on one knee to look beneath it, but the space was empty.

He heard Vianello come into the room behind him. 'Did you find anything else in her bedroom?' Brunetti asked.

'No. Nothing much. Except that she liked nice underwear and expensive sweaters.'

Getting to his feet, Brunetti went back to the chest. He pulled out the top drawer and pointed to the cellophane packets on top. 'They're all in different sizes, and nothing's opened.' Vianello stepped up beside him and looked into the drawer. 'Same with the tights,' Brunetti went on. 'And there are sweaters – no cashmere there – and a pair of pyjamas in the bottom drawer, and they all look like they've just been washed.'

'What do you make of it?' Vianello said. He shrugged and confessed, 'I've no idea.'

'Guests bring their own clothing,' Brunetti insisted. Vianello said nothing. 'Certainly their own underclothing.'

Brunetti and Vianello went back to the room where the woman's body had been found. From the doorway, Brunetti saw that the bloodstain had not been wiped away and thought what it would be for the family to come into this room and find it. In all these years of moving amidst the signs left by death, he had frequently wondered how it would feel to wipe away the last traces of a former life, and how a person could bear to do it.

With the woman's body gone, Brunetti could concentrate

enough to study the room for the first time. It was larger than he had at first thought. To the right he saw a sliding door and, beyond it, a small kitchen with wooden cabinets and what looked like Moroccan plates and tiles on the walls.

The kitchen was too small to hold a table, so it had been placed in the larger room, a utilitarian rectangle with four wooden chairs. It took a moment for Brunetti to realize that the room was virtually void of decoration. There was a beige rug of some sort of fibre on the floor, but the only decoration on the walls was a medium-sized crucifix that looked as if it had been mass produced in some non-Christian country: surely Christ was not meant to have such rosy lips and cheeks, nor was there anything much to justify his smile.

A dark brown sofa sat on the other side of the room, its back to the windows that looked out on to the *campo* and the illuminated apse of the church. There must once have been a door in the wall to the right of the sofa, but during one of the restorations that had been done to this building over the centuries, someone had decided to brick it up. Whoever had done the most recent restoration had removed some of the bricks and plastered over the back of the opening, added shelves, and turned it into an inset bookcase.

A desk with a typewriter stood not far from the sofa, it too facing away from the window. Brunetti stared at it to be sure he was seeing what he thought he was. Yes, an old Olympia portable, the sort of thing his friends had taken off to university decades ago. His own family had been unable to provide him with one. He sat at the desk and placed his fingers above the keys, careful not to touch them. He had to turn his head sharply to see out the window, and after orienting himself with the bell tower of the church, he realized that in the daylight the ignored view from these third floor windows must extend all the way north, as far as the mountains.

From behind him, he heard the sounds of Vianello opening

and closing drawers in the kitchen, then the whoosh of the opening refrigerator. He heard the rush of flowing water and the clink of a glass. Brunetti found the noises comforting.

Even though the desk appeared to have been checked for prints, from habit he slipped on plastic gloves and opened the single drawer at the centre, searching for he didn't know what. He was relieved to find disorder: unsharpened pencils, some paper clips swirling around on the bottom, a topless pen, a single cufflink, two buttons, and a blue notebook, the sort of thing used by students and, like the notebooks of so many students, empty.

He pulled out the drawer and set it beside the typewriter. He bent and looked into the empty space, but nothing was hidden, nor, when he held it up, could he see anything taped to the bottom of the drawer. Feeling not a little foolish and certain that Marillo's men had already done all of this, Brunetti knelt and stuck his head under the desk, but there was nothing taped there, either.

'What are you looking for?' Vianello asked from behind him.

'I don't know,' Brunetti admitted, pushing himself to his feet. 'It's all so orderly.'

'Isn't that supposed to be a good thing?' Vianello asked.

'In theory, yes. I suppose,' Brunetti admitted. 'But . . .'

'But you don't want to accept that she could have died of a heart attack or a stroke, the way Rizzardi suggested.'

'It's not that I want anything,' Brunetti said tersely, 'but you saw the mark.'

Instead of answering, Vianello let out a heavy breath, making a noise that could mean anything as easily as it could mean nothing. Brunetti was unwilling to mention the feeling he had had in the corridor for fear that Vianello would dismiss it as foolishness.

'There's no sign that anyone went through this place,' Vianello said. He glanced at the clock that hung beside the refrigerator. 'It's almost three, Guido. Could we lock the door and tape it and continue this tomor . . . later today?'

The name of the hour fell on Brunetti's shoulders like a heavy garment, bearing him back towards the tiredness he had felt even before his dinner with Patta and Scarpa.

He nodded, and the two men moved through the house, turning off lights. They chose to leave the shutters open, as they had found them: enough light filtered in from the *campo* to allow them to move through the apartment even after they had turned out most of the lights. Brunetti opened the door of the apartment and switched on the light in the stairway. Vianello pulled out a roll of red and white tape and used it to draw an enormous X across the door. Brunetti locked it and pocketed the keys, which he had taken from the table by the door. They had found no address book. There had been only a simple phone with no stored numbers, and it was now too late to bother the woman upstairs to ask about the dead woman's family. Brunetti turned away from the apartment and headed down the stairs.

'The woman upstairs said she was in a hotel in Palermo for five days. I'll check that,' Brunetti said.

As they passed the door to the apartment below, Vianello tilted his head towards it. 'The people in there heard us going up and down, so if they had anything to tell us, they probably would have.' Then, before Brunetti could comment, he added, 'But I'll come back later today and ask them. You never know.'

Outside, the Inspector phoned the station at Piazzale Roma and asked them to send a boat to pick him up at the Riva di Biasio stop. Brunetti knew it would be faster to walk, so he shook hands with his assistant and turned towards home.

5

By the time Brunetti awoke from a troubled sleep, everyone in the house had already left, and for half an hour he drifted in and out of wakefulness, recalling Signora Giusti's exclamation, 'She was a good neighbour,' and the pasty red goo that had seeped into the white hair of that good neighbour. His selective memory found Marillo's embarrassed reticence and replayed Rizzardi's cool thoroughness. He turned on to his back and looked at the ceiling. Is that what he would want someone to say about him, someone who had lived near him for a number of years? That he had been a good neighbour? Nothing more to be said about a person after years of acquaintanceship?

After a time, he went out into the kitchen, grumbling at the day, and found a note from Paola. 'Stop grumbling. Coffee on stove. Just light it. Fresh brioche on counter.' He saw the second and the fourth, did the first and the third. While the coffee was brewing, he went to the back window and looked off to the north. The Dolomites were clearly visible, the same mountains that Signora Altavilla had turned her back on and that Signora Giusti would see from her fourth-floor windows.

Though Brunetti was the son, grandson, great-grandson – and more – of Venetians, he had always found greater comfort in the sight of mountains than in that of the sea. Each time he heard of the approaching Something that was going to wipe the slate clean of humankind or read about the ever-escalating number of ships filled with toxic and radioactive waste scuttled by the Mafia off the coast of Italy, he thought of the majestic solidity of mountains, and in them he found solace. He had no idea how many years man had left to him, but Brunetti was sure that the mountains would survive whatever was to come and that something else would come after. He had never told anyone, not even Paola, about this idea nor of the strange consolation he took from it. Mountains seemed, he thought, so very permanent, while the sea, ever changing, was to him visibly disturbed by what happened to it; further, it was a more evident victim of the damage and depredations of man.

His thoughts had just moved to the continent-sized mass of garbage and plastic that was floating in the Pacific Ocean when the sound of bubbling coffee pulled him back to a more modest reality. He emptied the pot into his cup, spooned in sugar, and pulled a brioche from the bag. Cup in one hand, brioche in the other, he returned to the contemplation of the mountains.

This time it was the telephone that grabbed his attention. He walked into the living room and, mouth busy with his brioche, answered with his name.

'Where are you, Brunetti?' Patta shouted down the line.

When he had been younger and more prone to acts of prankish resistance, Brunetti would have answered that he was in his living room, but the years had taught him to interpret Patta-speak, so he recognized these words as a demand that he explain his absence from his office.

He swallowed the last of the brioche and said, 'I'm sorry to be delayed, sir, but Rizzardi's assistant said that the doctor was going to call me.'

'Don't you have a *telefonino*, for God's sake?' his superior demanded.

'Of course, sir, but his assistant said the doctor might want me to go and talk to him at the hospital, so I'm waiting for his call before I leave home. If I get to the Questura and have to go back to the hospital, it will waste—'

Even as Brunetti became aware that he was talking too much, Patta interrupted him. 'Stop lying to me, Brunetti.'

'Sir,' Brunetti said, careful to replicate the tone with which Chiara had answered Paola's last comment on her choice of clothing.

'Get down here. Now.'

'Yes, sir,' Brunetti said and replaced the phone.

Showered and shaved and much restored by having drunk the equivalent of three coffees, added to which was the sugar-high provided by two pastries, Brunetti left his apartment feeling strangely cheerful, a mood that was reflected everywhere in one of those glorious sunny days when autumn and nature unite to pull out all the stops and give people something to cheer about. Though his spirit begged him to walk, Brunetti went only as far as the Rialto stop, where he boarded a Number Two heading towards Lido. It would save only a few minutes, but the tone of Patta's voice had encouraged speed.

He had not had time to buy a newspaper, so he contented himself with reading the headlines he saw around him. Another politician caught on video in the company of a Brazilian transsexual; further assurances by the Minister of the Economy that all was well and getting better and that the reports of factory closings and unemployed workers were calculated exaggerations, a deliberate attempt on the part of the Opposition to instil fear and mistrust in the people.

Another unemployed worker had set himself ablaze in a city centre, this time Trieste.

He looked up from the headlines as they passed in front of the university. He saw nothing new there, either. How nice it would be if, one day, just as he was passing below the windows, Paola could fling one of them open and wave to him, perhaps call his name, shout out that she loved him absolutely and always would. He knew he would stand his ground and shout the same things back to her. The man next to him turned the page of his newspaper, and Brunetti turned his eyes back to the *Gazzettino* and the news that was never new. Teenage driver lost control of his father's car at two in the morning and slammed right into a plane tree; old woman cheated out of her pension by someone claiming to be an inspector from the electric company; frozen meat in large supermarket filled with worms.

He got out at San Zaccaria and walked along the water, spirits whisked up and about by the sight of the motion of the wind on the waves. He turned into the front door of the Questura a few minutes before ten and went directly up to Patta's office. His superior's secretary, Signorina Elettra Zorzi, was behind her computer; she was bedecked, like unto the lilies of the field, in a blouse that had to be silk, for the pattern in gold and white would have been wasted on any lesser fabric.

'Good morning, Commissario,' she said formally as he came in. 'The Vice-Questore is quite eager to have a word with you.'

'No less so than I, Signorina,' Brunetti answered and went over to knock on the door.

A bellowed '*Avanti!*' caused Brunetti to raise his eyebrows, Signorina Elettra her hands from the keys.

'Oh my, oh my, oh my,' she said by way of warning.

'I am just going inside and may be some time,' Brunetti said in English, to her consternation.

Inside, he found Patta in his no nonsense commander-ofarmed-men mode, one with which Brunetti was amply familiar. He adjusted his posture accordingly and walked to the seat Patta indicated in front of his desk.

'Why wasn't I called last night? Why was I kept in the dark about this?' Patta's voice was irate, but calm, as suited an official with a hard job to do and no help from the people around him, certainly not from the one in front of him.

'I informed you about the death when I left our dinner, Dottore,' Brunetti said. 'By the time we finished our initial investigation, it was after three in the morning, and I didn't want to disturb you at that hour.' Before Patta could say, as he usually did at this point, that there was no time, night or day, when he was not prepared to assume the responsibilities of his office, Brunetti said, 'I knew I should have done it, sir, but I thought a few hours would make no difference and we'd both be better able to deal with things if we had a decent night's sleep.'

'You certainly seem to have done so,' Patta was unable to stop himself from saying. Brunetti ignored the remark or at least allowed no response to it to show on the bland face he raised to his superior.

'You seem to have no idea of who the dead woman is,' Patta said.

'The woman upstairs said her name was Costanza Altavilla, Dottore,' Brunetti said in what he tried to make sound like a helpful voice.

Barely managing to suppress his exasperation, Patta said, 'She's the mother of my son's former veterinarian; that's who she is.' Patta paused to allow the significance of this to register on Brunetti, then added, 'I met her once.'

It was seldom that Patta left Brunetti utterly without words, but Brunetti had, over the years, developed a defensive response even to that rare event. He put his most serious expression on his face, nodded sagely a few times, and let out a long, and very thoughtful, 'Hmmmm.' He did not understand why, time after time, Patta was deceived by this, as he was again. Perhaps his superior had no coherent memory, or perhaps he was incapable of responding to outward manifestations of extreme deference in any other way, as an alpha dog is incapable of attacking a dog that flips over and shows its soft underbelly and throat.

Brunetti knew that there was nothing he could say. He could not risk saying 'I didn't realize that,' without Patta's hearing sarcasm, nor could he ask Patta to explain a relationship the importance of which he must obviously think self-evident. And, to the degree that he valued his job, he could not express curiosity about the fact that Patta's son had a veterinarian rather than a doctor. He waited, head tilted to one side in the manner of a very attentive dog.

'Salvo used to have a husky. They're very delicate, especially in this climate. He was plagued with eczema because of the heat. Dottor Niccolini was the only one who seemed able to do anything to help him.'

'What happened, sir?' Brunetti asked, honestly curious.

'Oh, Salvo had to give the dog away. It became too much trouble for him. But he formed a good opinion of the doctor and certainly would want us to help him in any way possible.' There was no doubt about it: Brunetti heard the sound of real human concern in Patta's voice.

Even after all these years, Brunetti had not learned to predict when Patta, in some unguarded moment, would give evidence of fellow feeling with humanity. He was always unmanned by it, seduced into the suspicion that trace elements of humanity were still to be found in his superior's soul. Patta's recidivism into his ordinary heartlessness had not broken Brunetti of his willingness to be deceived.

'Is he still here?' Brunetti asked, wondering if Patta had contacted Signora Altavilla's son but unwilling to ask.

'No, no. He got a job somewhere else. Vicenza. Verona. I forget which.'

'I see,' Brunetti said, nodding as if he understood. 'And is he still working as a veterinarian, do you think?'

Patta lifted his head, as if he'd suddenly detected a strange odour. 'Why do you ask?'

'We have to contact him. There was no address book in the apartment, and I couldn't go upstairs at that hour to ask the woman who lives there. But if he's still a veterinarian, he should be listed in one of those two cities.'

'Of course we should contact him,' Patta said with quickly manufactured irritation, quite as if Brunetti had opposed the idea. 'I hardly thought I'd have to explain something that simple to you, Brunetti.' Then, to prevent Brunetti from getting to his feet, he continued, 'I want this settled quickly. We can't have people in this city thinking they aren't safe in their homes.'

'Indeed, Vice-Questore,' Brunetti said instantly, curious to know who might have suggested to Patta that Signora Altavilla's death might lead to thoughts of safety. 'I'll have a look, and I'll call Signora Giusti . . .'

'Who?' Patta asked suspiciously.

'The woman upstairs, sir. She seems to have known the dead woman quite well.'

'Then she ought to know how to get hold of the son,' Patta said.

'I hope so, Dottore,' Brunetti said and started to get to his feet.

'What do you intend to do about the press?' Patta asked him, voice cautious.

'Have they been in touch with you, sir?' Brunetti asked, settling back into his chair.

'Yes,' Patta answered and gave Brunetti a long stare, as if he suspected that either he or Vianello – or quite possibly Rizzardi – had spent the rest of the early morning hours on the phone to reporters.

'What have they asked?'

'They know the woman's name, and they've asked about the circumstances of her death, but nothing more than they usually ask.'

'What have you told them, sir?'

'That the circumstances of her death are already under examination and we expect a report from the *medico legale* some time today or tomorrow.'

Brunetti nodded in approval. 'Then I'll see about getting in touch with the son, sir. The woman upstairs will surely know how to find him.' Then, before Patta could ask, Brunetti said, 'She was in no condition to answer questions last night, sir.' When Patta did not answer, Brunetti said, 'I'll go and speak to her.'

'About what?'

'About her life, about the son, about anything she can think of that might provide us with reason for concern.' He mentioned nothing about Palermo, nor did he say Vianello was going to speak to the neighbours below, fearing that Patta would jump to the conclusion that Signora Giusti was involved in her neighbour's death.

'"Concern", Brunetti? I think it might be wiser to get the results of the autopsy before you begin to use words like "concern", don't you?' Brunetti found himself almost comforted by the return of the Patta he knew, the master of evasion who so ably managed to deflect all attention that was not entirely positive or laudatory. 'If the woman died a natural death, then it doesn't concern us, and so I think we ought not to use that word.'

Instantly, as if he feared the press would somehow get hold of this remark and pounce upon its callousness, Patta amended it for those silent listeners, 'Professionally, I mean, of course. At the human level, her death is, as is anyone's, terrible.' Then, as if prodded by his son's voice, he added, 'And doubly so, given the circumstances.'

'Indeed,' Brunetti affirmed, resisting the impulse to bow

his head respectfully at the sibylline opacity of his superior's words, and allowing a moment to pass in silence. 'I believe there's nothing we can say to the press at the moment, sir, certainly not until Rizzardi has told us what he found.'

Patta fell upon Brunetti's uncertainty hungrily. 'Then you think it was a natural death?'

'I don't know, sir,' Brunetti answered, keeping to himself the mark near the woman's collarbone. If the physical evidence did point to a crime, it would fall to Patta to reveal this news, thus reaffirming his role as chief protector of the safety of the city.

'When we have the results, you should be the one to speak to the press, sir. They'll certainly pay more attention to anything that comes from you.' Brunetti wrapped the fingers of his right hand into a fist. Not even a beta dog had to continue lying on its back for so long, he told himself, suddenly tiring of his role.

'Right,' Patta said, restored to his good humour. 'Let me know what Rizzardi tells you as soon as you see him.' Then, as an afterthought, 'And find her son. His name is Claudio Niccolini.'

Brunetti wished the Vice-Questore good morning and went to the outer office to speak to Signorina Elettra, certain that she would easily find a veterinarian of the name Claudio Niccolini somewhere in the Veneto.

6

It proved far easier than he had imagined: all Signorina Elettra did was enter 'Veterinarian' and search the Yellow Pages for both cities, and she quickly found the number of the office of Dott. Claudio Niccolini in Vicenza.

Brunetti went back to his office to make the call, only to learn that the doctor was not in the office that day. When he gave his name and rank and explained that he had to speak to the doctor about the death of his mother, the woman with whom he was speaking said that Dr Niccolini had already been informed and was on his way to Venice, in fact was probably already there. The reproach in her voice was unmistakable. Brunetti offered no explanation for the delay in his call and, instead, asked for the doctor's *telefonino* number. The woman gave it to him and hung up without further comment.

Brunetti dialled the number; a man answered on the fourth ring. '*Sì?*'

'Dottor Niccolini?'

'*Sì. Chi parla?*'

'This is Commissario Guido Brunetti, Dottore. First, I want to offer my condolences for your loss,' Brunetti said, paused, and then added, 'I'd like to speak to you about your mother, if I might.' Brunetti had no idea what his authority was, since he had gone to the woman's home almost by default, and he had certainly not been given any formal assignment to look into the circumstances of her death.

The other man took a very long time to answer, and when he did he blurted out, 'Why . . .' and then stopped. After yet another seemingly interminable pause, he said, fighting to control his uneasiness, 'I didn't know the police were involved.'

If that's what he thought, Brunetti decided it was best to let him go on believing it. 'Only because the first call came to us, Dottore,' Brunetti said in his blandest bureaucratic voice. Then, switching registers to that of the beleaguered official, much put upon by the incompetence of others, he added, 'Usually the hospital would send a team, but because the person who reported the death called us, instead, we were obliged to go.'

'Ah, I see,' Niccolini said in a calmer voice.

Brunetti then asked, 'May I ask where you are, Dottore?'

'I'm at the hospital, waiting to speak to the pathologist.'

'I'm already on my way there,' Brunetti lied effortlessly, then added, 'There are some formalities; this way I can attend to them and also speak to you.' Without bothering to wait for Niccolini's reply, Brunetti said, 'I'll be there in ten minutes,' and snapped his phone closed.

He didn't bother to check if Vianello was in the officers' squad room but left the Questura quickly and started towards the hospital. As he walked, he mulled over Niccolini's tone as much as his words. Fear of involvement with the police was a normal response in any citizen, he realized, so perhaps the nervousness he had heard in the man's voice was to be expected. Added to this, Dottor

Niccolini was speaking from the hospital, where the body of his dead mother lay.

The beauty of the day interrupted his reflections. All it needed was the tang of burning leaves to recreate in his memory those lost days of late-autumn freedom when he and his brother, as children, had roamed at will on the islands of the *laguna*, sometimes helping the farmers with the last harvests of the year and wildly proud to be able to take home bags filled with the fruit or vegetables with which they had been paid.

He crossed Campo SS. Giovanni e Paolo, conscious of how perfect the light would be today for the stained-glass windows of the basilica. He went into the Ospedale. The vast entrance hall devoured most of the light, and though he passed through courtyards and open spaces on the way to the *obitorio*, the enclosing walls destroyed the sense that he was in the open air.

A man stood in the waiting room outside the morgue. He was tall and heavy-boned, with the body of a wrestler at the end of his career, muscle already beginning to lose its tone but not yet turned to fat. He looked up when Brunetti came in, saw but failed to acknowledge the arrival of another person.

'Dottor Niccolini?' Brunetti asked and extended his hand.

The doctor was slow in registering Brunetti, as if he had first to clear his mind of other thoughts before he could accept the presence of another person. 'Yes,' he finally said. 'Are you the policeman? I'm sorry, but I don't remember your name.'

'Brunetti,' he said.

The other man took Brunetti's hand more from habit than desire. His grip was firm but definitely fleeting. Brunetti noticed that his left eye was minimally smaller than the other, or set at a different angle. Both were deep brown, as was his hair, already greying at the temples. His nose and mouth were surprisingly delicate in a man of his stature, as though designed for a smaller face.

'I'm sorry to meet you in these circumstances,' Brunetti said. 'It must be very difficult for you.' There should be some formulaic language for this, Brunetti thought, some way to overcome awkwardness.

Niccolini nodded, tightened his lips and closed his eyes, then turned quickly away from Brunetti, as if he had heard something from the door to the morgue.

Brunetti stood, his hands behind him, one hand holding the other wrist. He became aware of the smell of the room, one he had smelled too many times: something chemical and sharp that tried, and failed, to obliterate another, this one feral and warm and fluid. Across from him, on the wall, he saw one of those horror posters that hospitals cannot resist displaying: this one held grossly enlarged pictures of what he thought were the ticks that carried encephalitis and borreliosis.

Speaking to the man's back, Brunetti could think of nothing but banalities. 'I'd like to express my sympathies, Dottore,' he said before he remembered that he had already done so.

The doctor did not immediately answer him, nor did he turn. Finally, in a quiet, tortured voice, he said, 'I've done autopsies, you know.'

Brunetti remained silent. The other man pulled a handkerchief from the pocket of his trousers, wiped his face and blew his nose. When he turned, his face looked for a moment like the face of a different man, older somehow. 'They won't tell me anything – not how she died or why they're doing an autopsy. So all I can do is stand here and think about what's happening.' His mouth tightened into a grimace, and for a moment Brunetti feared the doctor was going to start to cry.

There being no suitable rejoinder, Brunetti allowed some time to pass and then went over and, without asking, took Niccolini's arm. The man stiffened, as though Brunetti's touch was the prelude to a blow. His head whipped around and he stared at Brunetti with the eyes of a frightened animal. 'Come, Dottore,' Brunetti said in his most soothing voice. 'Perhaps you should sit down a moment.' The other man's resistance disappeared, and Brunetti led him over to the row of plastic chairs, released his arm slowly and waited while the doctor sat down. Then Brunetti angled another chair to half face him and sat.

'Your mother's upstairs neighbour called us last night,' he began.

It appeared to take Niccolini some time to register what Brunetti was saying, and then he said only, 'She called me this morning. That's why I'm here.'

'What did she tell you?' Brunetti asked.

Niccolini's hands, almost against his will, began to pull at one another. The sound, rough and dry, was strangely loud. 'That she'd gone down to tell *Mamma* she was home and to get her post. And when she went in, she found . . . her.'

He cleared his throat and suddenly pulled his hands apart and stuffed them under his thighs, like a schoolboy during a difficult exam. 'On the floor. She said she knew when she looked at her that she was dead.'

The doctor took a deep breath, looked off to Brunetti's right, and then went on. 'She said that when it was all over and they'd taken her away – my mother – she decided to wait to call me. Then she did. This morning, that is.'

'I see.'

The doctor shook his head, as if Brunetti had asked a question. 'She said that I should call you – the police. And when I did, they – I mean you – I mean the person I spoke to at the Questura – he said that I had to call the hospital to find out anything.' He pulled out his hands and folded them in his lap, where they remained motionless. He studied them, then said, 'So I called here. But they wouldn't tell me anything about it. All they did was tell me to come here.' Then he added, 'That's why I was surprised when you called me.'

Brunetti nodded, as if to suggest that the police were not involved, all the while considering how very intent Niccolini was on distancing the police from his mother's death. But what citizen would not do the same? Brunetti tried to free his head of suspicion and of a bureaucracy capable of inviting this man to this place at this time, and said, 'I apologize for the confusion, Dottore. In these circumstances, it must be doubly painful.'

Silence fell between them. Niccolini returned his attention to his hands, and Brunetti decided it would be wiser to say nothing. The circumstances, the location, the awfulness in course in the other room – all of these things oppressed them and weakened their desire to speak.

It was not too long, though Brunetti had no idea of how much time elapsed, before Rizzardi, having changed from his lab jacket into his usual suit and tie, appeared at the door. 'Ah, Guido,' he said when he saw Brunetti. 'I wanted to . . .' he began, but then noticed the other man, and Brunetti watched him realize that this had to be a relative of the woman whose autopsy he had just finished. Seamlessly, he turned his attention to him and said, 'I'm Ettore Rizzardi, *medico legale.*' He went over and extended his hand. 'I'm sorry to see you here, Signore.' Brunetti had seen him do it countless times, but each time it was new, as though the doctor had only this moment discovered human grief and wanted to do his best to comfort it.

Niccolini got to his feet and clung to Rizzardi's hand. Brunetti saw Rizzardi's lips tighten at the force of the other man's grip. In response, the pathologist moved closer and put his left hand on the man's shoulder. Niccolini relaxed a bit, then gasped for air, tightened his lips and bent his head back. He took a few deep breaths through his nose, then slowly released Rizzardi's hand. 'What was it?' he asked, almost begged.

Rizzardi seemed not at all disturbed by Niccolini's tone. 'Perhaps it would be better if we went to my office,' the pathologist said calmly.

Brunetti followed them towards Rizzardi's office, at the end of the corridor on the left. Halfway there, Niccolini stopped and Brunetti heard the veterinarian say, 'I think I have to go outside. I don't want to be in here.' It was obvious to Brunetti that Niccolini was having trouble breathing, so he moved past Rizzardi and led the other two men through the various halls and courtyards, back to the main entrance and out into the *campo*, where he discovered that the beauty of the day lay in wait for them.

Returned to the sun and to the live world, Brunetti was overcome by a craving for coffee, or maybe it was sugar he wanted. As the three of them descended the low steps of the hospital and started across the *campo*, Niccolini put his head back again and let the sun wash over his face in a gesture Brunetti found almost ritualistic. They stopped near the statue of Colleoni, Brunetti eyeing with longing the row of cafés on the other side of the *campo*. Without asking, Rizzardi broke away from them and headed towards Rosa Salva, then turned and waved them both into motion.

Inside, Rizzardi ordered a coffee, and when the others joined him, they nodded to the barman for the same. People stood around, eating pastry, some already eating *tramezzini*, or drinking coffee, others having a late-morning *spritz*. How wonderful, and yet how terrible, to emerge from there and enter here, amidst the hiss of the coffee machine and the click of cups on saucers, and come face to face with this reminder of what we all know and feel uncomfortable knowing: that life plugs along, no matter what happens to any of us. It puts one foot in front of the other, whistling a tune that is dreary or merry by turn, but it always puts one foot in front of the other and moves on.

When the three coffees were on the bar in front of them,

Rizzardi and Brunetti ripped open envelopes of sugar and stirred them into their cups. Niccolini stood looking at the cup as though uncertain just what it was. It was not until he was nudged by a man reaching past to replace his cup and saucer on the counter that he took a packet of sugar and poured it into his coffee.

When they were finished, Rizzardi put money on the counter, and the three men went back into the *campo*. A little boy, seeming no higher than Brunetti's knee, whizzed past on a scooter, pushing with one foot, screaming with the wild thrill of it. A moment later, his father pounded past, out of breath and shouting, 'Marco, Marco, *fermati*.'

Rizzardi walked to the railing surrounding the base of the statue of Colleoni and leaned back against it, looking down Barbaria delle Tole, the basilica on his left. Brunetti and Niccolini arranged themselves on either side of him. 'Your mother died of a heart attack, Dottore,' Rizzardi said with no introduction, eyes looking straight ahead of him. 'It would have been very fast. I don't know how painful it was, but I can assure you that it was very quick.'

Behind them they could hear Marco's continued shouts and his delight at the day and the discovery of speed.

Niccolini took a deep breath in which Brunetti heard the relief anyone would feel at the doctor's words. The three men listened to the voice of the child and the antiphon of the father's caution.

Niccolini cleared his throat and said, his voice hesitant, raw, 'Signorina Giusti – my mother's neighbour – said she saw blood.' That said, he stopped, and when Rizzardi did not answer, he asked, 'Is that true, Dottore?' Brunetti looked at Niccolini's hands and saw that they were drawn into fists that shook with tension.

The little boy screamed as he whizzed past them, and when he reached the other end of the *campo*, Rizzardi turned to Brunetti, as if asking him to contribute in some way, but

Brunetti offered no help, curious to know how the pathologist would answer Niccolini.

Rizzardi reached back to grab the top of the railing and propped his weight against it. 'Yes, there was some physical indication to explain that, but nothing inconsistent with a heart attack,' Rizzardi said. The doctor's lapse into medical jargon, Brunetti noticed, made no mention of the faint mark he had seen on Signora Altavilla. He excluded the possibility that the pathologist thought it meaningless: had that been the case, Rizzardi would surely have mentioned it, only to dismiss it.

Brunetti turned to see how Niccolini would respond to this non-answer, but he merely nodded to acknowledge that he had heard. Rizzardi continued, 'If you like, I could try to explain to you exactly what happened. In the medical sense, that is.' Seeing Rizzardi's affable smile, Brunetti realized the pathologist had no idea of Niccolini's profession, nor of the medical training that would have prepared him for it, and so could have no idea of the effect his condescension might provoke.

Niccolini asked in a very soft voice, 'Could you be more specific about this "physical indication"?'

His tone, not his words, caught Rizzardi's attention. The pathologist said, 'There were signs of trauma.' Ah, Brunetti found himself thinking: now we come to the mark on her throat.

Niccolini considered this and then said, his voice struggling for neutrality, 'There are many kinds of trauma.'

Brunetti decided to intervene before Rizzardi began to simplify the meaning of the term and further antagonize Niccolini. 'I think you should know that Dottor Niccolini is a veterinarian, Ettore.'

Rizzardi took a moment to respond, and when he did it was evident that the news pleased him. 'Ah, then he'll understand,' he said.

Both Rizzardi and Brunetti heard Niccolini gasp. He wheeled towards the pathologist, one hand involuntarily closing into a fist, face blank with shock.

Rizzardi stepped away from the railing and held up his hands, palms outward in an instinctive gesture of self-protection. 'Dottore, Dottore, I meant no offence.' He patted repeatedly at the air between him and Niccolini until the other man, looking stunned at his own behaviour, lowered his hand. Rizzardi said, 'I meant only that you'd understand the physiology of what I said. Nothing more.' Then, more calmly, 'Please, please. Don't even think it.'

Was Niccolini so upset that he had heard Rizzardi's remark as a comparison between animal and human anatomy? But how could he be expected to be cool and rational in the presence of the man who had performed the autopsy?

Niccolini nodded a few times, eyes closed, his face flushed, then looked at Rizzardi and said, 'Of course, Dottore. I misunderstood. It's all so . . .'

'I know. It's all so terrible. I've spoken to many people. It's never easy.'

The men returned to silence. A beagle came out of one of the shops near the end of the *campo* and relieved itself against a tree, then went back into the shop.

Rizzardi's voice summoned Brunetti's attention away from the dog. 'I can only repeat that your mother died of a heart attack: there's no question of that.' Brunetti had listened to the doctor enough times in the past to understand that Rizzardi was telling the truth, but Brunetti could see his face now, so he knew there was also something the doctor was not saying.

Rizzardi continued. 'And to answer your question: yes, there was blood at the scene. Commissario Brunetti saw it, as well.' Niccolini turned to Brunetti for confirmation, and Brunetti nodded, then waited to see how Rizzardi would explain it. 'There was a radiator not far from where your mother was found, and it is not inconsistent with the evidence that she hit her head as she fell. As you know, head wounds often bleed a great deal, but because death would have come so quickly after her heart attack, she would not have bled for long, and that too is consistent with what we observed at the scene.' With every sentence he spoke, Rizzardi's language moved closer and closer to the officialese of printed reports and committee minutes.

Like a man coming up for air, Niccolini asked, 'But it was the heart attack that killed her?' How many times, Brunetti wondered, did he need to hear this?

'Beyond question,' Rizzardi said in his most official voice, and at the sound of it, the mild squeak of discomfort with which Brunetti had listened to his previous evasions was suddenly transformed into a klaxon of doubt. Brunetti had no idea what the doctor was lying about, but he was now convinced that he was.

Niccolini imitated the pathologist's former position, and leaned back against the railing.

A sound resembling a war whoop caught their attention, and all of them turned and looked towards the far end of the campo, where Marco swirled in ever-narrowing circles around one of the trees. Brunetti, watching the narrowing gyre of the boy's play, wondered at Niccolini's behaviour. He would understand misery or grief or an explosion of tears. During his career he had seen the opposite, as well: cold-hearted satisfaction at the death of a parent. Niccolini seemed nervous and paralysed at the same time. Why else force Rizzardi to repeat his judgement that the death had been natural?

Rizzardi pushed back the sleeve of his jacket and looked at his watch. 'I'm sorry, Signori, but I have an appointment.' He reached to shake hands with Niccolini and said a polite goodbye. He told Brunetti that he would send him the written report as soon as he could and told him to call if he had any questions.

Niccolini and Brunetti watched silently as the pathologist walked across the *campo* and disappeared into the hospital.

7

When Rizzardi was gone, Brunetti asked, nodding in the direction of the hospital, 'Is there anything else you have to do in there?'

'No, I don't think so,' Niccolini answered, shaking his head as if to remove the idea or the place. 'I signed some papers when I went in, but no one told me I had to do anything else.' He looked at the hospital, then back at Brunetti, and added, 'They said I can't see her until this afternoon. Two o'clock.' Then, speaking more to himself than Brunetti, he said, 'This shouldn't have happened.' He looked up then and said, as if he feared Brunetti had reason to doubt it, 'She was a good mother.' Then, after a pause, 'She was a good woman.'

Despite the years – decades – he had spent as a policeman, Brunetti still wanted to believe this to be true of most people. Experience suggested that they were good, at least until they were put into unusual or difficult situations, and then some – many, even – changed. Brunetti surprised himself by thinking of prayer: 'lead us not into temptation'. How intelligent of whoever had said that – was it Christ himself? –

to realize how easily we were tempted and how easily we fell, and how wise we are to pray to be spared temptation.

'. . . you think they'll . . .' he heard Niccolini say and returned his attention to the other man. Instead of finishing the phrase, the veterinarian raised his hand in the air, palm towards the sky, then let it fall to his side, as if resigned to the fact that the heavens had little interest in what had happened to his mother.

Brunetti's lack of attention had been temporary. He very much wanted to listen to whatever the doctor had to say and so, glancing at his watch, he suggested, 'Dottore, if you'd like, we could have something to eat together.' He paused, then said, 'But if you'd like to be by yourself,' Brunetti went on, involuntarily raising both palms and shifting his body backwards, 'I understand.'

Niccolini's glance was level and direct. Then he too looked at his watch: his eyes stayed on it for some time, as if he were trying to figure out what the numbers meant.

'I have an hour,' he finally said. Then, very decisively, he added, 'Yes.' He looked around the *campo* for a familiar point and said, 'I don't know what to do until then, and the time will pass more quickly.' He looked back at the bar where they had had a coffee. 'It's all different,' he said.

'The bar? Or the *campo*?' Brunetti asked. Or perhaps Niccolini was talking about life. Now. After.

'All of it, I think,' Niccolini said. 'I don't come to Venice much any more. Just to visit my mother, and that's so close to the station that I don't see other parts of the city.' He looked around him, his eyes as stunned by what they saw as those of a tourist, exposed to this for the first time. He turned and pointed back towards the church of the Miracoli. 'I went to elementary school at Giacinto Gallina, so I know this neighbourhood. Or I knew it.' He waved his hand towards one of the bars. 'Sergio's gone, and the bar's Chinese now. And the two old people who used to run Rosa Salva: they're gone, too.'

As if encouraged by the name of the bar, Niccolini began to walk towards it. Brunetti fell into step beside him, assuming that his invitation had been accepted. By silent assent, they chose a table outside, one without an umbrella so they could better enjoy the remnants of the autumnal sun left to them. There was a menu on the table, but neither of them bothered with it. When the waiter came, Brunetti asked for a glass of white wine and two *tramezzini*: he didn't care which. Niccolini said he'd take the same.

In the first months after Brunetti's mother had fallen complete victim to the Alzheimer's that was to lead to her death, she had stayed in the old people's home a bit further along Barberia delle Tole, but Brunetti, no matter how much he wanted Niccolini to talk about his mother, was not willing to try to win his fellow feeling and goodwill by offering up his own mother's suffering as a way to encourage him to speak.

They waited in silence, strangely relaxed in each other's company. 'Did you come to see her very often?' Brunetti finally asked.

'Until a year ago, I did,' Niccolini said. 'But then my wife had twins, and so my mother started to come out to see us.'

'In Vicenza?'

'Lerino, really; it's where they were from originally, my parents. She'd come out on the train and I'd pick her up.' The waiter came with the glasses of wine. Brunetti picked his up and took a sip, then another. Niccolini ignored his and continued speaking. 'We have another child, a daughter. She's six.'

Brunetti thought of the joy his mother had taken in her grandchildren and said, 'She must have been happy with that.'

Niccolini smiled for the first time since they met, and grew younger. 'Yes. She was.' The waiter came and put the sandwiches in front of them.

'It's strange,' Niccolini said, picking up his glass but ignoring the sandwiches. 'She spent her whole life with children, first as a teacher and then with me and my sister, and then with other children when she went back to teaching when we both were in school.' He sipped at his wine, then picked up a sandwich and studied it. He set it back on the plate.

Brunetti took a bite of his first sandwich, then asked, 'What was strange, Dottore?'

'That when she retired, she stopped working with children.'

'What did she do, instead?' Brunetti asked.

Niccolini studied Brunetti's face before he asked, speaking very slowly, as if searching through his vocabulary for the right words, 'Why do you want to know all of this?'

Brunetti took another sip of wine. 'I'm interested in women of my mother's generation.' Then, with a glance in Niccolini's direction, before he could object, Brunetti added, 'Well, close in age to her generation.' He set his glass on the table and continued. 'My mother didn't work: she stayed home and took care of us, but once, years ago, she told me she would have loved to have been a teacher. But there was no money in her family, so she went to work when she was fourteen. As a servant.' Brunetti said it boldly, in defiance of all those years when he had denied this simple truth, wishing that his parents had been other than they were, richer than they were, more cultured than they were. 'So I'm always interested in those women who got to do what my mother wanted to do. What they made of the chance.'

As if now convinced of the legitimacy of Brunetti's interest, Niccolini went on. 'She began to work with old people. Well, older people. In fact,' he said, pointing with his chin, 'she started down there.' Anyone in Venice would know he meant the old people's home, the *casa di cura*, only a hundred metres away.

'Started how?' Brunetti asked. 'Doing what?'

'Visiting. Listening to them. Bringing them out here into the *campo* when the weather was good.' This, too, was a phenomenon with which everyone in the city was familiar: tiny old people curved into their wheelchairs and covered up with blankets, regardless of the season, wheeled into the sunlight by friends or relatives or, increasingly, women of Eastern European appearance, who brought them into the *campo* to spend a part of what remained of their lives in company with what remained of life beyond their tiny, cramped rooms.

Brunetti wondered if this man's mother could have been one of the people who helped his own, but no sooner did the thought come than Brunetti dismissed it as irrelevant.

'When the weather was bad, she read to them or listened to them.' Niccolini leaned forward and again picked up the sandwich. He took a bite and set it back on the edge of the plate. 'She always said how much they liked to be able to tell younger people about what life had been like when they were younger and what they had done and what the city was like: sixty years ago, seventy.'

'People don't have to be in the *casa di cura* to start doing that, I'm afraid,' Brunetti said and smiled, thinking of the hours he had already spent lamenting the changes that had taken place in the city since the time when he was a young man. 'I think it's part of being Venetian.' Then, after a moment, 'Or part of being human.'

Niccolini pushed himself back in his chair. 'I think it's worse for older people. The changes are so much more obvious for them.' Then, as so many people did when this subject arose, he sighed deeply and waved a hand in a meaningless circle.

'You said she started here,' Brunetti said. 'Where else did she visit them?'

'That place down in Bragora. That's where she was

working. Still.' Hearing himself say that word, Niccolini looked down at his hands.

Brunetti remembered hearing about it, years ago: one entire floor of a *palazzo* in Campo Bandiera e Moro, run by some order of nuns who, though they were rumoured to charge the highest prices in the city, were also said to provide the best care. There had been no beds free when he was looking for a place for his mother; he had not thought about the place since then.

A sudden intake of breath forced him to look across at Niccolini. 'Oh, my God,' the doctor said. 'I'll have to tell them.' Niccolini's face flushed red, and his eyes began to glisten. He leaned forward and, elbows propped on the arms of his chair, covered his mouth and nose with his hands.

Brunetti looked at his watch. It was almost two.

'I can't call them. I can't do this on the telephone,' Niccolini said, shaking his head to dismiss the possibility.

Tentatively, Brunetti asked, 'Would you like me to speak to them, Dottore?' Niccolini's eyes flashed at him. 'I know two of the sisters there,' Brunetti quickly added. Well, he had spoken to them years ago, so in a certain sense he did know them. 'It's not far from the Questura.' Brunetti didn't know how hard to press here and didn't want to seem too interested. 'Of course, if you'd rather do it yourself, I understand.'

The waiter walked past their table and Brunetti asked for the bill. In the minutes that elapsed while the waiter went inside to get it, Niccolini kept his eyes on his half-filled glass of wine and the uneaten sandwiches.

Brunetti paid the bill, left a few euros on the table, and pushed back his chair. Niccolini got to his feet. 'I'd like you to do it, Commissario. I don't know if I'm going to be able . . . ' he began but let his voice drift off, powerless to give a name to what it was he was unable to do.

'Of course,' Brunetti said, careful to keep his words to a minimum. He reached over and took the doctor's hand.

Before he could speak, the doctor took his hand and pressed it to the point of pain and said, 'Don't say anything. Please.' He released Brunetti's hand and walked across the *campo* towards the hospital.

8

Brunetti reached down and picked up one of the sandwiches on the plate. Embarrassed to be seen eating while standing, he sat down again and finished it, then went into the bar and had a glass of mineral water. He realized that he had failed to call Paola to tell her he would not be home for lunch. He paid and stepped outside to make the call. He dialled their home number and hoped she would understand that he had been, in a sense, hijacked by events.

'Paola,' he said when she answered with her name, 'things got away from me.'

'So did a *rombo* cooked in white wine with fennel.'

Well, at least she was not angry. 'And baby potatoes and carrots,' she went on relentlessly, 'and one of those bottles of Tokai your informer gave you.'

'I wasn't supposed to have told you that.'

'Then pretend you didn't hear me say I know who you got them from.'

Perhaps he was not going to get off so lightly. 'I had to meet the son of that woman who died last night.'

'It wasn't in the paper this morning, but it's already in the online version.'

Brunetti was not comfortable with the cyber age, still preferring to read his newspapers in paper form; the fact that a newspaper such as the *Gazzettino* now existed in cyberspace was to him a cause of great uneasiness. 'What will become of people who are exposed to the *Gazzettino* twenty-four hours a day?' he asked.

Paola, who often took a longer and more measured view than did Brunetti, said, 'It might help to think of it as toxic waste we don't ship to Africa.'

'Assuredly. I hadn't considered that. I'm at peace with my conscience now,' Brunetti said. Then, curious to learn how the story was being played, he asked, 'What are they saying?'

'That she was found in her apartment by a neighbour. Death was apparently caused by a heart attack.'

'Good.'

'Does that mean it wasn't?'

'Rizzardi's being dodgier and more noncommittal than usual. I think he might have seen something, but he didn't say anything to the woman's son.'

'What's he like, the son?'

'He seems a decent man,' Brunetti said, which had certainly been his first impression. 'But he couldn't disguise his relief that the police aren't showing any interest in his mother's death.'

'Is it you who isn't doing the showing?' she asked.

'Yes. He seemed bothered that I wanted to speak to him, so I had to pass it off as a procedural formality because we were the ones who received the call.'

'Why would he be nervous? He can't have had anything to do with it.' Hearing her speak so categorically, Brunetti realized that he too had dismissed this possibility *a priori*. The world offered a cornucopia of variations on the theme of homicide; wives and husbands killed one another with staggering frequency, lovers and ex-lovers existed in a state of undeclared warfare; he had lost count of the women who had killed their children in recent years. But still his mind stopped short of this: men don't kill their mothers.

He let himself wander off in pursuit of these thoughts. Paola remained silent, waiting. Finally he admitted, 'It could just as easily be nothing. After all, he's had a terrible shock, and after I talked to him, he had to go back to the hospital to identify her.'

'*Oddio*,' she exclaimed. 'Couldn't they have found someone else?'

'A relative has to do it,' Brunetti said.

For a few moments neither of them spoke, then he pulled them both away from these things and said, 'I should be on time tonight.'

'Good.' And she was gone.

The best way to get to the rest home was to walk past the Questura: the map in his brain offered other possibilities, but they were all longer. He could go by and pick up Vianello to come along with him, so that he could tell him about Niccolini and how the presence of the other man had stopped Rizzardi from telling him whatever it was he had wanted to say about the autopsy.

He pulled out his phone and dialled Vianello's number, told him where he was and that he would pass by to get him in five minutes or so. The sun had passed its zenith, and the first *calle* he turned into was beginning to lose the warmth of the day.

As he walked alongside Rio della Tetta, Brunetti was cheered, as always happened when he walked here, by the sight of the most beautiful paving stones in Venice. Of some colour between pink and ivory, many of the stones were almost two metres long and a metre wide and gave an idea of what it must have been to walk in the city in its glory days. The *palazzo* on the other side of the canal, however, provided proof that those days were gone for ever. There was a way to recognize abandonment: the flaking dandruff of sun-blasted paint peeling from shutters; rusted stanchions holding flowerpots out of which trailed the desiccated memory sticks of flowers; and water-level gates hanging askew from their rust-rotten hinges, moss-covered steps leading up and into cavernous spaces where only a rat would venture. Brunetti looked at the building and saw the slow decline of the city, while an investor would see only opportunity: a studio for foreign architects, yet another hotel, perhaps a bed and breakfast or, for all he knew, a Chinese bordello.

He crossed the small bridge, down to the end, left, right, and there ahead of him he saw Vianello, leaning against the railing. When he saw Brunetti, Vianello pushed himself upright and fell into step with him. 'I spoke to the people who live on the first floor,' the Inspector said. 'Nothing. They didn't hear anything, didn't see anyone. They didn't hear the woman upstairs come home, didn't hear anything until we started to show up. Same with the old people on the second floor.'

'You believe them?'

With no hesitation, Vianello said, 'Yes. They've got two little kids, so I doubt they'd hear much of anything. And the old people are pretty much deaf, anyway.' Then he added, 'They said she had people to stay with her. Always women. At least the ones they've seen.'

Brunetti gave him an inquisitive glance, and Vianello said, 'That's all they said.'

As they continued walking, Brunetti said, 'Her son told me Signora Altavilla volunteered in that *casa di cura* down in Bragora, so I thought we should talk to the sisters about her. He said she went there to talk to – but really to listen to – the old people.'

'That's far more useful, don't you think?' Vianello asked.

'Hmm?'

'Seems to me, the older people get, the less interest they have in the world around them, and in the present, and so the more they want to think about the past and talk about the past. And maybe live in the past.' He paused, but when his superior remained silent, Vianello continued. 'It's certainly that way with most of the old people I know, or knew: my grandmother, my mother, even Nadia's parents. Besides, if you think about it, why should they be interested in the present? For most of them, it's filled with health problems, or money problems, and they're getting weaker and weaker. So the past is a better place to spend their time, and even better if they've got someone to listen to them.'

Brunetti was forced to agree with him. It had surely been the case with his parents, though he wasn't sure if they – his father returned from the war a broken, unhappy man and his mother eventually lost to Alzheimer's – were reliable examples. He thought of Paola's parents, Conte and Contessa Falier – anchored in the present and curious about the future – and Vianello's theory fell apart.

'Are we doing this,' Vianello asked, keeping perfectly in step with Brunetti, 'because of that mark?'

Brunetti fought the impulse to shrug and said, 'Rizzardi's at his uncommunicative best. He told the son she died of a heart attack – so I suppose that's true – but he didn't say anything about the mark. And we couldn't talk.'

'You got any ideas?' Vianello asked.

This time Brunetti permitted himself the shrug, then said, 'I'd like to learn something about her, then see what Rizzardi decides to tell us.'

As they reached the top of Ponte San Antonin, Brunetti pointed with his chin at the church and said, 'My mother always used to tell me, whenever we passed here, about some time in the nineteenth century – I think it was – that a rhinoceros – or maybe it was an elephant – she told me both versions – somehow ended up trapped inside the church.'

Vianello stopped and stared at the façade. 'I never heard anything about that, but what could a rhinoceros have been doing, walking around the city? Or an elephant, for that matter.' He shook his head, as if at yet another tale of the strange behaviour of tourists, and started down the steps on the other side. 'I was at a funeral there once, years ago.' Vianello stopped walking and looked at the façade with open surprise. 'Isn't that strange? I don't even remember whose funeral it was.'

They continued, following the curve to the right, and Vianello said, returning to what Brunetti had told him, 'It makes you understand why nothing's ever clear, a story like that.'

'You mean the rhinoceros? That was or wasn't there? And that was or wasn't a rhinoceros?'

'Yes. Once it gets said, someone will believe it and repeat it, and then hundreds of years later, people are still repeating it.'

'And it's become the truth?'

'Sort of,' Vianello answered, sounding reluctant. They walked in silence for some time, and then he observed, 'It's pretty much the same today, isn't it?'

'That stories aren't reliable?' Brunetti asked.

'That people invent stories, and then after a time there's no telling what's true and what isn't.'

They turned into the *campo*, and the sun came back to work in front of them, lifting their mood. The trees still had their leaves, a number of people sat on the benches beneath them, and the open vista soothed their eyes.

They crossed the *campo* without speaking. Brunetti couldn't remember which door it was, though he knew it was in the line of buildings to the right of the church. He stopped at the first row of bells and read the list, but only family names were given. On a panel next to the second door he found '*Sacra Famiglia*' and rang the bell.

It was almost a full minute before a female voice, old and wavering, asked who it was. 'Brunetti,' he said, adding, 'I'm a friend of Signora Altavilla's . . .' He prevented himself from continuing the lie, or at least the full lie, by concluding, '. . . son.'

'She's not here,' the voice said, sounding querulous, though that might have been nothing more than the speaker-phone. 'She didn't come in today.'

'I know that, Suora,' Brunetti said. 'I'd like to speak to the Mother Superior.'

The voice said something neither he nor Vianello could hear, and then the door snapped open. They stepped into a large entrance hall, its pavement laid out in the orange and white chequerboard pattern so common to buildings of this epoch. Nothing more than dimness entered through the grillwork of a row of windows at the back of the building. They ignored the elevator and took the staircase to the right of it. A small old woman stood at the only door on the first floor: her clothing spoke of her vows before her size and stance spoke of her age.

She nodded as the two men approached, then put out her hand. Both of them had to angle down their arms, almost as though they were shaking hands with a child: she came to their chests and actually had to put her head back to look into their eyes. 'I'm Madre Rosa,' she said, 'Mother Superior here. Suora Grazia said you wanted to speak to me.' She stepped back inside the door to get a better look at them. 'I have to say I don't like the look of you.'

Her face remained unmoved as she spoke, and her accent revealed even more strongly its origins far south of Venice.

One of the tenets of the mental identikit Brunetti possessed held that southerners, even the children, always recognized policemen, and so he asked, smiling as he did so, 'Is that because we're men or because we're big, or because we're policemen?'

She stepped back further and nodded to them to enter. She closed the door after them and said, 'I know already that Costanza's dead, so any policeman who comes saying he's a friend of hers is lying in order to get information. That's why I don't like the look of you. I don't care how big you are.'

Brunetti was struck with a sudden sympathy for the people he had outwitted in questioning and admired this woman, who had made child's play of his attempt; further, he admired her directness in telling him her feelings. 'I'm not a friend of her son's, either, Madre,' he confessed. 'But I did just speak to him, and he asked me to come and tell you what happened.'

The nun did not respond to his frankness but turned and led them into what must once have been the over-furnished sitting room of a private apartment. From the back, she appeared even smaller; Brunetti noticed she favoured her right leg when she walked. The sofas and chairs were covered with thick brown velvet and had feet carved to look like the paws of lions. A closer look revealed that many of the toes were missing, and some of the chairs had grease spots on the backrests and bald spots on the arms, with some of the patches surrounded by horizontal tears in the fabric. The baldness was repeated on the enormous Kashan that covered the floor from wall to wall.

The nun pointed to two of the easy chairs and gingerly took her place facing them on a hard wooden chair, careful not to bend her right leg. Their chairs had sagged with age and use to such a degree that their heads, when they sat down, were on a level with hers.

Brunetti leaned to his side to reach for his wallet in order to show her his warrant card, but she forestalled him by saying, 'I don't need to see it, Signore. I know policemen when I see them.'

Brunetti abandoned the attempt and tried to sit upright, but his position was so constricting that he got to his feet and sat on the arm of the chair. 'I was called last night when Signora Altavilla's body was found, and I went to her apartment. I spoke to her neighbour,' he said, and the nun nodded, suggesting that she knew the woman and her closeness to Signora Altavilla or that she knew about the phone call.

'The autopsy that was performed this morning . . .' he began and saw the nun's eyes contract. ' . . . suggests that she died of a heart attack.' He paused and looked in her direction.

'Suggests?' Madre Rosa asked.

'There was a cut on her forehead, which the pathologist thinks must have happened when she fell. I was there last night and saw that she had fallen close to a radiator: that might explain it.' She nodded, understanding, but not necessarily believing.

Brunetti noticed then something he had not seen since he was a boy in elementary school: she reached under her long white scapular and pulled up the string of rosary beads she wore at her side. She held them as she looked at him, then let one of them slip through her fingers, and then another. He had no idea if she was praying or merely touching them to give herself strength and comfort. Finally she said only, 'Might explain?'

Brunetti, as he always did when people caught him in prevarication, gave an easy, relaxed smile. 'We won't know what happened until the physical evidence from her apartment is examined.'

'And you won't know it then, either, will you?' she asked. 'Not for sure, that is.'

Brunetti watched Vianello cross and uncross his legs, then he got to his feet, as well. He put his hands on his hips and bent backwards, and when he came forward again, he said, 'Madre, if we could use one of these chairs for people we're questioning, I think we'd save a great deal of our time. And have a great deal more success.'

She tried to stop herself from smiling, but she failed. Then she surprised them both by saying, in purest Veneziano, '*Ti xe na bronsa coverta.*' Hearing her so effortlessly go from her accented Italian to perfectly pronounced dialect surprised both of the men into answering smiles. Her assessment was accurate: Vianello was much like the embers in a covered brazier. One never knew what brightness lurked there or what light might break forth from his invisible silence.

Almost as if she disapproved of the way the mood had lightened and wanted to put an end to that, she erased her smile. She glanced between them, and Brunetti saw the wariness return to her face. 'What is it you'd like to know about Costanza?' she asked. The raising of her guard had aged her: she stiffened her back against the muscles that had allowed her to lean forward, and her face sagged tiredly.

Vianello imitated Brunetti by sitting on the thick arm of his chair. He took his notebook from his side pocket, opened his pen, and prepared to take notes. 'We don't know anything at all about her, Madre Rosa,' Brunetti said. 'Her neighbour and her son both praised her.'

'I don't doubt that,' she said.

When it seemed she had no more to say, Brunetti went on, 'I'd like to know something about her, Madre.' Again he waited for the nun to say something, but she did not.

'Was she popular with the people here?' he asked, waving his hand to encompass the entire home.

The nun answered almost at once. 'She was generous with her time. She was retired, I think in her mid-sixties, so she had a life of her own, but still she listened to them. She took some of them out for walks, down to the *riva*, even on to the boats if they wanted that.' Brunetti gave no hint of the surprise with which her sudden loquacity filled him.

Neither man responded, so she added, 'Sometimes she'd spend the morning watching the boats go by while they talked, or sit with them in their rooms here and listen to them.

She'd let them talk to her for hours, and she always paid attention to what they said. Asked questions, remembered what they'd told her on previous visits.' She waved a hand towards the door of the room in imitation of Brunetti's gesture. 'It makes them feel important, to think that what they say is interesting and that someone will remember it.' Brunetti wondered if she included herself among those who would listen to and remember their stories, or if it would make her feel important to have someone remember what she said.

'Did she treat them all the same way?' Brunetti asked.

He saw that she wasn't prepared for this question and didn't like it when she heard it. Perhaps she disapproved of friendships with the old people; perhaps she simply disapproved of friendships. 'Yes. Of course,' she said; Brunetti noticed that she clenched the rosary in her fist: no more easy flow of beads.

'No special friends?' Brunetti enquired.

'No,' she said instantly. 'Patients aren't friends. She knew the danger of that.'

Confused, Vianello asked, 'What danger?'

'Many of them are lonely,' she said. 'And many of them have families that are waiting for them to die so they can have their money or their homes.' She waited for a moment, as if to see if they would be shocked that a nun could speak with this bleak clarity. In the face of their silence, she continued, 'So the danger is that they will become too attached to people who treat them well. Costanza . . .' she began but did not finish whatever it was she intended to say. Instead, she changed back to her original subject and said, 'They can be very difficult, old people.'

'I know,' Brunetti agreed, omitting any reference to how he had learned this truth. Then, after a short pause, he said, 'But I'm afraid – and I say this with all respect – that you haven't told us very much about her.'

Madre Rosa gave a wry grimace. 'I shouldn't say this,

Signore, and I hope the Lord will pardon me for having thought it, but if you knew how difficult many of the people here can be, perhaps you'd understand. It's very easy to be kind to people who are kind themselves or who are appreciative of kindness, but that is not always the case.' From the tired resignation with which the nun said this, Brunetti realized hers was the voice of long experience. He also realised that this was all she was going to say.

Brunetti and Vianello exchanged a look and, as if by mutual agreement, got to their feet. In a way, Brunetti's thoughts also shook themselves out and stood up straight. They had come all the way down here, and all this woman had done was speak of Signora Altavilla's patience and had been anything but forthcoming in doing so. For their purposes, they had learned next to nothing about Signora Altavilla, though peace be on her soul. 'Thank you, Madre,' Brunetti said, not sure whether he should offer his hand to her or not. She made the decision for him, confining herself to a nod, first to him and then to Vianello, her hands safely tucked under her scapular, then turned and led them towards the front entrance.

She paused at the door as she said, 'I hope you'll convey my condolences to her son. I never met him, but Costanza spoke about him from time to time and always had good things to say.' Then, as if answering some unspoken question on their part, she added, 'It sounds as though he's inherited her terrible honesty.'

'What do you mean by that, Madre?' Brunetti asked.

It took her a long time to answer, so long that she had to shift her weight to her left side as she stood there. When she finally spoke, she answered with a question. 'You hear I'm from the South, don't you?'

Both men nodded.

'We have different ideas about honesty than you do up here,' she said obliquely.

Vianello smiled and said, 'To say the least of it, Madre.'

She had the grace to return his smile and spoke to the Inspector as she continued. 'Just because our ideas are different doesn't mean we don't have as great a respect for honesty as you do, Signori.'

Neither man spoke, curious to learn where this was going to lead. 'But we are . . .' she stopped and glanced from one face to the other. 'How can I say this? We are more frugal with the truth than you are.'

Frankly curious, Brunetti asked, 'And why is that, Madre?'

Again, to get a better look at them, she stepped back awkwardly. 'Perhaps because it costs us more to be honest than it does you,' she said. Her accent had become more pronounced. She went on, 'So we've come to value reticence, as well.'

'Are you talking about Signora Altavilla?' Brunetti asked.

'Yes. She believed that one should always tell the truth, regardless of the cost. And I assume, from some of the things she told me, that she taught this to her son.'

'Do you think that's an error?' Brunetti asked with real curiosity.

'No, gentlemen,' she said and smiled again, a smaller smile. 'It's a luxury.'

She reached behind her and opened the door; she held it as they passed through, and they heard it close as they started down the steps.

9

As they emerged into the sunlight, Vianello said, 'I never know what to do in situations like this.'

'Situations like what?' Brunetti asked, starting across the *campo* and back towards the Questura.

'When someone pretends to know less than they do.'

Brunetti turned to the left and towards the church. 'Hmmm,' he muttered, letting Vianello know that he agreed.

'All that talk about honesty,' Vianello said. He stopped at the top of the bridge and rested his forearms on the parapet. He stared down at a boat moored to the side of the canal and continued, 'It's clear she knows – or suspects – more than she's willing to let on. She's a nun, so she probably believes it's not right to raise unfounded suspicions or pass on gossip.' Then, in a lower voice, he added, 'Though I can't imagine a convent where that doesn't happen.'

Brunetti let that pass, waiting.

'She's a southerner,' Vianello said. 'And a nun.' Brunetti grew alert to hear just what sort of generalization was coming. Vianello went on, 'So that means she wanted us to know or suspect something but couldn't bring herself to say it directly.'

Brunetti had to agree. Who knew what went on the mind of a nun, much less one from the South? They drank discretion with the first taste of mother's milk and grew up with frequent examples of the consequences of indiscretion. He remembered the recent shock-video of a very ordinary, very casual, daytime murder in Naples: one shot, then the second to the back of the head, while people continued about their business. No one saw anything; no one noticed a thing.

It was hard-wired into them: to talk indiscreetly or say anything that might cause suspicion was to endanger not only yourself but everyone in your family. This was the Truth, no matter how many years a person had spent in a convent in Venice. Brunetti was as likely to sprout angel wings and fly off to Paradise as Madre Rosa was to speak openly to the police.

'She made truth sound like a handicap, didn't she?' Vianello shoved himself away from the parapet. He raised his arms and let them fall to his sides in a gesture of complete confusion, but before Brunetti could speak, they were interrupted by the ringing of his phone.

'Guido? It's me,' Rizzardi said.

'Thanks for calling.'

Wasting no time, Rizzardi went on: 'The mark on her throat,' he said, but then stopped. When Brunetti said nothing, the pathologist continued, 'It could be a thumbprint.'

Brunetti tried to imagine where the other fingers could have been when the thumbs were on her throat, but he permitted himself only, 'Ah.' And then, "Could be"?'

Rizzardi ignored the provocation and continued. 'There are three faint marks that are probably bruises on the back of her left shoulder, and two on her right. And another one – barely visible – in front.'

Brunetti tilted his head to the side and trapped the phone

against his shoulder. He raised his cupped hands in front of him, then he positioned his thumbs and bent his hands into claws. 'Are the marks in the right places?' he asked, not thinking it necessary, with Rizzardi, to say more than that.

'Yes,' the pathologist answered, then slipped back into his usual mode to continue, 'They are not inconsistent with her having been grabbed from the front.'

'"Not inconsistent"?' Brunetti asked.

Ignoring this, Rizzardi asked, 'You remember the cardigan she was wearing?'

'Yes,' Brunetti answered.

'It would have cushioned a lot of the force: that could explain why the marks are so diffused.'

'Could it be anything else?' Brunetti asked, wondering if Rizzardi's caution was like an accent, and he would never lose it.

'In the mouth of a clever defence attorney, those marks on her back,' Rizzardi began, his speculation about a possible court case sufficient to tell Brunetti how convinced he was that Signora Altavilla had been the victim of violence, regardless of how unwilling he was to say it directly, 'could have happened when she fell against a radiator, or she had been trying to give herself a back massage and squeezed too hard, or she lost her balance and fell against the door when she was letting herself into the apartment—'

Brunetti cut him off. 'Ettore, don't tell me what it could be. Tell me what it is.'

Rizzardi behaved as if Brunetti had not spoken and went on, 'I know lawyers and you know lawyers who would argue she fell against the door five times, Guido.'

Unable to bridle his anger, Brunetti snapped, 'I can figure out for myself what could have happened. For God's sake, just tell me what did happen.' There followed a long pause, during which Brunetti considered that he might have gone too far. People did not talk to Rizzardi that way.

'Someone grabbed her from the front, and it's possible they shook her,' Rizzardi said with a clarity that surprised Brunetti. No hesitation, no rhetorical self-protection, no compromise. When had the pathologist ever been this clear?

'Why do you say that?'

'There's something else.'

'What?'

'There's a very faint injury to her third and fourth vertebrae. And some haemorrhaging in the muscles and ligaments around them.'

Brunetti refused to ask, bent on forcing Rizzardi to say it.

'So someone could have shaken her.'

'Or?'

'Or it could have happened when she fell. The blow to her head was very hard, and she hit the radiator. I saw that last night.'

'Or she was pushed,' Brunetti said.

'I can't say that,' Rizzardi told him.

Brunetti felt as though Rizzardi had a ration of frankness, and now he had used it up.

Finally the doctor said firmly, 'Nothing is going to change the fact that the cause of death was a heart attack.' Again, a pause that Brunetti did not interrupt, and then Rizzardi said, 'Her heart was in bad shape, and a shock of any sort could easily have sent her into fibrillation.'

Brunetti was aware of Vianello at his side, unable to disguise his curiosity.

'Did your men find propafenone in her apartment?' the doctor asked.

Brunetti had not seen a written report of the results of the search, so he avoided answering and asked, 'What's that?'

'It's used for fibrillation; which is what killed her. A shock would bring it on.'

If you burn down a house and don't know there's a person inside, are you guilty of murder? If you kidnap a diabetic and

77

don't give them insulin, are you responsible for their death? And if you frighten a person with a weak heart? Rizzardi was right, this was a defence lawyer's playground.

'I'll check. They will have listed everything,' Brunetti said, though that was never a sure thing. 'Anything else?'

'No. Aside from the heart, she was healthy for a woman in her mid-sixties.' Rizzardi paused for a long time. 'But it was a ticking bomb, so maybe it didn't matter how healthy she was.' Brunetti heard a click, and the doctor's voice was gone.

Brunetti switched off his phone and put it in his pocket. Turning to Vianello, he said, 'She died of a heart attack. But he found signs that someone might have shaken her. That might have caused it.'

Vianello gave him an appreciative look. 'You got Rizzardi to say that?'

Ignoring him, Brunetti said, 'So we take a closer look at her life.'

Sounding almost angry, Vianello said, 'She sounds like a decent person, not the sort who'd get threatened or shaken. Or killed. Good people shouldn't be killed like that.'

Brunetti thought about this for some time, and then said, 'Would that that were true.'

10

When he got to his office, Brunetti found nothing. That is, he found nothing from the crime squad: no photos of Signora Altavilla, no photos of the apartment or list of the objects found in it. He sat at his desk and thought about some of those objects, trying to find a way to see them as reflective of her life.

The apartment and the things in it had given no clue to her financial status. There had been a time, decades ago, when a mere address might resolve any doubt. San Marco and the *palazzi* on the Canal Grande bespoke prosperity, while to live in Castello was to confess to poverty. But vast amounts of money had migrated to the city; thus any building and any address could now be the newly restored home of luxury and excess, while the former owners or tenants reversed the path of generations and moved to the mainland, leaving the city to those who could afford it.

Brunetti ran his memory through the rooms. The furniture had been of good quality, all of it from some epoch between the old and the antique. There had been few books, few decorative objects: he could not remember a single painting. The whole place spoke of simplicity and of a pared-down life. What lingered most strongly in his memory was the placement of the sofa and the table: what sort of person would turn away from the view of the church and the mountains? Not only for herself but for guests who came to the apartment? He knew not everyone was addicted to beauty, but to choose to look at that boring room instead of both man-made and natural beauty made no sense to Brunetti and made him uneasy about a person who would make such a choice.

What to make of the unopened packets of cheap under-wear in the drawers of the spare bedroom? A woman who bought cashmere sweaters of the quality of the ones in her drawers, regardless of her age, would not wear cotton underwear like that, or else his ideas about women were more mistaken than Paola occasionally said they were.

And why the three different sizes? Niccolini's daughter, should she visit her grandmother, could hardly be old enough to wear even the smallest size; besides, parents were usually careful to send along the proper clothes when their children spent the night away from home. It might be that friends came to visit or perhaps sent their daughters to stay for a time in Venice. And the unopened toiletries in the bathroom? A person did not prepare for unexpected visits with that kind of thoroughness. It was her home, after all, not a hotel or lodging house.

He left his desk and went downstairs. Over the course of the years, he had discussed many topics with Signorina Elettra, though female lingerie was not among them. She was standing at her window when he came in, arms folded, looking across the canal at the same view that greeted him from his own windows: the façade of San Lorenzo looked no less decrepit from one floor below.

She turned and smiled. 'Can I be of help, Commissario?'

'Perhaps,' Brunetti said and walked over to her desk. He

leaned back against it and crossed his legs. Light streamed through the window, not only from the sun but from its reflection on the water in the canal below. He saw her thus in profile and realized that the outline of her features was less sharp than he remembered its being. Her chin was less clear-cut, her skin on her cheekbone less tightly drawn. He noticed, too, the small wrinkles on the outer side of her eye. He looked away and studied the church.

'Have you any idea what it means if the drawers in the guest room of an apartment hold unopened packages of women's underwear, but in three different sizes?' She looked at him, and he saw her brow contract in confusion. 'And tights and sweaters, also in different sizes.' Then, recalling who he was speaking to and knowing this detail would make a difference, he added, 'All plain cotton, the sort of thing you'd buy at a supermarket.'

She unfolded her arms and raised her chin, glancing back at the church. Her attention on the façade, she asked, 'Is this in a man's apartment or is it in the apartment you went to last night?'

'It's what we found in Signora Altavilla's apartment, yes,' he answered. 'Why do you ask?'

Attention still directed at the church, as if consulting with it to find an answer, she said, 'Because in a man's apartment, it would suggest one thing; in a woman's, something entirely different.'

'What would it suggest in a man's?' he asked, though he suspected he knew.

She turned to face him and answered, 'In a man's, it would suggest fresh underwear for a woman – or for the women – he brought home for the night,' she said, pausing to consider the sound of this. Then she added, sounding less certain, 'But then it probably wouldn't be simple cotton, would it? And it wouldn't be in another room. Not unless he was very strange indeed.'

81

Presumably, then, she considered it not at all strange for a man to keep women's underwear in differing sizes in his home, so long as it was expensive and kept in his bedroom. For a moment, Brunetti wondered what other information had been closed off to him by the vows of matrimony. But he confined himself to asking, 'And in a woman's?'

'There's nothing to preclude the same explanation,' she said, surprising him with how ordinary she managed to make it sound. But then she smiled and added, 'But more likely it would suggest she brought the women home for some more prosaic reason.'

'Such as?' he asked.

'Such as to protect them from the sort of men who would invite them home for one night,' she said in a tone that suggested she might be serious.

'That's a puritanical vision of things.'

'Not necessarily,' she said levelly. Then, in a more accommodating voice, she went on, 'It's more likely she's helping illegal refugee women, letting them stay with her – safely – while they look for work or find a place to live.' She paused, and he watched her run through possibilities. 'Or it could be that she wanted to protect them from other people.'

'Such as?'

'Any man who thought he had a right over them. A boyfriend. A pimp.'

He gave her a level look but did not say anything. Brunetti toyed with her idea and, after a while, found that he liked the feel of it. To test it, he said, 'Do you think she could organize that on her own? After all, where would she find out about them or be put in touch with them?'

As a knight would first swing into the saddle of his horse before lifting his lance, Signorina Elettra returned to the chair behind her computer. She hit a few keys, studied the screen, and hit a few more. Brunetti pushed himself away from the desk and turned to watch. After some time she waved a hand to him and said, 'Come and have a look.'

He moved behind her and looked at the screen. He saw the usual photomontage of a woman, her face turned away from the viewer, the menacing shadow of a man lurking behind her. A headline declared 'Stop Illegal Immigration.' Below it were a few sentences, offering support and help and providing an 800 telephone number. He did not read the full text, but he did take out his notebook and write down the number.

'You remember what the President said last year?' Signorina Elettra asked him.

'About this?' he asked, indicating the screen and what it held.

'Yes. Do you remember the number he gave?'

'Of victims?'

'Yes.'

'No, I don't.'

'I do,' she said, and Brunetti could all but hear her adding that she remembered because she was a woman and he did not because he was a man. But she said nothing else, and Brunetti did not ask.

'Would you like me to do anything, sir? Call them?'

'No,' he said too quickly; he saw that she was surprised by the answer as well as by the speed with which he gave it. 'I'll do it.' He wanted to say something more to cover up the force of his response to her proposal, but that would be to draw attention to it.

'Anything else, Commissario?' he heard her asking.

'No, thank you, Signorina. The number's enough.'

'As you will, Dottore,' she said and bent her head over the screen.

Walking up the steps, Brunetti was assailed by uneasiness about his strong rebuff of Signorina Elettra's offer; she was so obviously superior to most of the people who worked at the Questura that she deserved far better of him. Inventive and clever, she was also well versed in the law and would have been an ornament to any police department lucky enough to hire her as an officer. But she was not, and he should not permit her to present herself as a police officer when asking questions or requesting information on the phone. It was bad enough that he turned a blind eye to the various acts of cyber-piracy in which he knew she engaged; indeed, acts which he encouraged her to commit. There was a line somewhere between what she could and could not be permitted to do: Brunetti's dilemma was that the line he drew was never straight and was never drawn in the same place twice.

On his desk, delivered there he had no idea how, Brunetti found the autopsy report as well as the one from the scene of crime team. He stacked the papers in the centre of the desk, pulled his reading glasses from their case in his pocket, slipped them on, and started to read.

Rizzardi, a quiet man and not at all given to vanity or boasting, could not resist the temptation to show off in two fields: his dress and his prose. Understated, subtle in colour, his suits and overcoats, even his raincoat, were of such a quality as to make Brunetti suspicious of his sources of income; his prose was of a grammatical precision and inventiveness of expression Brunetti despaired of finding in any of the other reports he read. It was not unusual for the pathologist to describe an organ as being 'captive within the tendrils of small veins', or to describe the 'starburst' of cigarette burns on the back of a victim of torture. Indeed, the report of the first autopsy Rizzardi had done at Brunetti's request had described the slash marks on the victim's stomach, from which he had bled to death, by saying, 'The wounds are reminiscent of Fontana when he worked in red.'

There were no flourishes, however, in his report on Signora Altavilla. He described the condition of her heart, making it clear that the cause of death had been uncontrollable fibrillation. He described the injury to the vertebrae and surrounding tissue and described the cut on her forehead, saying that they were not inconsistent with a bad fall soon before her death. Brunetti put his report aside long enough to open the technicians' report, where he found reference to the presence of blood and skin tissue on the radiator in the sitting room, blood of the same type as Signora Altavilla's.

Rizzardi also described 'a grey mark,' 2.1 centimetres in length and close to the left of the collarbone of the dead woman. The marks on her shoulders were 'barely visible', as banal an expression as Brunetti had ever known the pathologist to use.

He read quickly through the rest of the report: signs of her having given birth at least once, the seam left by a broken left wrist, a bunion on her right foot. Rizzardi presented the physical information without comment. Brunetti knew that, in a police department led by Vice-Questore Giuseppe Patta, physical evidence this inconclusive was likely to lead to the conclusion of natural death.

Brunetti placed the technicians' preliminary report on top of Rizzardi's and read through it carefully this time. He noticed a certain willingness to cater to Patta's preference for non-interpretation. Aside from the blood on the radiator, the examination of the house suggested nothing beyond 'normal domestic use'.

Then, on the last page, came a hammer blow to any hope Brunetti might have had of conducting an investigation. Propafenone was found in the medicine cabinet in Signora Altavilla's bathroom. Thus proof of a pre-existing condition validated Rizzardi's posthumous diagnosis of death by heart fibrillation.

Brunetti set the report on top of Rizzardi's and carefully tapped at the sides of the papers until they were aligned. He folded his hands and placed them in the middle of the top sheet. He studied his thumbs, noticed that the right-hand cuff of his shirt was beginning to fray, then looked away from it and out the window.

The reports would please Patta: that was a given. But they would also please – Brunetti was equally certain of this – Niccolini. No, that was the wrong word: too strong. Slowly, as though it were a film he could view at will and at leisure, Brunetti played over his meeting with the veterinarian.

His emotion, really, might more accurately be called relief, the same emotion Brunetti had seen on the faces of people when hearing the verdict 'Innocent' read out. But innocent of what? No stranger to pretence and emotional forgery, Brunetti did not doubt the intensity of Niccolini's pain. He recalled the doctor's face after he blurted out that he too had performed autopsies. And, remembering that scene, Brunetti grew indignant that he could have been left there, while he knew what was being done in the nearby room.

He unfolded his hands and dialled the internal number for the officers' squad room, asked to speak to Vianello. When the Inspector answered, Brunetti said, 'I think we should go back and have another look at her apartment.'

'Now?' asked an audibly reluctant Vianello.

'Why?'

'It's almost seven,' the Inspector began. Surprised, Brunetti looked at his watch and saw that it was so. 'You think we could leave it until tomorrow morning?' Vianello asked. Before Brunetti could answer, the Inspector said, 'I'll call this Signora Giusti and tell her we'll be there – what time should I say?'

Brunetti was tempted to ask Vianello if he was making a suggestion or giving an order. Instead, he said, 'Ten would be fine.'

11

They took the Number One but chose to sit inside, where Brunetti told Vianello about the contents of both Rizzardi's and the technicians' reports. He also gave him his general impression of Niccolini as a man made uncomfortable by unsaid things.

As the boat passed in front of the Piazza, Brunetti looked to the right and asked, 'It never becomes ordinary, does it?' Before Vianello could answer and as though the Inspector had removed it from his drawer while he was out of the office, Brunetti added, 'Where'd yesterday go?'

'We walked,' Vianello said.

'What?'

'It's not like the movies, where you get in a car and speed to where you're going, siren blaring. You know that. We walked, and then we walked back. So it took a long time. And the old nun, even if she didn't want to tell us anything, she still took a fair amount of time doing it. We're not in New York, Guido,' he said and smiled to show the vast relief with which he greeted that fact.

As if to argue in favour of Vianello's assertion, they were strafed by a sudden burst of light reflected from the windows of the buildings on the left side of the canal. Their eyes followed the origin of the dazzle to the row of buildings: beige, ochre, something between yellow and brown, pink; and then the windows: pointing up and pirouetting at the top, pushing aside twisted columns in order to let in more light. Then, barely seen at the waterline, the enormous cubes of stone from which the city leaped up towards the heavens.

'We should have had Foa take us,' Brunetti said, still unsettled by how swiftly the previous day had passed. Spurred by his restlessness, they got off at San Silvestro and walked: it would take the same time if they waited to get off at San Stae, but at least this way they were moving.

As they walked, Brunetti explained that he wanted to take another look at the place. 'And talk to the neighbour,' he added as they walked down the bridge from San Boldo, turned into Calle del Tintor and towards the *campo*.

Brunetti was wearing the same jacket and pulled the keys from his pocket. The largest of the three opened the street door, and the one next to it fitted the lock on the door to the apartment, where Vianello's tape was still in place. Brunetti pulled it loose on one side and let it hang free before opening the door.

Inside, he noticed the envelopes he had seen the night before, leafed through them, and saw that they were all – including a registered letter – addressed to Signora Giusti. He slipped them into the pocket of his jacket. During the next half-hour, they found nothing more than they had the night before save for receipts for bills that had been paid through the post office and bank records stretching back five years. Looking through them, Brunetti saw an entirely normal pattern: her pension arrived each month, along with a second payment from what might have been her widow's pension. The first amount reflected the fact that she had chosen to retire early; the second one was more substantial and raised her monthly income to a sum on which a single person could live very comfortably. This would be even easier – Brunetti saw no sign that she had been paying rent through the bank – for a woman living in an apartment she owned.

One thing that caught Brunetti's attention were the tiny nails, lonely nails that had lost their paintings. There were two in the corridor, under them only rectangles of paint minimally whiter than the paint on the wall. In the smaller bedroom, now that Brunetti knew to look, he saw another phantom painting and, above it, the nail.

By mutual consent, they decided to go upstairs. When they left, Vianello reattached the tape as best he could while Brunetti stood, keys in hand, waiting to lock the door. After he did, he held the keys in the palm of his hand and showed them to Vianello and said, 'I wonder what the third one's for.'

'Perhaps a storeroom downstairs?' the Inspector suggested.

Brunetti started up the stairs. 'We can ask Signora Giusti.'

The woman opened the door to her apartment while they were still on the final flight of steps. 'I heard you moving around down there,' she said by way of greeting, then remembered to put out her hand and say good morning. She looked less agitated now, and Brunetti was surprised to realize that she no longer seemed as tall. Perhaps it had something to do with the relaxation of her body or her shoulders. She had also moved closer to the loveliness he had imagined before.

Brunetti introduced Vianello, and she let them into the apartment, which Brunetti thought had relaxed as much as she had. The table in the living room held two newspapers, one of them open to the Culture section, the other obviously gone through and sloppily closed. Beside it stood an empty glass and a plate that held the skin and core of an apple as well as the knife that had peeled it. The cushions on the sofa were dented; one lay on the floor.

In the front room Brunetti was again struck by the sense of drama created by the thrust of the apse seen from this height and angle, as if the church were caught in the high seas and heading towards them. Her furniture, two chairs and a sofa, were angled to look out at the church and the *campo* and the mountains beyond. She sat at the end of the sofa, leaving them the two chairs, a table between them. She did not bother asking if they would like anything to drink.

Brunetti removed the envelopes from his pocket and placed them on the table. Signora Giusti glanced at them but made no move to touch them. Looking at him, she nodded her thanks, sober-faced. Brunetti still had the keys in his hands, and he held them out to her. 'There's a third key on the set you left downstairs, Signora. Could you tell me what it's for?'

She shook her head. 'I have no idea. I asked her that same thing, when she gave me the keys, and she said it was . . .' She paused and closed her eyes. 'It was strange what she said.' Vianello and Brunetti remained quiet to give her the time to remember. After a moment, she looked up and said, 'She said something about its being a safe place to keep a key.'

She met their puzzled expression with one of her own. 'No, it doesn't make any sense to me, either, but that's what she said, that it would be a safe place.'

'When did she give you these keys, Signora?'

She was surprised by his question, as though it displayed some special power on his part. 'Why do you ask?'

'Simple curiosity,' Brunetti said. He had no idea how long either woman had lived there, so he had no idea how long it had taken before they trusted one another sufficiently to exchange the keys to their homes.

'I've had a set of her keys for years, but a week ago she asked for them back for a day, said something about wanting to have copies made.' She pointed to the keys as though looking at them would make the two men understand. Then she leaned over and touched them, saying, 'But look at them.

One's red and one's blue. They're just cheap copies, probably doesn't even cost a euro to have them made.'

'And so?' Brunetti asked.

'And so why would she copy these when she has the master keys? When she gave them back to me, the third key was on the ring, too, and that's when she said that, about its being a safe place to keep it.' She looked at each of them in turn, searching for some sign that they found this as puzzling as she did.

'Did she know where you kept them?' Brunetti asked.

'Of course. I've kept them in the same place for years, and she knew where that was,' she said, pointing towards a room that was probably the kitchen. 'There. In the second drawer.' Brunetti stopped himself from saying that was precisely where a competent housebreaker would look.

'Do you have storerooms on the ground floor?' Brunetti asked. 'Is one of them hers?'

She shook the idea away. 'No, they belong to the appliance store near the pizzeria and to one of the restaurants in the *campo*.'

He noticed that Vianello had silently managed to take out his notebook and was busy writing.

'Could you give me some idea of the sort of life she led, Signora?'

'Costanza?'

'Yes.'

'She was a retired teacher. I think she retired about five years ago. Taught little children. And now she visits old people who are in rest homes.' As if suddenly aware of the dissonance between events and the present tense, she put her hand to her mouth.

Brunetti let the moment pass and then asked, 'Did she have guests?'

'Guests?'

'People who came to stay with her. Perhaps you met them

on the stairs, or perhaps she told you that you would see strangers coming in, just so you'd know and not be concerned.'

'Yes, I'd see people on the steps, occasionally. They were always very polite.'

'Women?' Vianello asked.

'Yes,' she said casually, and then added, 'Her son came to see her.'

'Yes, I know. I spoke to him yesterday,' Brunetti answered, curious about her reluctance to discuss the female visitors.

'How is he?' she asked with real concern.

'When I spoke to him, he seemed battered by it.' This was no exaggeration; Brunetti suspected it stated the reality that lay behind Niccolini's reserve.

'She loved him. And the grandchildren.' Then, with a small smile, 'And she was very fond of her daughter-in-law, too.' She shook her head, as if at the discovery of some exception to the rule of gravity.

'Did she speak of them often?'

'No, not really. Costanza – you have to understand – was not by nature a talkative person. It's only because I've known her for years that I know any of this.'

'How many years?' Vianello interrupted to ask and held up his notebook as if to suggest he was simply doing what the pages told him to do.

'She was living here when I moved in,' she said. 'That was five years ago. I think she'd been here for a few years before that, since her husband died.'

'Did she say why she moved?' Vianello asked, eyes on what he was writing.

'She said the old place – it was near San Polo – was too big, and that once she was alone – her son was married by then – she decided to find somewhere smaller.'

'But stay in the city?' Vianello asked.

'Of course,' she said and gave Vianello a strange look.

'Let me go back to something,' Brunetti said. 'About her guests.'

'Guests,' she repeated, as if she had quite forgotten having been asked the question before.

'Yes,' Brunetti said with his easiest smile. Then he went on, 'Well, perhaps you wouldn't be so much aware of them, up here. I can ask the people downstairs: they're more likely to have noticed.' He cleared his throat, as if preparing to change the subject and ask another question entirely.

'As I told you, occasionally people did stay. Women,' she said. 'Occasionally.'

'I see,' Brunetti said, sounding only faintly interested, 'Friends?'

'I don't know.'

Vianello looked up and said, with an easy smile, 'Everyone wants to come and stay in Venice. My wife and I are always being asked if the sons or daughters of friends can stay, and our kids always have friends they want to invite.' He shook his head at the thought, as though he were the concierge of a quiet bed and breakfast in Castello – conveniently located out of the crowded city centre – and not an *ispettore di polizia*. The news of these requests surprised Brunetti. Considering the young age of his children and the fact that all of Vianello's friends lived in Venice, what the inspector said was very unlikely, but, apparently convinced by his own story, Vianello went on to conclude, 'That's probably who they were,' and bent his head over his pages.

'Perhaps,' Signora Giusti said uncertainly.

Sensing her hesitation, Brunetti abandoned his casual tone and spoke with the seriousness he thought this matter warranted. 'Signora, we simply want to understand what sort of woman she was. Everyone we speak to says she was a good person, and I have no reason not to believe it. But that doesn't give me any real understanding of her. So anything you can tell me might help.'

'Help what?' she asked with a sharpness that surprised Brunetti. 'What is it you're really asking about? You're the police, and nothing good ever comes of getting mixed up with you. Since you came in here, you've been mixing truth with what you think I want or need to hear, but what you've never said is why these questions are important.'

She paused, but it was not to try to calm herself, nor to listen to anything either one of them might try to say. 'I looked at the newspapers, and they're saying she died of a heart attack. If that's true, then there's no need for you to be here, asking these questions.'

'I can understand your concern, Signora, living in the same building,' Brunetti said.

She raised both hands to her temples and pressed against the side of her head, as if there were too much noise or too much pain. 'Stop it, stop it, stop it. Either tell me what's going on or get out of here, the two of you.' By the time she finished, she was almost shouting.

Training warred against instinct; Brunetti's experience of human nature came up against his feelings of human sympathy. Caution won. Once someone knew something, you were no longer in control of it, for they were free to do with it what they pleased, and what they pleased need not be what pleased you, and often was not.

'All right,' he said, forcing his body to relax into an easier posture, one reflective of honesty. 'The cause was a heart attack; there's no question of that. But we would like to exclude the possibility that someone might have created conditions favourable to it.'

She bristled at the jargon and said, 'What does that mean?'

Calmly, as though he had not noticed her reaction, he went on, 'It means that someone might have . . .' and here he paused and gave every appearance of pausing to assess her trustworthiness before he went on, 'frightened her or threatened her.'

94

More calmly, she asked, 'Is this an official investigation?'

He lapsed into the truth. 'No, not really. Perhaps it's for my peace of mind, or her son's. But I'd like to exclude the possibility that she was . . . that she was forced or frightened into death. I want to know if someone menaced her in any way, and I thought you might know something.'

'Does it make a difference?' she asked instantly.

'To what?'

'Legally,' she said.

Without telling her about those small marks on Signora Altavilla's neck and shoulders, Brunetti had no answer to give her.

She got up and went over to the front window that looked into the *campo* and at the thrusting church. Back still to them, she said, 'From down on the ground, when I go out the door, I see the church, and it looks one way: heavy, locked into the ground. But from up here, it looks almost as if it had wings.' She paused for a long time; Brunetti and Vianello exchanged a glance.

'Same church. Different angle,' she said and again lapsed into silence.

'Like Costanza,' she said after a long pause, and Brunetti and Vianello exchanged a quicker glance. 'When I first saw the women on the stairs, I had no idea who they were. I knew they weren't cleaning women because we use the same one, Luba. But I couldn't ask Costanza. Because she was such a private person. But they'd be there, and I'd see the same ones a few times. In the beginning, as I said, I really didn't notice them. And then I did, but they never caused any trouble, were always very polite, so I just sort of got used to them.'

'Until?' Brunetti asked, sensing that he was meant to ask and that she needed help to tell this story.

'Until I found one of them on the steps, well, on the landing in front of Costanza's door: I was coming up the steps, and there she was. Costanza wasn't home – I rang her bell – and this girl was lying there. At first I thought she might be drunk or something. I don't know why I thought that; they'd always been very quiet.' She looked away, and Brunetti could see her thinking about what she had just said. 'Maybe it's because they'd all looked poor, and it was my bourgeois prejudice coming out.' They watched her shoulders rise in an unconscious shrug. 'I don't know.

'I couldn't just leave her there, so I tried to help her get up. She was moaning, so I knew she wasn't unconscious. That's when I saw her face. Her nose was pushed to one side, and there was a lot of blood down the front of her coat. At first I didn't notice it because the coat was black and I hadn't really seen her face until I got her to sit up.'

Signora Giusti turned around and folded her arms across her chest. 'I asked her what had happened, and she said she had fallen on the street. So I said I was going to call an ambulance and take her to the hospital.'

'Was she Italian?' Vianello asked.

'No, I don't know where she was from. The East somewhere, I'd say, but I'm not sure.'

'Did she speak Italian?'

'Enough to understand what I said and to tell me about falling. "*Cadere. Pavimento.*" That sort of thing. And enough to understand "*ospedale*".'

'What did she do?'

'When she heard me say that, she panicked. She grabbed my hand and said "*Prego, prego,*" again and again. "*No ospedale.*" Things like that.'

'What happened?' Brunetti asked.

'I heard – we both heard – the door open. The front door downstairs.' She closed her eyes, remembering the scene. 'The woman – she was really still a girl. Couldn't have been much more than a teenager, really – she panicked. I've never seen anyone do this, just read about it. She crawled over to the corner and pushed herself into it. She pulled her coat up over her head as if she thought that would hide her or make her invisible. But she kept moaning, so anyone would know she was there.'

'And then?'

'And then Costanza came up. She didn't say anything, just stopped at the top of the steps. The girl was moaning again by then, like an animal. I started to say something, but she held up a hand and said the girl's name, Alessandra or Alexandra, I don't remember which, and then she said that everything was all right and there was nothing to be afraid of, the same sort of thing you'd say to children when they wake up in the night.'

'And the girl?' Vianello asked.

'She stopped moaning, and Costanza went over and knelt down beside her.' She looked at them, surprised to be remembering something now. 'But she didn't touch her. She just said her name a few more times and told her everything was fine and not to worry.'

'Then what?' Brunetti asked.

'I stood up and Costanza said, "Thank you," as though I'd just given her a cup of tea or something. But it was clear that she was telling me to leave, so I did. I went back up to my apartment.'

'Did you ever see the girl again?'

'No. Never. Then, after a few months, there was another one, but I never spoke to any of them again – there might have been two or three more that I knew about.'

'Did Signora Altavilla ever refer to it or say anything to you about it?'

'No. Nothing. It was as though it had never happened, and after a time it felt that way, too. I'd say hello to her – Costanza – on the steps, or she'd ask me in for a cup of tea, or she'd come up here if I suggested it. But neither of us ever said anything about it.' She looked back and forth between them, as if asking them to understand. 'You know how it is. After a time, something that's happened, even if it isn't very nice, if you just don't talk about it, it sort of goes away. Not that you forget about it, not really, but it isn't there any more.'

Brunetti recognized the familiarity of this, and Vianello said, 'It's the only way life can go on, really, if you think about it.'

At this, Brunetti glanced at Signora Giusti and their eyes met. She nodded, and Brunetti found himself nodding in return. Yes, it was the only way life could go on.

12

'Did you ever find out what she was doing?' Brunetti finally asked.

'It doesn't take much to understand, does it?'

'What do you mean?' Brunetti asked.

'I think she was using her apartment as some sort of safe house for . . . well, for women at risk.' Then, before he could ask, she explained, 'From their boyfriends or their husbands, or in the case of these women from the East, for all I know, from the men who own them.'

'Own?' Vianello asked.

'You're a policeman. You should be able to figure it out,' she said, surprising them both with the blunt challenge. Then she went on in a calmer voice, 'What else could they be, if not prostitutes? That woman, Alessandra or Alexandra, she wasn't Italian, she barely spoke the language. I doubt she was anyone's wife. But I know she was frightened, terrified that whoever broke her nose would come back and finish the job. That's probably why she disappeared.'

'Can you remember,' Brunetti began, 'anything that your

neighbour said in all this time – since you noticed the women coming into the house – that would suggest she felt in danger?'

In a voice that strove for patience, she said, 'I told you, Commissario, Costanza was a very private person. She wouldn't say anything like that. It wasn't her way, her style.'

'Even as a joke?' Vianello interrupted to ask.

'People don't joke about things like this,' she said sharply.

Brunetti was of a different mind entirely, having had plenty of evidence of the human capacity to joke at anything, no matter how terrible. It seemed to him an entirely legitimate defence against the looming horror that could afflict us. In this, he was a great admirer of the British; well, of the British who were, with their wry humour in the face of death, their gallows humour – they even had a word for it – defiant to the point of madness.

'Signora,' Brunetti said in a voice meant to restore tranquillity, 'did you draw conclusions on your own?' Before she could ask, he said, 'Here I'm asking for your general feeling or impression of what might have been going on.'

For some reason, his question calmed her visibly. Her shoulders grew less stiff. 'She was doing what she thought was right and trying to help these poor women.' She raised a hand, then turned and left the room and was quickly back, carrying a small piece of paper, the familiar receipt for a bill paid in the post office. She handed it to Brunetti and sat again in her place on the sofa.

'Alba Libera,' he read, wondering what Free Dawn she was involved with.

'Yes,' she said, raising a hand as if to wave away the banality of the title. 'They probably wanted to have a title that would not call attention to itself.'

'And who are they?' Brunetti enquired: it was not the organization Signorina Elettra had found.

'It's a society for women. You can see it's a non-profit,' she said, pointing to the letters that followed its name.

Brunetti restrained his impulse to say that those letters were no guarantee of fiscal probity and, instead, asked, 'What do they do?'

'What Costanza did. Help women who run away, or who try to run away. They have a helpline, and they take it in turn to answer. And if they think there's real danger, then they find a place for them to stay.'

'And then what?' asked the ever-practical Vianello.

Signora Giusti failed to control the coolness of the glance with which she greeted his question. 'Taking them in's a start, wouldn't you say?' she asked. Then she added, 'They try to find them a place to live in a different city. And a job.' She started to say something, stopped, then continued, 'And sometimes they help them change their names. Legally.'

Brunetti nodded. 'How do people give them money?' he asked. 'That is, how did you learn about them?'

She lowered her head and looked attentively at her hands. 'I opened a piece of Costanza's mail,' she said in a low voice. 'It was a mistake. Over the years, we've fallen into the habit of collecting the post from the box downstairs. There's only one for all four apartments. She and I take one another's so it doesn't get confused with the mail for the people on the other floors. Or picked up by their kids. That's happened a few times. So whichever of us comes in first,' she explained, and Brunetti noted how easily she had fallen back into the present tense, 'collects the mail. I put hers on the mat in front of her door, and she puts mine on the table beside her door. But one time – it must have been a year or two ago – I brought one of her envelopes up here by mistake and opened it while I was opening my own. There was a leaflet inside, and I read it through. Pretty terrible stuff. At the end there was one of these payment slips,' she said, leaning over and touching the receipt. 'And when I looked at it, I saw that her name was on it.' She stopped and looked down at her hands, the very picture of a guilty schoolgirl. 'And then I saw that her name was on the envelope.'

'What did you do?' Vianello asked.

'I waited for her to come in, and when I heard her, I went downstairs and gave her the envelope and explained what had happened. She gave me a strange look: I'm not sure she believed me, not really. But she pulled the leaflet out of the envelope – I'd put it back in so it looked as if I hadn't read it – and said I might like to have a look at it.'

She looked back and forth at their faces. 'So I took it, and then I sent them some money, and now I do it every six months or so. They need it, God knows.'

'I see,' Brunetti said. Suddenly his stomach growled. As happens in that situation, everyone pretended they had not heard it. He leaned forward and took out his wallet. He removed one of his visiting cards and wrote his *telefonino* number on the back. 'Signora,' he said, 'this is my own number. If you remember anything or anything happens that you think I should know, please call me.'

Without glancing at the card, she set it on the arm of the sofa and got to her feet. She led them to the door and shook hands with them, wished them good day and closed the door as soon as they were outside the apartment.

'Well?' Vianello asked, as they started down the steps.

'More proof that people don't trust us,' Brunetti said.

'You and me or the police in general?' Vianello asked as they reached the last flight.

'The police,' Brunetti answered and pulled open the door of the building, letting them out into the light of the day. 'I think she did trust you and me. Or else she wouldn't have told us about this Alba Libera thing.' Then, after a pause, Brunetti asked, 'Silly name, isn't it?'

Vianello shrugged. 'You mean because it's boastful?'

Brunetti nodded, adding, 'No more so than Opus Dei, I suppose.'

Vianello laughed and ran both hands through his hair, as if ridding himself of the events of the morning. 'I'll take the 51,' the Inspector said. 'It's faster.'

For a moment, Brunetti was confused, but then he understood: Vianello simply was not opting to accompany him back the way they had come, towards Rialto, where the Inspector could get the One to take him towards Castello. Like Brunetti, he was eager to get home for lunch, and the boat that went back behind the island and down to the Celestia stop was the faster way to do it.

'Later, then,' Brunetti said and turned towards home. As his feet took care of navigation, Brunetti turned his imagination to what they had just heard. Calle Bernardo took him out into Campo San Polo, but he was blind to everything and everyone he passed, trying to picture the young woman with the bloody face crouched on the landing he had just crossed. He tried not only to picture her there but to imagine what had put her there or where she might have gone after Signora Giusti found her.

The existence of the man who had beaten the girl – Brunetti entertained no doubt as to the aggressor's sex – was the first evidence that Signora Altavilla's desire to help the unfortunate might have led to something other than sweetness and harmony. At this thought and his recognition of the cynicism with which he phrased it, Brunetti gave an involuntary grunt, something he did when he was surprised by his own worst thoughts.

If her son had known about the arrival and departure of these girls and women, it might explain his nervousness. He might have cautioned his mother against sheltering the women in her own home: Brunetti found it hard to think of a son who would not so warn his mother. But he lived in Lerino, she in Venice, and so he could exercise little real control over what she did or did not do, whom she did or did not receive in her own home.

He found himself in front of his own house, stopped there in the manner of a wind-up toy that had run into a wall but kept trying to move forward, still preoccupied with Signora Giusti's story about the women going into and out of the apartment and with the memory of Dottor Niccolini standing outside the door of the mortuary. And, like tinnitus, he felt the low rumble of Patta's need to do as little as possible to upset the public.

Someone came up behind him and said good afternoon. Brunetti turned and said hello to Signor Vordoni, who put his key into the lock and pushed open the door, waiting for Brunetti to precede him. Brunetti muttered his thanks and went in, then held the door for the older man, closed it quietly after him, and made a business of checking their mailbox to delay having to go up the stairs with him.

As he knew it would be, the box was empty, but by the time he had flipped it closed and turned his key in the lock, Signor Vordoni had disappeared. Brunetti started up the steps, all but heedless of the smells of lunch that greeted him on every landing.

He opened his own door, and at the scent of what must be something concerning pumpkin and something else that involved chicken, he rediscovered his interest in aromas and the food that produced them.

In the kitchen he found Paola at the table, intent on a magazine: one of the habits she had developed over the years was to read soft-covered material only in the kitchen, books in her study and in bed. 'The university on strike?' he asked as he bent down to kiss her. She turned as he spoke, so he ended up kissing her right ear instead of the top of her head. Neither minded.

'No,' she answered. 'Only one of my students showed up, so I cancelled the class and came home.' She let the magazine slip on to the table, where it fell open at the article she was reading. Brunetti glanced down and saw what looked like an agitated white cloud covering the top half of the left page. 'What's that?' he asked, picking it up and holding it at the distance his eyesight now dictated. She passed her reading glasses to him; he closed one earpiece and held the lenses up to his eyes. 'Chickens?' he asked. He took a closer look. Chickens.

He dropped the magazine on the table and handed her back her glasses. 'What's it about?'

'It's one of the usual horror articles, the sort of thing you wish you hadn't started reading but then can't stop once you begin. About what's done to them.'

'Chickens? Horror chickens?' he enquired, listening to the sound of crackling from the oven, a sure portent of what was roasting inside.

'It's something Chiara brought home and told me to read.' Paola rested her head on her hand and asked, 'Do you think that's another sign that they've grown beyond your control?'

'What?'

'When they stop asking you to read things and start telling you to read them?'

'It could be,' he said and went over to the refrigerator in search of something that would dull the horror of the chicken. Lying in one of the drawers at the bottom he saw a few bottles of Moët. 'Where'd the champagne come from?' he asked.

'One of my students,' she answered.

'Students?'

'Yes. He passed his final exam a few days ago, and he sent me a few bottles.'

'Why?'

'I oversaw his thesis. It was brilliant, about the use of the imagery of light in the late novels.' Suddenly alert, Brunetti realized this was the moment crucial for intervention. If he did not act immediately, head her off, stop her, he was faced with a yet-to-be-determined period of time listening to what a student had written, under the direction of his lady wife, about the use of light imagery in the late novels of Henry James. Considering the fact that he had recently endured a meeting with Vice-Questore Giuseppe Patta and yesterday had had only three *tramezzini* – one stolen – for lunch, he decided that no time was to be lost.

'How many bottles did he send you?' he asked, stalling for time.

'A few cases.'

'What?'

'A few cases. Three or four, I don't remember.'

This, Brunetti knew, was the consequence of being born into a noble family that was possessed not only of pedigree but of great wealth: you lost count of the cases of Moët that a student sent you.

'That's a bribe,' he declared in his bad cop voice.

'What?'

'A bribe. I'm shocked you'd accept it. I hope you didn't give him a high grade on this thesis.'

'As high as I could. It was brilliant.'

Brunetti buried his face in his hands and moaned. He pulled out one of the bottles and took two glasses from the cabinet. He put the glasses on the table, making a lot of noise as he set them down, then turned his attention to the bottle, ripping off the gold foil. He aimed the cork at the far corner and pushed it off: the explosion shot through the house and warmed his heart.

He had disturbed the bottle, and so the champagne foamed out and ran across his hand. Quickly, he poured some into the first glass, which it overran, then into the second, where the same thing happened. Two small puddles spread round the glasses.

'Quick, quick,' he said, handing her a glass. Saying nothing else, he tapped his glass against hers, said '*Cin, cin,*' and drank deep. 'Ah,' he said, at peace with the world once more. With another quick swig, he emptied the glass.

'What's the matter with you?' Paola asked, then picked up her glass and took a sip after she said it. 'What are you doing?'

'Destroying the evidence.'

'Oh, you are a fool, Guido,' she said, but she laughed while she said it and the bubbles went up her nose and made her cough.

Lunch was, perhaps because of the bubbles or the laughter or some combination of the two, an easy, comfortable meal. Chiara seemed satisfied when her mother assured her that the chicken was a free range, bio chicken, that it had lived a healthy, happy life, and Brunetti, a man sworn to keep the peace, did so by not enquiring just how one was meant to tell if a chicken had been happy or not.

Chiara, of course, did not eat any of the chicken, but her vegetarian principles were sufficiently assuaged by her mother's assurances as to the lifestyle of the chicken to cause her not to provoke the other members of the family with her comments upon the profoundly disgusting act they were engaged in by eating said chicken. Her brother Raffi, unconcerned as to the chicken's happiness, cared only for its flavour.

Later, when they went into the living room to drink their coffee, Brunetti, profoundly happy that no one had asked him about Signora Altavilla, asked, 'What do they do to those chickens?'

'Not the one we ate, I hope you understand,' Paola said.

'So it wasn't a lie?'

'What wasn't?'

'That it was a bio chicken?'

'No, of course not,' Paola said, not indignant but perhaps ready to be, if provoked.

'Why?'

'Because the others are filled with hormones and chemicals and antibiotics and God knows what, and if I get cancer, I want it to be because I drank too much red wine or ate too much butter, not because I ate too much factory meat.'

'You really believe that?' he asked, curious, not sceptical.

'The more I read,' she began, turning on the sofa to face him, 'the more I believe much of what we eat is contaminated in some way.' Before he could comment, she said it for him. 'Yes, Chiara's a bit gone on the subject, but she's right in principle.'

Brunetti closed his eyes and slid down on the sofa. 'It's exhausting, always worrying about these things,' he said.

'Yes, it is,' Paola agreed. 'But at least we live in the North, so we're less at risk.'

'"At risk"?' he asked.

'You read the articles, you know what they've been doing down there,' she said. He glanced aside and saw her pick up her glasses and, apparently unwilling to talk about such things so soon after lunch, return her attention to the book she had brought from her study.

He sat up again and returned his attention to his own book, Tacitus' *Annals of Imperial Rome*, a book he had not read for at least twenty years. And which he was now reading with the attention of a man a generation older than the one who had read it last. The savagery of much of what Tacitus described seemed fitted to the times in which Brunetti found himself living. Government sunk in corruption, power concentrated in the hands of one man, public taste and morals debased almost beyond recognition: how familiar it all sounded.

His eyes fell upon this sentence: 'Fraudulence, attacked by repeated legislation, was ingeniously revived after each successive counter-measure.' He replaced his bookmark and closed the book. He decided that he would not return to work that afternoon but would instead engage in an act of fraudulence and go for a long walk, perhaps in the company of his lady wife.

13

The next morning, Paola brought him coffee in bed and gave him that day's edition of the *Gazzettino*, she equally persuaded of its lesser toxicity when confined to paper. Brunetti sipped at his coffee then set it on his night table, the better to free his hands for the reading of the paper. Sometime in the last years, even the *Gazzettino* had given in to the necessities of cost and was printed in the reduced size most newspapers now favoured. Even though the smaller-sized edition was easier to read in bed, Brunetti – just as he missed the typeface he had read for decades – missed the older, full-sized paper that demanded it be read with outstretched arms. He recalled the many times his reading of that invasive larger edition had provoked angry nudges and comments from the people sitting beside him on the vaporetto. But still he missed it, perhaps because its very size made the reading of it a quasi-public act: there was no way to limit its encroaching on the space of other people. This new version was too private an affair.

The story about Signora Altavilla's death had all but

disappeared from the papers. Elderly woman found dead of a probable heart attack: what sort of news was that? The best the editors could do was work it for some residual pathos: they mentioned her widowhood as well as the son and three grandchildren she left. He turned to the notices of mourning and found two, one from her son and family and one from the Alba Libera organization.

He read a few more articles and then, interest in the paper exhausted, got up, shaved and showered, and went into the kitchen, where he found Paola with *La Repubblica* spread on the table in front of her, chin propped in her palms.

Hearing him come in, she said, 'I was never able to read *Pravda*, but I wonder if all other newspapers are simply variations on it.'

'Probably,' he said, going over to the sink to refill the coffee pot.

'When I was studying in England,' she went on, 'I got accustomed to newspapers that had a part for news and a separate part for editorials.' She saw she had his attention, so she picked up the paper from the bottom and flapped the pages, as if she were trying to shake crumbs off a tablecloth. 'There's no difference here. It's all editorializing.'

'The other one's no better,' he said. 'And remember, *La Repubblica* has a good reputation.'

She shrugged this away and said, her disappointment real, 'I'd expect better from it.'

'That's foolish,' Brunetti said and put the coffee pot on the stove.

'I know it is, but that doesn't stop me from hoping.' Then, folding the paper closed, she said, 'The pan's in the sink,' leaving it to him to heat the milk for his coffee.

'You find out anything about that woman's death?' she asked as the coffee began to plunk against the top of the pot.

'Rizzardi says the physical cause was a heart attack,' he said, knowing Paola would jump on his prevarication.

'And *La Repubblica* has a good reputation,' she said.

'What's that supposed to mean?' he asked, though he suspected he knew.

'In logic, the error is called the Appeal to Authority,' she confused him by saying. 'You tell me Rizzardi says it was a heart attack with the same voice you say it's a good newspaper. You're citing authorities, but you don't believe them.' She waited for him to comment, but when he did not, she added, 'Something's bothering you; my guess is it's this woman's death, and that means you probably don't believe Rizzardi, or, more likely, he's being more Jesuitical than usual, and you know it.' She smiled at him and held out her cup for more coffee. 'That's what it's supposed to mean.'

'I see,' he said, pouring more coffee for her, and then for himself. He added milk and spooned in some sugar, then came to sit opposite her. When he saw that he had her attention, he said, 'There were what look like bruises on her throat and shoulders.' He reached his hands towards her to show her what he meant.

'Squeezing someone's shoulder doesn't cause them to have a heart attack,' she said calmly, as if this were an entirely normal conversation to have over coffee and the morning paper.

'It does if that person has a history of heart fibrillation and is taking propafenone.'

'Which is what?' Paola asked.

'A medicine against it.' He allowed her a few moments and then added, 'So, if a person were taking that for heart trouble, being grabbed and roughed around might cause them to go into fibrillation, and that's what Rizzardi thinks might have caused her death. But the vertebrae were injured.' He realized he was slanting the argument, and so he said, 'She fell and hit her head, as well. Against a radiator. That could have done it.'

'Could have?'

He gave her a level glance and took a few sips of coffee. 'The chicken or the egg,' he could not stop himself from saying, then added reluctantly, 'The fibrillation. The other is only a possibility, a speculation.'

'Yours or his?' she asked.

'Both.'

Paola sipped at her cup in turn, then swirled the coffee around a few times and drank the last of it. 'What does Patta say?'

Brunetti had the grace to smile. 'Nothing new there. He wants it settled, and I'm sure he's happy as a lark with the obvious explanation: heart attack. And that's the end of that.'

'But it's not for you?' she asked.

This time it was Brunetti who toyed with his cup. He got up and emptied the pot into it, added sugar and milk, and drank it quickly. 'I don't know. I can't say that, not really. There's something about it that makes me uncomfortable. It looks like she was giving refuge to women who were running away from dangerous men, and the nun at the *casa di cura* where she worked was overly discreet when talking about her.'

'Guido,' she said with every sign of patience, 'there doesn't exist the cleric you think capable of telling the simple truth.'

'That's not true,' he shot back. Then, more slowly, 'There have been some.'

'Some,' she repeated.

'You've never trusted them, either,' he added.

'Of course I don't trust them. But I don't question them in situations where people might lie: dead people or what might have killed them, please remember. I discuss the weather with them when I meet them at my parents' place. The rain is an especially fascinating topic: too much or too little. They like absolutes. But it's not the same thing.'

'And do you trust them when they talk about the weather?' he asked.

'If I'm near a window and look outside,' she answered, got to her feet and said she had to go to the university.

After she was gone, Brunetti glanced through the newspaper she had left on the kitchen table, but he was unable to concentrate on anything he read. He mulled over what he had just said to Paola, aware that his instinctive remarks reflected his real feelings about the death of Signora Altavilla. The nun knew more than she had said, and he needed to find out more about Alba Libera.

He went into the living room and dialled Signorina Elettra's office number. But then he remembered that it was Tuesday and she would still be at the Rialto Market, selecting the flowers for Vice-Questore Patta's office, and for her own. He dialled her *telefonino* number. She answered with a languid '*Sì*, Commissario?' and Brunetti was again struck by the unfair psychological advantage given to the person who could see who was calling.

'Good morning, Signorina,' he said blandly. 'I'd like to ask you to do something for me.'

'Certainly, Signore, as soon as I get to the office.'

'Oh, aren't you there?' he asked with false surprise.

'No, sir, I'm at the market. It's Tuesday, you know.' He was her superior; she was not at work and was not likely to be there for another hour, at best. She had probably requisitioned a police launch to take her to the market to buy flowers, or had arranged for one to pick her up and carry her – and the flowers – back to the Questura, a clear violation of the rules concerning the abuse of office. It was his responsibility to reprimand her and see that this abuse of office would not be repeated.

'If I got there in five minutes, could you give me a ride to work?' he asked.

'Of course,' she said. 'Or I could have Foa stop at the end of your *calle* and pick you up there.'

It took a second for Brunetti to regain his breath, and then all he said was, 'No, that's too much trouble. I'll meet you at the flower stalls.' He replaced the phone, went back into the bedroom to get his jacket, and left the apartment.

It took him only a few minutes to get to the market, past the fish on his left, their tangy smell something he had always loved. When he glanced up from a large squid, he saw Signorina Elettra standing, arms filled with flowers, just in front of the stand, which really wasn't a stand, just a line of large plastic buckets set in a row and each one bursting with flowers. Buying the flowers at the stall instead of at Biancat, the florist, was Signorina Elettra's contribution to Vice-Questore Patta's latest demand that all unnecessary spending at the Questura be stopped.

Brunetti had never been good at remembering the names of flowers. Iris he knew because he so often bought them for Paola, and carnations and roses were easy to spot. But those small ones with the bright crinkly petals: he'd forgotten their name, so too the bold round ones the size of oranges with the thousands of spiky petals. Gladioli he recognized, but that had never made him like them, and the scent of lilies always made him feel faintly ill.

'Good morning, Commissario,' she said with a bright smile when she saw him approach. She wore a cobalt blue silk jacket, and against it the red and yellow flowers seemed somehow brighter. She handed him three bouquets, which were quickly replaced in her arms by more from the woman selling them. While he waited, Signorina Elettra detached an arm for long enough to pass her some notes. No receipt was given in return: second crime of the morning.

'Office equipment?' he asked, nodding at her flowers, trying to ignore his own.

'Oh, Commissario,' she said with every indication of surprise, 'you know I couldn't live with myself if I thought for an instant that I was doing something improper with regard to the finances of the Questura.' When she realized that Brunetti was not going to play straight man, she said, 'I just happen to have a receipt for some colour cartridges for a printer. I'll submit it: the amount is about the same.'

He didn't want to know. He didn't want to know. This way, the flower seller did not pay taxes on the sale, and someone gave Signorina Elettra a receipt for some private purchase, and the Questura paid for the flowers, magically transformed into colour cartridges. Before he got on to the boat and also made improper use of it, Brunetti decided to stop counting crimes.

Foa appeared from the left and took the flowers from Signorina Elettra. Sure enough, on the other side of the market, a police launch was moored to the *riva*, motor running, another uniformed officer at the wheel. Foa handed the flowers to his colleague, jumped down into the boat and helped Signorina Elettra take her place, then reached up and accepted the flowers from Brunetti, leaving him to step into the boat himself.

Brunetti held open the door of the cabin, then joined her inside. When they were seated and the boat was heading under the Rialto, he said, 'Signorina, do you know anything about an organization called Alba Libera?'

Her eyes widened in dawning understanding. 'Of course, of course. I just didn't think of them.'

He nodded in response and said, 'She was a member; well, at least a supporter. And from what her neighbour said, she had women stay with her.'

'That explains the underwear,' she said.

Brunetti allowed time to pass before he asked, 'Do you know anything about them?'

She gave him a level look, then let her eyes drift off to the buildings they were passing. Finally she looked back at him and said, 'A bit.'

'Might I ask you what that bit is?'

'Just as you said, Signore, they provide safe places for women to stay.'

'Women at risk?' he asked.

'Any woman who contacts them and is in need.'

'Is that all she has to say?'

'I'm sure they ask for proof.'

'What would that be?' he enquired in a level voice.

'Police reports,' she said. A long pause, and then, 'Or hospital reports.'

'I see,' he said. 'You sound familiar with them.' He tried to speak in a judicious, neutral tone.

She smiled. 'I give them money every year,' she said. 'But because I work where I do, I've never offered to have one stay with me, and I'm not involved in any way.'

Brunetti nodded and said, 'That's probably wise.' Then he asked, 'But you know the people who are?'

'Yes,' she said, sounding not at all eager to say so.

'Could you . . .' he began, not sure how to phrase his request. 'Could you introduce me to them?'

'And vouch for you?' she asked with a smile.

'Something like that.'

'Now?'

'When we get to the Questura,' he said. Then he asked, 'Do they know where you work?'

'No,' she said, waving the question away with her hand. 'Just that I work for the city.'

'Better that way,' Brunetti said.

'Yes.'

14

When they got to the Questura, Foa and his companion seemed happy to help Signorina Elettra with the flowers, so Brunetti went directly to his office. There were some reports and papers on his desk, most of them bureaucratic, and he spent some time looking through them.

The only thing that caught his interest was a request for information about a Romanian woman, one of whose names Brunetti recognized. They had arrested her at least a dozen times, each time under a different pseudonym, with a different place and date of birth. She had, it seemed, now turned up in Ferrara, where she had been arrested in the train station while trying to steal the purse of an off-duty policewoman. She refused to give any information other than her name, but in her pocket there was a receipt for a coffee from a bar in Castello, so the police in Ferrara had thought to contact them, sending the name she was using, photo, and fingerprints.

He called down to the archive, giving the alias she had used in Ferrara and the name he thought was on her file.

When he heard the names, the archivist laughed and said, 'And I thought we were rid of her.'

'We are, but I'm afraid Ferrara is not,' Brunetti said. 'Could you send them a copy of the file?'

'And so now she'll get a letter from them, telling her to leave the country within forty-eight hours?' Tomasini asked. Then, after a moment's reflection, he said in a completely serious voice, 'I think what we should do is declare ourselves an art cooperative and ask to be allowed to exhibit at the Biennale. All they have to do is give us the Italian pavilion.'

'Who's "us"?'

'Everyone here, but me especially because I've got all the documents and the copies of the letters.'

'What would you do with them?' Brunetti asked.

'Paper the walls of the entire pavilion. Not in any order; not chronological or alphabetical or according to crime. We'd just mix up a few thousand of them and paste them on the walls, all those letters telling the same people, time after time, that they have forty-eight hours to leave the country because of the crime they've committed. And we call it something like, "*Italia Oggi*."'

All joking fled from the archivist's voice as he asked, 'It's the right title, isn't it? This *is* Italy today.' When Brunetti did not answer, the younger man repeated, 'Isn't it?'

'Fabio,' Brunetti said in a level voice, 'send the file to Ferrara, all right?'

'*Sì*, Dottore,' he answered and replaced his phone.

The ecologists never tired of saying that the city was going to be under water in a number of years: though the number of years changed, no one questioned the prediction. When, Brunetti wondered, would the entire country be under papers? The walls in the rooms at the back of the ground floor were already lined with metal racks filled with files that reached from the floor to ten centimetres short of the ceiling. The *acqua alta* of three years ago had destroyed the first two shelves, long before they had been put into the computerized system, and so that part of the record of criminal behaviour had effectively been destroyed. Maybe Tomasini was on to something: surely the walls of a Biennale exhibit could be no less evanescent than the files downstairs.

His phone rang. 'I've spoken to them, Commissario,' Signorina Elettra said. 'Shall I come up and tell you?'

'Yes. Please.'

She arrived preceded by flowers. 'I'm afraid I went a bit overboard this morning, Dottore,' she said as she came in. 'So I'd like to leave some here, if you don't mind.' They were tall things that looked like daisies, white and yellow, and they brought some cheer into the room. She set the vase on his desk, stood back and studied them, and then moved the vase over to the windowsill. Satisfied, she came back and sat in one of the chairs in front of his desk.

'I got the *telefonino* number of the woman who runs it,' she said, placing a piece of paper on his desk. 'Maddalena Orsoni. She's very bright.'

'Bright enough to what?' Brunetti asked.

'To wonder why the police are interested in Signora Altavilla. And her death.'

'If I say it's only routine?'

'She won't believe you,' Signorina Elettra said quickly. 'She's been dealing with the authorities for years, and with the social services, and with the men these women are hiding from. So she can spot a liar at ten metres, and she isn't likely to believe you.'

'And if I'm not lying about her death?'

'Commissario, even I suspect you're lying.'

Brunetti thought about trying to bluster but abandoned the idea. He waited for her to continue.

'Remember, Signore, the only habitual liar I have to deal with is Lieutenant Scarpa, so I've really not developed the skill. Maddalena has,' she said. Once again, with her embedded comment on the Lieutenant, she had left Brunetti uncertain how to deal with her criticism of a superior.

'If you think I shouldn't talk to her, then how can I ask her about Signora Altavilla?' he asked, preferring to avoid the subject of Lieutenant Scarpa.

She smiled at his question and said, 'I'm afraid we've been talking at cross-purposes, Commissario. I'm not suggesting that you don't speak to her. Just that you don't lie to her. If you treat her honestly, then she'll do the same.'

'You know her that well?' he asked.

'No. But I know people who do.'

'I see,' he said, choosing not to enquire about that, either. He pulled the piece of paper towards him, held up a hand to stop her from getting to her feet, and dialled the number.

On the third ring, a women answered with a neutral, '*Sì?*'

'Signora Orsoni,' he said, 'this is Commissario Guido Brunetti.' He gave her a chance to ask, as many people would, why the police were calling, but she said nothing.

'I'm calling about someone who worked for your organization, Alba Libera.' Again, she said nothing. 'Costanza Altavilla.'

This time Brunetti determined not to say anything else and waited until she asked, 'In what way can I be useful to you, Commissario?' Her voice was low, with no indication of age, nor was there a discernible accent. She was a woman who spoke precise Italian and that was all he could judge.

'I'd like to talk to you about Signora Altavilla.'

'For what purpose?' she asked, sounding neutral, curious, but nothing more.

Burning his bridges, Brunetti said, 'To see if there is reason to take a closer look at her death.'

Her response was delayed a few moments, but then she asked, voice still revealing nothing, 'Does that mean that the press report was wrong and it wasn't a heart attack, Commissario?'

'No, there's no question that the heart attack was the cause of her death,' he said. Then, when that had registered, he added, 'I'm curious about the possible circumstances of the heart attack.'

He glanced at Signorina Elettra, who did her best to give every appearance of taking no extraordinary interest in his side of the conversation.

'And you'd like to speak to me?' she asked.

'Yes.'

'I'm not in the city at the moment,' she said.

'When will you be back?'

'Perhaps tomorrow.'

'And if I told you it was urgent that I speak to you?' Brunetti asked.

'I'd say what I'm doing is also urgent,' she said, not offering an explanation.

Stalemate. 'Then I'll call you again,' Brunetti said, quite pleasantly, as if he were inviting her to lunch.

'Good,' she said and hung up.

He replaced the phone, looked at Signorina Elettra, and said, 'Too busy to see me.'

'I'm told she is not one to undervalue herself, Maddalena,' she said.

15

'You've read the reports?' Brunetti asked, his interest in and respect for her habit of reading all official documents with attention and scepticism overcoming any scruples he might have about her civilian status.

Signorina Elettra nodded.

'And?'

'The technicians were thorough,' she said. Brunetti thought it best to forgo comment, which encouraged her to add, 'The marks on her throat and back and the trauma to her back caught my attention.'

'And mine,' Brunetti said, deciding to follow the path of caution and say nothing about what Rizzardi had told him in private.

Her look was sharp, but her voice was calm when she said, 'What a pity such things fail to rouse the doctor's.'

'That's usually the case,' Brunetti admitted.

'Indeed.' From her inflection, he had no idea if she were making a statement or asking a question about Rizzardi's opinion. She continued: 'You spoke to the nuns at the *casa di cura* in Bragora.' This time there was no doubt about the question.

'Yes.'

'And?' she asked, showing that two could play at Monosyllable.

'And the nun with whom I spoke regarded her highly. The Mother Superior seemed forthcoming, but . . .' he began and then drifted off, uncertain how to admit to his worst prejudice. She gave him no help, and so after a while he was constrained to continue. 'But she's from the South, so I sensed a certain . . .'

'Reticence?'

'Yes,' he said. 'Vianello was with me.'

'That usually helps,' she said. 'With women.'

'Not this time. Perhaps because there were two of us. And we're big.'

She looked across at him as though examining him for the first time. 'I've never thought of either one of you as being particularly big,' she said, then looked at him again. 'But perhaps you are. How small was she?'

Brunetti, keeping his palm horizontal, brought it up to the centre of his chest.

Signorina Elettra nodded. He watched the animation leave her face and her eyes shift focus, two things he'd noticed in the past when her attention was captured by something. He knew enough to wait for her to come back to the conversation. When she did, she said, 'I've often thought that nuns have a different reaction to men.'

'Different in what way or from whose?' he asked.

'Different from women who . . .' she paused, obviously unable to find the proper formulation '. . . from women who find them attractive.'

'Do you mean in a romantic way?'

She smiled. 'How delicately you put it, Commissario. Yes, "in a romantic way".'

'What's different?' Brunetti asked.

'We're less frightened of them,' she said instantly but then added, 'Or maybe it's that we're more likely to trust them because we're more familiar with how their minds work.'

'You think women do understand us?'

'It's a survival skill, Commissario.' She smiled when she said it, but then her face grew serious and she said, 'Maybe that really is the difference, because we live with men and deal with them every day and fall in love with them, and out of love with them. I think that must minimize our sense of the alien.'

'Alien?' Brunetti asked, unable to hide his surprise.

'Different, at any rate,' she said.

'And nuns?' he asked, drawing her back to what had started her down this path.

'One whole area of interaction is closed down. Call it flirting if you want, Dottore. I mean that whole area where we play back and forth with the idea that the other person is attractive.'

'You mean nuns don't feel this?' he asked, wondering at her use of the word 'play'.

She gave a small shrug. 'I have no idea if they do or they don't. For their sake, I hope they do because if you manage to stifle that, then something's gone wrong.' Abruptly she got to her feet, both surprising him and, he realized, disappointing him that she did not want to continue with this subject.

'You said the nun was reluctant to talk to you,' she said, standing behind her chair. 'If it wasn't because of her feelings about men – and I think it would be hard for anyone to find Vianello threatening – then maybe it is because she's a southerner or because there's something she doesn't want you to know. I'd never want to exclude that possibility.' She smiled and was gone, leaving Brunetti to consider why she had not said she thought it would be hard for anyone to find him threatening.

He looked up and saw Lieutenant Scarpa at his door. Brunetti did his best to disguise his surprise and said, 'Good morning, Lieutenant.' He could never look at the Lieutenant without the word 'reptile' coming into his mind. It had nothing to do with the Lieutenant's appearance, for indeed he was a handsome man: tall and slender, with a prominent nose and broad-spaced eyes over high cheekbones. Perhaps it had to do with a certain sinuosity in the way he moved, a failure to pick his feet up fully when he walked, which caused an undulant liquidity in his knees. Brunetti was reluctant to admit that he attributed it to his own belief that inside the man there was nothing but the icy chill found in reptiles and the far reaches of space.

'Have a seat, Lieutenant,' Brunetti said and folded his hands on his desk in a gesture of polite expectation.

The Lieutenant did as he was requested. 'I've come to ask your advice, Commissario,' he said, smoothing out the consonants in his Sicilian way.

'Yes?' Brunetti asked with rigorous neutrality.

'It's about two of the men in my squad.'

'Yes?'

'Alvise and Riverre,' Scarpa said, and Brunetti's sense of danger could have been no stronger had the man hissed.

Brunetti put a look of mild interest on his face, wondering what those two clowns had done now, and repeated, 'Yes?'

'They're impossible, Commissario. Riverre can be trusted to answer the phone, but Alvise isn't even capable of that.' Scarpa bent forward and placed his palm on Brunetti's desk, a gesture he had no doubt taught himself to make when he wanted to imitate sincerity and concern.

Brunetti could not have more strongly agreed with this assessment of the two men. Riverre, however, had a certain knack in getting adolescents to talk: no doubt by dint of fellow feeling. But Alvise was, in a word, hopeless. Or in two, hopelessly stupid. He recalled that Alvise had spent months working on a special project with Scarpa a few years ago: had the poor fool stumbled on something that might compromise the Lieutenant? If so, he had been too stupid to realize it, or surely the entire Questura would have known about it the same day.

'I'm not sure I agree with you, Lieutenant,' Brunetti lied. 'Nor that I know why you've chosen to come to me about this.' If the Lieutenant wanted something, Brunetti would oppose it. It was as simple as that.

'I'd hoped that your concern for the safety of the city and the reputation of the force would encourage you to try to do something about them. That's why I've come to ask your advice,' he said, and then, the echo arriving with its usual tantalizing delay, ' . . . sir.'

'I certainly appreciate your concern, Lieutenant,' Brunetti said in his blandest voice. Then, getting to his feet, he added, trying to sound sorry about the fact, 'But, unfortunately, I'm late for an appointment and must leave now. But I'll certainly consider your comments and . . .' he began and then – to show that he was equally capable of making use of the echo – paused before adding, 'and the spirit that animates them.'

Brunetti came around his desk and paused beside the Lieutenant, who had no choice but to get to his feet. Brunetti guided Scarpa out of his office, turned to close the door, something he seldom did, and then led the way downstairs. Brunetti nodded to the Lieutenant and crossed the lobby, not bothering to stop and talk to the guard. Outside, he decided to continue to Bragora and see if he could speak to any of the old people Signora Altavilla had befriended, convinced that listening to old people talk about their pasts, no matter how exaggerated their memories, would be vastly preferable to hearing the truth – especially from the likes of Lieutenant Scarpa – about Alvise and Riverre.

He thought he would take the longer route to Bragora and crossed the bridge into Campo San Lorenzo. Up close, Brunetti saw that the sign stating the date when the restoration of the church had begun had been bleached clean by the sun. He could no longer remember when they were supposed to begin – surely it was decades ago. People at the Questura said the work had actually started, but that was before Brunetti's time, and so he had only rumour to rely upon. During the years he had stood at his window and studied the *campo*, he had seen the restoration of the *casa di cura* begin, continue, and even finish. Perhaps that was of greater importance than the restoration of a church.

He turned right and left a few times and found himself again passing the church of San Antonin. Then down the Salizada and out into the *campo*, where the trees still invited passers-by to sit for a while in their shade.

He crossed and rang the bell at the *casa di cura*. He announced himself and said he had come to speak to Madre Rosa. This time, a different nun, even older than Madre Rosa, waited for him at the door at the top of the stairs. Brunetti gave his name, entered, and turned to close the door himself. The nun smiled her thanks and led him to the room where he had already spoken to the Mother Superior.

Today Madre Rosa was sitting in one of the armchairs, a book open on her lap. She nodded when he came in and closed her book. 'What may I do for you today, Commissario?' she asked. She gave no indication that he should sit, and so Brunetti, though he approached her, remained standing.

'I'd like to speak to some of the people who knew Signora Altavilla best,' he said.

'You must realize that your desire makes little sense to me,' she said. When Brunetti did not respond, she added, 'Nor does your curiosity about her.'

'It makes sense to me, Madre,' he said.

'Why?'

It was out before he thought about it. 'I'm curious about the cause of her heart attack.' Before the nun could ask him anything, Brunetti said, 'There's no question that she died of a heart attack, and the doctor assures me it was very fast.' He saw her close her eyes and nod, as if in thanks for having been given something she desired. 'But I'd like to be sure that the heart attack was . . . was not brought on by anything. Anything unpleasant, that is.'

'Sit down, Commissario,' she said. When he did, she said, 'You realize what you've just said, of course.'

'Yes.'

'If the cause of her heart attack – may she rest in peace – was, as you say,' she began, pausing a moment before allowing herself to repeat his word, 'unpleasant, then there must be a reason for that. And if you've come here to look for that reason, then it's possible you think you'll find it in something one of the people she worked with told her.'

'That's true,' he said, impressed by her quickness.

'And if that *is* true, then that person might equally be at risk.'

'That's certainly possible, as well, but I think it would depend on what it is they told her. Madre,' he continued, deciding he had no choice but to trust her, 'I've no idea what happened, and I feel foolish saying that all I have is a strange feeling that something is wrong about her death.' Conscious of having said nothing about the marks on her body, Brunetti wondered if it were worse to lie to a nun than to any other sort of person: he decided it was not.

'Does that mean you are not here . . . how to say this? That you are not here officially?' She seemed pleased to have found the word.

'Not at all,' he had to admit. 'I want only to bring some peace of mind to her son,' he added. It was the truth, but it was not the whole truth.

'I see,' she said. She surprised him by opening the book in her lap and returning her attention to it. Brunetti sat quietly for a time that spread out and became minutes, and then more minutes.

At last, she held the book closer to her face, then appeared to read aloud: '"The eyes of the Lord are in every place, beholding the evil and the good."' She lowered the book and looked at him above the pages. 'Do you believe that, Commissario?'

'No, I'm afraid I don't, Madre,' he said without hesitation.

She set the book on her lap, leaving the pages open, and surprised him again, this time by saying, 'Good.'

'Good that I said it or that I don't believe it?' Brunetti asked.

'That you said it, of course. It's tragic that you don't believe it. But if you had said you do, you would have been a liar, and that's worse.'

Like Pascal, she knew the truth not by reason, but by the heart. But he made no mention of this, merely asked, 'How do you know I don't believe it?' he asked.

She smiled more warmly than he had seen her do so far. 'I might be a dried-up old stick, Commissario, and from the South, as well, but I'm not a fool,' she said.

'And the fact that I'm not a liar, what bearing does that have on this conversation?'

'It makes me believe that you are really interested in finding out if anything unpleasant – as you put it – might have been involved in Costanza's death. And since she was a friend, I am interested in that, as well.'

'Which means you'll help?' he asked.

'Which means I will give you the names of the people she spent most time with. And then you are on your own, Commissario.'

16

She gave him not only their names but their room numbers as well. Two women, one man, all in their eighties and one of them in indifferent mental health; that was the word she used: 'indifferent'. Brunetti had the feeling that she would not choose to elucidate that last remark, so he let it pass. He thanked her, asking if he could speak to them now.

'You can try to,' she said. 'It's lunchtime, and for many of our guests, that's the most important event of their day; it might be difficult to get them to concentrate on anything you ask, at least until after they've eaten.' Hearing her, he remembered a period in his mother's decline when she had become obsessively interested in food and eating, though she had continued to grow thinner, no matter what she ate. But soon enough she had simply forgotten what food was and had to be reminded, then almost forced, to eat.

She heard him sigh and said, 'We do it for love of the Lord and for love of our fellow man.'

He nodded, temporarily unable to speak. When Brunetti looked across at her, she said, 'I don't know how helpful they'll be if they know you're a policemen. It might be sufficient to say that you're a friend of Costanza's.'

'And leave it at that?' he asked with a smile.

'It would be enough.' She did not smile in return but said, 'After all, it's true, in a sense, isn't it?'

Brunetti got to his feet without answering her question. He leaned down and extended his hand. She squeezed it briefly, then said, 'If you go out the door here, turn left and at the end of the corridor, right, you'll be in the dining room.'

'Thank you, Madre,' he said.

She nodded and returned her attention to her book. At the door, he was tempted to turn and see if she was watching him, but he did not.

Brunetti did not have to use his professional skills to know that lunch was roast pork and potatoes: he had smelled them when he entered the building. As he passed by what must have been the door to the kitchen, he realized just how good roast pork and potatoes could be.

Six or seven tables, half of them small and set for only one or two persons, sat in front of the windows that looked out on the *campo*. There were a dozen or so people, some sitting in couples, one quartet, some alone. No table was empty. There were bottles of wine and mineral water on all of the tables, and the plates looked like porcelain. Heads turned as he entered the room, but soon two dark-skinned young women appeared behind him, dressed in a simplified version of the habit worn by Madre Rosa and the other sister. Hidden in the midst of the headcloth and veil of the first one were the almond eyes and long-arched nose of a Toltec statue. The lips carved into her mahogany face were surrounded by a thin line of lighter skin which exaggerated their natural redness. Brunetti stared at her until she turned in his direction; then he did what he did when a suspect gazed his way: he changed the focus of his eyes to long vision and panned around the room, as though she were not there or were not worthy of his attention.

The two novices went quickly around the tables, stacking the dishes in which pasta had been served. As they went past on the way to the kitchen, Brunetti saw deep green traces of pesto, a sauce he had never liked. The novices were quickly back, each carrying three plates that held pork, sliced carrots, and roasted potatoes. They served the people at the nearest tables, disappeared, then returned with more plates.

The hum of conversation that had broken off at the sight of him resumed, and the heads – most of them white but some defiantly not – bent over their lunch. Forks clicked against china, bottles against glass; the usual sounds of a communal meal.

The nun who had opened the main door suddenly appeared at his side and asked, 'Would you like me to tell you who they are, Signore?'

Assuming that she had been sent by the Mother Superior, Brunetti said, 'That would be very kind of you, Suora.'

'Dottor Grandesso is having lunch in his room today, Signora Sartori is over there, at the second table, in the black dress, and Signora Cannata is with the other people at the table next to her. She's the one with the red hair.'

Brunetti looked across the room and singled out the two women. Signora Sartori was hunched over her food, her left arm encircling her plate, almost as if she were trying to protect her dish from someone who wanted to snatch it from her. He saw her in profile: one high cheekbone with little flesh covering it, but with a plump pouch of skin hanging under her chin. Her lipstick was a violent red and veered beyond the line of her lips. Her skin, like the skin of old people who no longer see the light of day, had a slightly greenish cast, an effect intensified by the inky blackness of her shoulder-length hair.

She held her fork in her gnarled fist and shovelled up the potatoes. Brunetti noticed that her meat had arrived pre-cut in smallish pieces. While he watched, she finished her potatoes and then, just as quickly, the carrots. She took a piece of bread, broke it in half, and proceeded to wipe half of her plate clean, then the other side with the remaining piece of bread. As he watched, she went on to finish two more slices of bread, and when there was no more, she stopped and sat immobile. One of the novices took her empty plate away and received a sharp, angry look for doing so.

Brunetti walked towards the table where the woman with the red hair sat. The novices swept past him, setting a piece of apple cake in front of each of the three people at the table. Brunetti stopped a bit before the table and addressed the woman with the wispy red hair, 'Signora Cannata?'

She looked up at him with a smile in which he read automatic flirtatiousness. Her eyes blinked rapidly and she raised a palm to keep Brunetti at bay, as though she were a teenager and he the first boy who had paid her a compliment. Her nose was thin and finely drawn, the taut skin under her eyes a few shades lighter than the skin on the rest of her face. Her mascara had been applied with a heavy hand, as had her lipstick, traces of which were visible on her napkin and in small cracks running off from both sides of her mouth. She might have been sixty; she might have had a child of sixty.

The other people at the table turned to him, a man with thinning white hair and a suspiciously black moustache and a blonde woman whose face and what Brunetti could see of her chest appeared to be made of well-tanned leather. The woman's head and, when he looked, her hands moved erratically in the telltale tremor.

He nodded and smiled at them all. 'And you are?' the man with the moustache asked.

'Guido Brunetti,' he said, adding, careful to use a more sober tone, 'a friend of Costanza Altavilla.'

Their eyes did not change, though the blonde overcame the tremor for a moment to turn down the sides of her mouth and tilt her head to the side while she said, 'Ah, *povera donna*,' and the man shook his head and made a clicking noise with his tongue. Was this what happened, Brunetti wondered? Did we all reach a point in our lives when the death of other people didn't matter, and the best we could be expected to produce was a kind of formulaic sadness, the generic form of grief instead of the real? What he observed in them was something much more like disapproval than sadness. Shame on death for having shown his face at the window of our lives; shame on death for having reminded us that he was lurking outside and waiting for us.

'Oh, a friend of Costanza's,' Signora Cannata sighed.

'More of her son's, really. In fact, he asked me to come along to speak to the sisters,' he began, telling the truth, then quickly segued into the lie. 'He asked me, while I was here, if I'd try to speak to some of the people she mentioned and tell them how very fond she was of them.'

Hearing this, Signora Cannata placed her open palm on her chest, as if to ask, 'Who? Me?'

Brunetti gave her a beneficent smile and said, 'And I hoped I'd be able to take some words to her son, some sign of how much she was appreciated here.'

The man got to his feet abruptly, as if tired of all of this talk of affection and regard. The blonde stood, as well, and linked her arm in his. 'We're going out to get a coffee,' he said, to Brunetti or to Signora Cannata or, for all anyone knew, to the Recording Angel. He nodded to Brunetti, made no motion to shake his hand, and turned away from them, taking the woman with him.

Ignoring them, Brunetti asked, 'May I join you, Signora?' and at her smile and wave, sat in the chair to her left, where no one had been seated. He smiled in return and said, 'As you can well understand, Signora, her son is very troubled by this. You know how close they were.'

She raised her napkin, which Brunetti noticed was cloth and not paper, folded it to a clean patch, and made two dainty dabs at the corner of her left eye, then at the right. 'It's a terrible thing,' she said. 'But I suppose her son – he's a doctor, isn't he? – knew that she was not in good health.' Her mouth turned down at the sides and she said, 'It was a heart attack, wasn't it?'

'Yes, it was. At least the poor woman didn't suffer,' he said, doing his best to use the voice of piety he remembered hearing in his youth.

'Ah, thank God,' she said. 'At least for that.' Unconsciously, she placed her palm against her chest again; this time the gesture had nothing artificial about it.

'Her son told me that you were one of the people she mentioned frequently. And she said how much she enjoyed talking to you.'

'Oh, how very flattering,' Signora Cannata said. 'Not that I have much to talk about. Well, perhaps, when I was younger and my husband was still alive. He was an accountant, you know, helped so many important people in the city.'

Brunetti put his elbow on the table and propped his chin in his right palm, ready to sit there all afternoon and listen to the story of her husband's numerical triumphs. Signora Cannata did not disappoint: her husband had, during his working life, discovered a serious overpayment of tax for the owner of a shipping line, once helped a famous surgeon devise a private accounting system for foreign patients, and had also – though this whole business of computers was something he came to late in life – managed to design a computer system to do the complete billing and bookkeeping for his office.

Brunetti slipped into his most complimentary mode, nodding and smiling at every triumph she recounted, wondering how this woman could possibly have put anyone at risk, save herself from the violence of the people she bored.

'And how long have you been a guest here, Signora?' Brunetti asked.

Her smile grew more brittle as she said, 'Oh, I realized a

few years ago that I'd have much more freedom here. And be with people of my own age. Not with people of my son's generation, or even younger. You know how it is, how insensitive they can be,' she continued, widening her eyes to display honesty and open-hearted sincerity, to make no mention of human warmth to the point of excess. 'Besides, people prefer the company of their peers, who have the same memories and history.' She smiled, and Brunetti gave a nod so filled with agreement it served to shake him fully awake.

'Well,' he said, pushing himself with every sign of reluctance to his feet, 'I don't want to keep you any longer, Signora. You've been very generous with your time and I'm not sure how to thank you.'

'Well,' she said, putting on what she probably intended to be a flirtatious smile, 'one way would be by coming back to talk to me again.'

'Indeed, Signora,' Brunetti said and extended his hand. She took it and held it for a long moment, and Brunetti felt himself sink towards compassion. 'I'll try to do that.'

Her look was so clear he realized neither of them was fooled one bit by what he said, but both of them decided to stay in role until they were finished with the scene. 'I'll look forward to it,' she said, taking back her hand and folding it into the other in her lap.

Brunetti smiled. He knew he could not simply move to the other table and start talking to Signora Sartori, who appeared not to have moved since she had finished her cake. He left the room and went down the corridor towards the kitchen. One of the novices came out with a large tray and started towards him.

'Excuse me,' he began, uncertain what title to give her, 'could you tell me where I might find Dottor Grandesso?'

'Oh, he's at the back of the hall, Signore, down on the right. Last door.' She looked around Brunetti and pointed down the corridor, as if she feared he could not follow her instructions.

'Thank you,' he said and made off down the corridor. The

last door on the right was closed, so he knocked. He knocked again and then, hearing no response, slowly opened the door and called into the room, 'Dottor Grandesso?'

A noise answered. It might have been a word, though it might have been a grunt, but it was definitely a noise, so Brunetti took it as an invitation to enter. Inside, he saw what he at first took to be a skull propped on the pillow of the bed. But the skull had tufts of hair attached and a thin covering of grooved skin. There was a long, narrow form under the covers, and at the end of it a miniature bishop's mitre of feet. The eyes were still there, and they were turned in his direction. They did not blink and they did not move, merely opened up a conduit between him and a skull. Brunetti recognized the smell he had come to know in his mother's room.

'Dottor Grandesso?' Brunetti asked.

'Sì,' the skull answered without moving its lips, the single word pronounced in a voice that surprised Brunetti with its depth and resonance.

'I'm a friend of Signora Altavilla's son. He's asked me to come to speak to the sisters and to those of you who knew his mother best. If it doesn't upset you, that is.'

The eyes blinked. Or, more accurately, they closed and stayed closed for some time. When they reopened, they had somehow been transformed into the eyes of a living man, filled with emotion and, Brunetti was certain, pain. 'What happened?' he asked in that same deep voice.

As Brunetti approached the bed he was acutely aware of how Dottor Grandesso's eyes studied him; their scrutiny filled Brunetti with a sense of the man's oxymoronic vitality. 'She died of a heart attack,' Brunetti said. 'The autopsy results said it would have been immediate and whatever pain there was would have lasted only a short time.'

'Rizzardi?' the other man surprised Brunetti by asking.

'Yes. Do you know him?' Brunetti had not considered the possibility that this man's title was a medical one.

'I know of him. Or did, when I still worked. Solid man,' he said. The doctor's lips moved as he spoke, and his eyes paid careful attention to Brunetti, but the grooves in his cheeks remained motionless, and his expression was to be read only in his eyes.

What he said of Rizzardi was both description and praise, pronounced in a voice that should not have been able to emerge from that form. The doctor closed his eyes again, and that simple act transformed him, subtracting the spirit and leaving in its place nothing more than that ravaged head and the sticks below it, under the covers.

Not wanting to invade, Brunetti glanced away, but the window beside the bed gave out on a narrow *calle* and provided nothing more than a view of a wall and a shuttered window. He continued to look at them until the other man said, 'Did you know her?'

He looked back then, and saw animation and interest reborn. 'No. Only her son. I was with him while Rizzardi . . .' The sentence languished, Brunetti uncertain what to do with it.

'He asked me to come here to speak to the sisters,' Brunetti resumed. 'He said his mother was happy when she came here. I took it upon myself, after I spoke to the Mother Superior, to try to speak to the people she was especially fond of.'

'Did the son know our names?' he asked, and Brunetti heard the surge of hope in his voice.

He wanted to lie and tell the doctor that, yes, she had spoken to her son about the people she cared for most, but Brunetti couldn't bring himself to do it. Instead, he said, 'I don't know. I decided to try to speak to you after I talked to the Mother Superior. She gave me your name.'

The man in the bed turned his head aside when he heard this, surprising Brunetti with the motion. But his eyes did not close, and he did not repeat that complete disappearance of humanity Brunetti had observed.

He turned back; his glance met Brunetti's, and he asked in

a level voice, 'What is it you want to know?'

Brunetti considered for a moment whether he should perhaps ask what the man meant. But Dottor Grandesso held his glance, and Brunetti saw that this was a man who had no time to waste. The expression, so often used as a cliché, came to him with stunning force. The doctor had an appointment, not with him, and not one that anyone wanted to keep, but there was no avoiding it.

'I want to know if there is any reason a person might have wanted to do her an injury,' Brunetti said. Hearing himself say it, he felt a sudden chill, as though he had been asked to put a coin in this man's mouth to pay for his voyage to the other world or, worse, had given him some heavy burden to take with him.

'If I were somehow able to call Rizzardi, would he tell me that she died of a heart attack?' the doctor asked.

'Yes.'

Grandesso looked away from Brunetti, as if examining the shuttered window across the *calle* in search of what to say. 'You're not a religious man, are you?'

'No.'

'But were you raised believing?'

'Yes,' Brunetti had no choice but to admit.

'Then you remember the feeling when you came out of confession – when you still believed in it, I mean – and you felt elevated – if that's the right word – by being rid of your guilt and shame. The priest said the words, you said the prayers, and your soul was somehow clean again.'

Brunetti nodded. Yes, he remembered it and was wise enough to be glad he had had the experience.

The other man must have read Brunetti's face, for he continued. 'I know it sounds strange, but she had a capacity that reminded me of that. She'd listen to me. Just sit there and smile at me and sometimes hold my hand, and I'd tell her things I've never told anyone since my wife died.' He disappeared behind closed eyes, and when he came back, he said, 'And some things I never told my wife, I'm afraid. After that, she'd squeeze my hand, and I felt relieved at having been able, finally, to tell someone.' The doctor tried to raise a hand to make some sort of gesture but managed to lift it only a few centimetres from the bed before it fell back. 'She didn't ask, never seemed curious in any prurient sense: maybe it was the stillness in her that made me want to tell her things. And she was never judgemental, never showed surprise or disapproval. All she did was sit there and listen.'

Brunetti wanted to ask what he had told her but could not do it. He told himself it was respect for the doctor's situation, but he knew that some sort of religious taboo prevented him from daring to break the seal of that confessional, at least in the presence of one of the speakers. Instead, he asked, 'Do you think she listened to everyone the same way?'

Something that might have been a smile flashed across the doctor's face, but his mouth was too thin for it to register on his lips. 'Do you mean do I think that everyone talked to her?'

'Yes.'

'I don't know. It would depend on the person. But you know how old people love to talk, and love most to talk about themselves. Ourselves.'

He went on. 'I've seen her with them, and I think most of them would talk to her freely. And if they thought she could actually forgive them, then . . .' His voice trailed away.

Brunetti could resist his curiosity no longer. 'Did you?'

He struggled to move his head, but when he failed to do that, he said, 'No.'

'Why?'

'Because, like you, Signore,' the doctor said, and this time the smile did reach his lips, 'I don't believe in absolution.'

17

It suddenly occurred to Brunetti to wonder how this bed-ridden man had managed to see Signora Altavilla in the company of other people. 'Is this something you observed, Dottore?' he asked.

The doctor was some time in answering him. 'I haven't always been like this,' he replied simply, as if to declare that the time for explanations had run out, and fact was all he had time for now.

Brunetti remained silent so long that the doctor said, 'I think you'd be more comfortable if you sat.' Brunetti pulled a straight-backed chair to the side of the bed and did as he was told.

It was as if Grandesso, not Brunetti, had relaxed. His lids closed once, twice, but then they snapped open and he said, 'I've sat near her when people have told her things they might better have kept to themselves,' then, even before Brunetti could ask, he added, 'Doctors are in the business of keeping secrets.'

Smiling, Brunetti said, 'I'd guess you're good at that, Doctor.'

Dottor Grandesso started to smile in return, but then his face twisted in a vice of pain; the tendons of his jaw pulsed a few times, and Brunetti thought he could hear his teeth grind, but he wasn't sure. Tears emerged from the man's eyes and ran down the sides of his face. Brunetti was pulled halfway out of his chair, uncertain whether to take the Doctor's hand or to go for help, but then the other man's face relaxed. His jaws unclenched and his mouth fell open; he gasped a few times, then grew calmer, though he still fought to pull in enough air to breathe.

'Is there anything I can . . . ' Brunetti began.

'No,' he said between gasps. Then, 'Don't tell them. Please.'

Brunetti shook his head, unable to respond.

'No hospital,' the doctor gasped. 'It's better here.' His voice came in short spurts, punctuated by long breaths. He closed his eyes again, and this time his face relaxed and the tortured sound of his breathing quieted.

For an instant, Brunetti feared that the man had died before his eyes, he helpless to prevent it; then he heard another of those long breaths, but softer. He sat motionless and watched until he was sure the doctor was asleep. As quietly as he could, Brunetti got to his feet and backed towards the door. He went into the corridor, leaving the door open so that the sleeping man could be seen.

The corridor was empty; the clink of plates and the rushing sound of water came from behind the closed door of the kitchen. Brunetti leaned against the wall. He put his head back until it touched the wall and stood like that for a few minutes.

One of the dark-skinned novices emerged from the kitchen and headed in the other direction. Hearing her footsteps, Brunetti turned towards her. 'Excuse me,' he said and pushed himself away from the wall.

She smiled when she saw him. '*Sì, Signore?*' Then she asked, 'How is he?'

'Resting,' Brunetti answered.

Pleased to hear that, she started to turn away. Brunetti forced himself to ask, 'Could you tell me where I'd find Signora Sartori?', still uncertain how to address her. She wore the habit of a novice, so he could not call her 'Suora', and she had renounced the chance of being called 'Signorina'.

'Ah, I don't know if she's supposed to have visitors,' she said, then added, sounding uneasy, 'Only her husband visits her now. He says it will upset her to have other people in her room, and he doesn't want her bothered.' Brunetti wondered when 'now' had begun.

'Ah,' he said, giving voice to disappointment. 'Signora Altavilla's son asked me to try to speak to the people his mother was closest to and tell them how important they were to her,' he explained with the easy smile of an old friend of the family. He watched her face for signs of belief or sympathy, and when he saw the first signs, he added, 'He told me he was sure she would want them to know.'

'In that case, I suppose it's all right,' she said. She allowed herself to smile, revealing gleaming white teeth, their perfection augmented by the contrast to her dark skin. Brunetti wondered how anyone could be 'bothered' by Signora Altavilla's visits or how anyone could see them in this light. He gave no indication of his uncertainty, however, as the young woman asked him to follow her to Signora Sartori's room.

The door to this room was also open; she walked directly in without announcing either herself or the man who followed her. The woman he had seen eating with such solitary intensity now sat on a simple wooden chair in front of the room's single window. She was staring at the shuttered window opposite, or perhaps at the wall surrounding it: her face was inert, and again Brunetti saw it in profile. The flash of lipstick was still the same glaring red and appeared newly applied.

'Signora Sartori,' the novice said. 'I've brought you a visitor.' The woman remained intent in her contemplation of the wall.

'Signora Sartori,' she tried again, 'This gentleman's come to speak to you.' Still no response.

There was a noise behind them, and when they turned they saw the other dark-skinned novice – the one Brunetti now thought of as the Toltec statue – who, careful to keep both hands hidden under her scapular, said, 'Sister Giuditta needs your help in the kitchen.' She gave Brunetti a nervous smile, uncertain whether she should say something to him, as well.

At the news, the first novice pressed her hands together, glanced at Brunetti, then at her companion, then back to Signora Sartori. Brunetti puffed himself up with the air of casual command and said, 'Fine, then. You go and speak to Suora Giuditta, and I'll wait for you here.' To show how patient he was, as well as to assert his intention to remain in the room, he looked around and chose to sit on a chair to the left of the door, a safe, declared distance from the woman at the window.

In the face of this manifestation of male authority, both girls – for they were hardly more than that – nodded and left the room together, leaving him to Signora Sartori. Or her to him.

He sat quietly, trying to sense how aware, or unaware, she was of his presence, and as time passed he began to suspect that she was as sensitive to his presence as he to hers. He let more time pass. Occasionally people walked past the door, but because Brunetti was sitting to the side of it, no one noticed that he was there. No one stopped to look in, nor did anyone come in to speak to Signora Sartori. After ten minutes or so Brunetti began to suspect that the novices had forgotten about him or perhaps assumed that he had left.

He thought back to the tables in the dining room and his choice of seat. He had sat to Signora Cannata's left, the seat closest to Signora Sartori. How easily she could have heard everything they said, especially in the silence left by the departure of the other two people. So intent had she been on her food that it had not occurred to him at the time that she might have been intent on anything else, though he had said little to Signora Cannata, certainly nothing to raise interest or arouse curiosity.

The silence and the passing of time began to weigh on him, but he forced himself to remain both silent and still.

Her voice, when it came, was rough, the voice of someone no longer accustomed to speech. 'She was a good woman.' How many times was Brunetti to hear this? he wondered. He had never questioned it, and nothing he had heard about her made him suspect that it was not true. Events, however, had placed Signora Altavilla beyond criticism, and so it now mattered little whether she had been a good person or not, or who maintained that she was.

'She understood things. Why people do things.' She spoke a dialect so dense a non-Venetian would have struggled to understand what she said. She nodded in self-affirmation, then again and then again, but without looking in Brunetti's direction. In an entirely different voice, she said, 'We had to,' letting the last word die out in a terminal fall into silence.

'It's hard, sometimes, to know,' Brunetti ventured.

'We knew,' she said, quickly, defensively.

'Of course,' Brunetti agreed.

She turned to look at him then. 'Are you a friend of his?' she asked.

Brunetti settled for a noncommittal noise.

'Did he send you?' Like a bad actress, she squinched up her eyes as she asked this question, as if to show that she was both a suspicious and a clever person and would know if he lied. Seeing her whole face for the first time, he was surprised by its plumpness and the fullness of her mouth. Two deep vertical lines ran beside it; a third line, this one horizontal and in the middle of her chin, turned her face into a wooden puppet's, a resemblance that was augmented by the impassivity of her glance and her strangely round blue eyes.

'No, Signora, he didn't,' Brunetti said, with no idea who they were talking about. 'I came to see you, just as I came to see Signora Cannata: to tell you how important your friendship was to Signora Altavilla and how very fond of you she was.'

She must have preferred whatever she saw on the other side of the *calle*, for she turned her eyes back to it.

He let some more time pass. 'You told her what you did,' he said in an entirely conversational voice, phrasing it as something halfway between a question and a reminder.

His words seemed to strike a blow, for she hunched her shoulders and brought her fists together at the centre of her chest, but she did not turn to face him.

Casually, as though presenting some old adage about the behaviour of children, Brunetti said, 'I think it helps, to be able to tell people what we did and why we did it. Talking about it helps it to go away.' Speaking to her seemed to Brunetti like trying to order from a menu in a language he did not speak: he might see a familiar word or two, but he had no idea what was going to arrive after he spoke those words.

'Trouble comes,' she said to the window on the other side of the *calle*.

As if summoned by her words, a man walked through the door. He was older than she, well into his eighties, one of those common types seen in bars: short, stocky, nose thickened by decades of hard drinking, a bit askew from years of hard living. His sparse hair, dyed a dark mahogany, was longer on one side of his head; it had been carefully combed over his bald scalp and sealed in place by some sort of shiny gel that made his head look as though it had recently been painted or oiled, then streaked with dark paint.

He came in just as she spoke, his arrival an antiphon to her words. He stopped short, apparently at the sight of Brunetti on the chair near the door. 'Who are you?' he demanded angrily, as if Brunetti had been provoking him and he wasn't going to put up with it any longer. When Brunetti did not answer immediately, the man took a few steps towards him, stopped and planted his feet solidly, giving himself a firm base from which to launch an attack. 'I asked you who you are,' he said.

The broken veins in his cheeks and nose grew red, as if his anger had switched them on. 'What are you doing in here?' he demanded, looking at the woman, whose attention had remained on the window. His face softened when he looked at her, but she ignored him and he made no move to approach her. He turned back to Brunetti. 'Are you bothering her?'

Brunetti got slowly to his feet and adopted a look of mild relief. He bent down and carefully pulled at the knees of his trousers to show his concern that they should not wrinkle. 'Ah,' he said with relief he made audible, 'if you're the Signora's husband, perhaps you could give me the information.'

This confused the old man and he asked, 'Who do you think you are to ask me questions? And what are you doing here?' In the face of Brunetti's refusal to answer, he repeated, voice rising another notch, 'Have you been bothering her?' He stepped closer to the woman, placing the thickness of his body between her and Brunetti.

Brunetti reached into his pocket for his notebook. 'All I did was try to ask a question,' he said, allowing annoyance to slip into his own voice. 'But I realized I'd have to speak to someone else, Signore.' He pursed his lips and, making no attempt to disguise his irritation, said, 'I couldn't get any sense out of her.' A look between anger and pain crossed the old man's face. Brunetti licked a finger and turned a few pages, then pointed down at a page on which he had written, in preparation for a parent–teacher meeting that was to be held at Chiara's school the following week, a list of her teachers and the subjects they taught.

'I need the information about the years 1988 and 1989. There's nothing we can do until we have it.'

'Go to hell with your 1988, and take 1989 with you,' the old man said, pleased that he now had something specific to be angry about and pleased with his cleverness in expressing it.

Brunetti allowed surprise, then indignation, to play across his face. Then he took a long look at this noisy old man, as if seeing or hearing him for the first time. He stood up straighter and took a step towards him; there was no menace in the movement; though the old man leaned back from him, he did not move from his position in front of the woman.

Brunetti waved the notebook in the air between them. 'See this, Signore? See this notebook? It's got her entire work record, all those years. But not 1988 and 1989, so they haven't been credited to her account.' An exasperated Brunetti allowed himself to glance at the woman. 'So she's not being paid for them.' He allowed himself to sound as if, given the way this man had treated him, he was almost pleased with the fact.

'I asked her about those years,' Brunetti said, looking in her direction with an annoyance he tried, and failed, to disguise. He'd come all this way to try to solve a problem, and first the woman was mute, and now the man told him to go to hell. 'Like talking to a statue.' He leaned forward, and this time the old man did take one step backwards. 'And then I have to listen to you,' Brunetti said with angry disgust.

Brunetti drew a few deep breaths, as if enjoining himself to patience; but, like every bureaucrat, he had a point beyond which his patience was exhausted, and he had clearly passed it. 'Try to help people, and all you get is abuse.'

As he spoke, his voice angrier with every sentence, Brunetti kept his eyes on the old man. If Brunetti had stuck him with a pin, he could not have deflated more quickly. Strangely enough, this time the other parts of his face flushed red, while his cheeks and his nose turned an unhealthy white.

He cast a glance at the woman to see if she had been following, and Brunetti could almost smell his fear that she had heard and understood what his meddling had provoked.

The old man raised both hands in a placatory gesture towards Brunetti. 'Signore, Signore,' he said. All signs of aggression and anger had vanished. He pasted a thin smile on his face.

'No,' Brunetti said, snapping the notebook shut just under the other man's nose and jamming it back in his pocket. 'No. There's no use wasting my time on the likes of you. No use ever trying to do anyone a favour.' He forced his voice even louder and all but shouted, 'You can wait for official notice, the way everyone else does.'

He turned and walked quickly towards the door. The old man took one tentative step towards him, hands still raised, now in near-supplication. 'But Signore, I didn't understand. I didn't mean . . . She needs . . .' he almost bleated in the tone of a citizen who sees himself losing the chance to receive a payment from a government office and who knows he will now have to wait for the bureaucracy to volunteer to make the payment.

Brunetti, enjoying his indignation, left the room and walked quickly down the corridor. He made his way to the front door and left the *casa di cura* without seeing either of the novices or any of the sisters.

18

Returned to the street and free of the role of irritated bureaucrat, Brunetti considered, and then regretted, the rashness of his behaviour. There had been no need for his charade, his heavy-handed impersonation, but something in him knew that the man should be prevented from suspecting that the authorities were taking an interest in the nursing home or any of the people in it, and so he had acted without thinking and given in to his impulse towards secrecy: should he ever have to deal with the old man in his official capacity as a representative of the law, the situation could be legally complicated by his original misrepresentation. He had seen cases destroyed by less.

But what was he doing, even thinking in terms of a case? All he had was a choleric old man shouting at him and a woman of uncertain lucidity warning him of trouble to come. When was trouble not coming?

The old man had foreseen trouble in the presence of an unknown visitor in her room and had been suspicious that Brunetti had been asking questions. Why should this concern him? Brunetti cast his memory back over the scene. He had explained that it was impossible to get any information from her, and the man's anger had been dissipated only by the possibility that the woman would receive money.

Brunetti seldom permitted himself the luxury of disliking the people he met in the course of his work. He formed first impressions, surely, sometimes very strong ones. They were often correct, but not always. Over the years, he had come to accept that the negative ones were more distorting than the positive ones: it was too easy to follow the dictates of dislike.

But, of all the world, Brunetti most hated bullies. He hated them for the injustice of what they did and for their need to make others submit. Only once in his professional life had he lost control of himself, almost twenty years ago, during the questioning of a man who had kicked a prostitute to death. He had been captured because his three initials were embroidered on the linen handkerchief he had used to wipe the blood off his shoes and dropped not far from the woman's body.

Luckily, three officers had been detailed to question the man, an accountant who shared control of a string of girls with their pimp. When asked to identify the handkerchief, it did not escape the observation of any of the policemen that he wore an identical one in his breast pocket.

As soon as he realized the meaning and the consequences of the handkerchiefs, he had said, man to man, just one of the boys, and oh, so eager to show what a tough boy he was, 'She was just a whore. I shouldn't have wasted a linen handkerchief on her.' It was then that the younger, rawer Brunetti had jumped to his feet, already halfway across the table towards him. Wiser heads, and hands, had intervened, and Brunetti had been replanted solidly in his chair to wait out, silently, the interrogation.

Times had been different then, and his attempt had had no legal consequences. In today's legal climate, however, were the old man ever to be accused of a crime, the disclosure of Brunetti's true profession would be milk and honey to a defence attorney.

Mulling over all of this, Brunetti made his way back to the Questura. When he got there, he went directly to Signorina Elettra's room, where he found her reading: not a magazine, as was her usual habit in quiet moments, but a book.

She slipped a piece of paper between the pages and closed the book. 'Light workload today?' he enquired.

'You might put it that way, Commissario,' she said, placing the book to the side of her computer, the front cover facing downward.

He approached her desk and said, 'I met a woman today, one of the people that Signora Altavilla visited with at the *casa di cura*.'

'And I'd like you to see what we can find out about her,' she concluded, just as if she were channelling his thoughts, though she made no attempt to imitate his voice.

'It's that obvious?' he asked, smiling.

'You do get a certain predatory look,' she said.

'What else?'

'You don't usually limit yourself to that person, Signore, so I'm preparing myself to see what I can find, not only about her but about her husband and any children they might have.'

'Sartori. I don't know her first name, and I don't know how long she's been there. At least a few years, I'd guess. She has a husband who seems to have the default mechanism of anger. I don't know his name, and I don't know about children.'

'Do you think she's there as a private patient?' Signorina Elettra asked, confusing him with the question.

'I have no idea,' he said. He thought back to the room, but it was just a room in an old people's home. There had been no evidence of luxury, and he had not noticed any personal items. 'Why? What difference would it make?'

'If she's there as a public patient, then I'd start first with the state records, but if she's private, I'd have to access the records of the *casa di cura*.' The mere sound of the word 'access' falling from the lips of Signorina Elettra induced in Brunetti a state analogous to that of a rabbit under the gaze of a boa constrictor.

'Which is easier?' he asked, refusing to add 'to access' and wise enough not to use 'to get into'.

'Ah, the *casa di cura*, certainly,' she said, with the condescension of the heavyweight champion confronted by a nightclub bouncer.

'The other?' he asked, curious as always about the importance the state gave to the protection and accuracy of the information it possessed about its citizens.

His question elicited a sigh and a weary shake of her head. She made a tisking sound and said, 'With government offices, the problem's not about getting into the system – in most cases, a high school student could do it – it's about then being able to find the information.'

'I'm not sure I understand the distinction,' Brunetti admitted.

She paused, considering what example would be simple enough for a person of his limited talents. 'I suppose it's like a burglary, Signore. Getting into the house is easy, especially when the door is left on the latch. But once you get inside, you discover that the people live in a complete mess, with dirty dishes in the bedroom and old shoes and newspapers in the kitchen.' She saw his dawning understanding and went on. 'And they've lived that way since the house was built, so all that's happened as time passed and more things came into the house is that the mess has turned to complete chaos, and even finding the simplest thing – a teaspoon, for example – requires you to go through the whole house room by room, and search for it everywhere.'

Not that he needed to know, but because her explanation forced him to be curious: 'Is this the case in all public offices?'

'Mercifully not, Commissario.'

'Which are the best?' he asked, unaware of the ambiguity of his question.

'Oh,' she said. 'There's no best; it's only least bad.' Seeing that she had not satisfied him, she said, 'Finding out who has been given a passport is usually easy. And gun permits. Those records are quite orderly. But after that there's a great deal of confusion, and there's no hope of knowing who has a *permesso di soggiorno* or a work permit, or really understanding what the rules or criteria are for getting them.'

Since those all fell under the Ministry for which Brunetti worked, the news came as little surprise. He could not resist the temptation and asked, 'And the worst?'

'I'm not really competent to judge,' she said with admirably feigned modesty, 'but the ones I find it most difficult to, well, to navigate – however easy it is to get to the point where I can – are those which authorize people to do things, or perhaps it's better to say those agencies which are meant to protect us.' In response to his furrowed brow, she said, 'I mean those offices where they're supposed to check that nurses have the right documents and that they really did study where they say they did. Or, for that fact, doctors and psychiatrists and dentists.' She spoke with dispassion, the frustrated researcher reporting her findings. 'There's terrible negligence there. Getting into their system is easy, as I told you, but after that it's all very difficult.' Then, gracious and generous as ever, she added, 'For them as well, I'm sure, poor things.'

Brunetti's family occasionally watched a television programme that made public some of the worst cases of governmental negligence. For reasons he did not understand, his children found it wonderfully funny, while he and Paola cringed at the nonchalance with which its nightly revelations were greeted when presented to the authorities who had failed to prevent or detect abuses. How many fake doctors had the programme discovered, how many fake healers? And how many of them had been stopped?

Brunetti pulled himself away from these thoughts and said, 'I'd be very grateful for anything you could find about either her or her husband.'

'Of course, sir,' she said, not unrelieved to have an end called to their discussion of her cyber-explorations and their resulting discoveries. 'I'll see what I can find.' Then, efficiency itself, 'How far back should I go?'

'Until you find something interesting,' he said, trying to sound as if he were joking but fearing he did not succeed.

After this, Brunetti repaired to his office. Once at his desk, he was suddenly assailed by hunger, looked at his watch, and was surprised to see that it was well past three. He called home but no one answered: he hung up before the machine kicked in. Paola refused to carry a *telefonino*, and the kids, both probably already back at school, were not likely to be of any help. He could try her on her office phone, but she seldom answered it: her students knew where to find her, and any colleague who wanted to speak to her, as far as she was concerned, could walk down the hall to her office.

He thought of calling home again and this time leaving a message, but nothing he could say would change the fact that he had once again failed to show up for lunch and had not thought to call. The kids would hear about something like this for days had either tried it.

His phone rang, and he answered with his name.

'This is Maddalena Orsoni,' she said. 'It turns out that I came back sooner than planned.'

In most circumstances, Brunetti would offer some cliché about hoping this did not mean she had encountered any sort of difficulty, but she did not sound like the sort of woman to have much patience with cliché or sentiment, and so he said, 'Would it be possible for us to meet now?'

Neither of them, he noticed, made any reference to the

subject that concerned them. He was a public official in pursuit of information, yet he instinctively avoided asking any specific questions on the phone. How convenient Venice made it to have a conversation, to meet on the street, as if by accident, and go for a coffee; how easy to walk across town to have a drink and a chat.

'Yes,' she finally answered.

'A bar?'

'Fine.'

'I don't know where you are,' he said, adding, 'but I'm at San Lorenzo. So choose a place that's convenient for you; I'll meet you there.'

She took some time considering this and finally said, 'There's a bar just at the end of Barbaria delle Tole in Campo Santa Giustina, on the corner on the left as you come in from SS. Giovanni e Paolo. I can be there in ten minutes.'

'I'll see you there,' he said and replaced the phone.

19

What an odd place to meet. Could any *campo* be more out of the way than Campo Santa Giustina? Only someone heading towards San Francesco della Vigna or to the Celestia boat stop would pass through it, or someone like Brunetti who often walked for the simple pleasure of seeing or re-seeing the city. He recalled coming here, years ago, in search of the person rumoured to be able to repair dolls. Chiara's grand-parents had given her a porcelain-headed girl in a hoop skirt for Christmas, but the doll had lost an eye. Brunetti no longer remembered whether he had managed to find the eye, but he did remember the taciturn grey-haired woman who ran the Doll Hospital, looking as much like a patient as did the dolls she kept in the window. He had passed through the *campo* since then but had never veered over to look in the window to check up on new patients.

It took him only a short time to get there. Across the *campo* he recognized the dreary window of the second-hand clothing store. Like most Italians of his age, Brunetti disliked the idea of buying used clothing; indeed, used anything, unless it were, say, a painting. But who would be tempted, save by abject misery, to want anything in that window? Brunetti had not been to Bulgaria when it was still a Communist country, but he imagined its shop windows must have looked like this: dusty, sober, earth-coloured pleas that people pass by without looking.

He went into the bar. A dark-haired woman was the only client, sitting at a table near the window. He approached and asked, 'Signora Orsoni?'

She looked at him without smiling or extending her hand. 'Good afternoon, Commissario,' she said and nodded towards the seat opposite her.

He pulled the chair away from the table and sat. Before he could say anything, the barman approached their table and they asked for coffee; then Brunetti changed his mind and asked for a glass of white wine and a toast.

When the man moved away, they studied one another, each waiting for the other to speak. Brunetti saw a woman in her early fifties, with light eyes in surprising contrast to her dark hair and olive skin. She had made no attempt to colour the grey in her hair: that and the crow's feet around her eyes spoke of a lack of concern with maintaining the appearance of youth.

'I'm Maddalena Orsoni, Commissario. I set up Alba Libera, and I've run it since it began.'

'How long ago was that?' he asked, displaying no surprise at her refusal to engage in the usual social preliminaries to conversation.

'Four years.'

'May I ask why you started it?'

'Because my brother-in-law killed my sister,' she said. Though she must have given this same answer many times, Brunetti suspected she was curious about the effect of such brutal honesty. He acknowledged her statement, however, with only a nod, and she went on. 'He was a violent man, but she loved him. He said he loved her. There was always a reason for his violence, of course: he'd had a hard day; something was wrong with dinner; he saw her looking at another man.'

Hearing her recite this made him wonder how many times she had told this story, but it also reminded him of how often he had heard the same explanations given from men in justification of violence, rape, murder.

The barman came and served them. Brunetti couldn't bring himself to touch his toast, not while her words still echoed between them.

'Go ahead and eat,' she said, pouring some sugar into her cup. She stirred it slowly, watching it dissolve.

Brunetti's stomach, perhaps at the proximity to what was going to have to substitute for the lunch he had lost, growled. She smiled, finished her coffee and set the cup down. 'Please. Eat.'

He tried to do as he was told: the toasting had done nothing to improve the taste of processed white bread, nor had the heat managed to melt the processed cheese or bestow taste upon the cooked ham. Cardboard would have been worse, he supposed. He put the toast back on his plate and took a sip of wine. That, at least, was tolerable.

'She didn't want to call the police,' Signora Orsoni continued: Brunetti realized she had not finished telling the story of her sister. 'And then she was afraid to call them. He broke her nose, and then her arm, and then she did call them.' She looked at him, a level glance, appraising. 'They did nothing.' Brunetti asked for no explanation. 'There was no place she could go.' She caught his expression and said, 'Or would go. I was living in Rome, and she never told me anything was wrong.'

'Your family?'

'There were only two old great-aunts left, and they knew nothing.'

'Friends?'

'She was six years younger, and we were never at the same school together. So we didn't have any friends in common.' She shrugged this away. 'That's the way it was. It's not something women talk about, is it?'

'No, it's not,' Brunetti said and drank more wine.

'She was a lawyer,' Signora Orsoni said, giving a lopsided smile, as if asking him to believe, please, that she wasn't making this up, and who could believe that her sister could have been so stupid. 'After she finally called the police – after her arm – they took him away, but the prison was full, so he was given house arrest.' She paused to see what this representative of the legal system would have to say to that, but Brunetti remained silent.

'So *she* moved out, and then she got a separation, and when that didn't keep him away, she got an injunction against him. He had to stay at least a hundred and fifty metres from her.' Orsoni caught the barman's attention and asked for a glass of mineral water.

'She wanted to move away – they were both still living in Mestre. She had left him the apartment when she moved out, but her job was there, and . . .' Brunetti wondered how she would manage to say what she had to say, something he had heard many people say, after. 'And I suppose she didn't have any idea about him.' The barman brought the water. She thanked him for it and drank half, then set the glass down.

'One night he went to her new apartment with a gun, and he shot her when she opened the door. Then he shot her three more times, and then he shot himself in the head.' Brunetti remembered the case: four, five years ago.

'You came back?'

'Do you mean then, when she was killed?'

'Yes.'

'Yes, I came back. And I decided to stay and do something new. If I could.'

'Alba Libera?' he asked.

Perhaps hearing scepticism in the way he pronounced the name, she said quickly, 'Well, it *is* dawning liberty for most of these women.' Brunetti nodded, and she went on. 'It took me two years to set it up. I was already managing an NGO in Rome, so I was familiar with the system and knew how to get the permissions and money from the state.'

He liked the fact that she called it 'money' and did not bother with all the euphemisms people used. And now that she was talking about procedure and routine, the angry undertone had disappeared from her voice.

She went on. 'She should have gone to another city: she could have found work. The law couldn't protect her, but she didn't want to believe that. There was no safe house, no place where she could go and live and be with people who would try to protect her.'

Brunetti knew well how little chance a person in danger had of getting any sort of protection from the state. The current government was doing everything in its power to eviscerate the existing witness protection programme: there were too many people saying embarrassing things in court about the Mafia. These witnesses provided information, at least, in return for safety: imagine the chance of protection being offered to a woman who had nothing to offer the state in return.

Perhaps she too heard the tinge of outrage creeping into her voice. 'I think that's enough explanation. At least you know why I started it. We have a number of houses, most of them out on *terra ferma:* here in the city, we have some people who will give a room to the women we send them and not ask questions.'

'Are they safe here?'

'Safer than where they come from. Much.'

'Always? They don't get found?'

'It happens,' she said, pushing her glass to one side

without picking it up. 'Last year, near Treviso, there was a case.'

Brunetti searched his memory but could come up with nothing. 'What happened?'

'Her boyfriend found out where she was – we never learned how he did or who told him – and came to the home where she was living and asked for her.'

'What happened?'

Her face softened, as if to announce that there would be some lessening of misery in this story. 'The old woman she was staying with – she's almost ninety – said she didn't really understand what he was talking about, she lived alone, but told him he looked like a nice boy, so she invited him in to have a coffee. She told me she left him alone in the living room while she went to the kitchen.'

She saw Brunetti's fear for the old woman, and for the younger one, so she explained, 'She's a wily old thing, told me her parents had a Jewish friend live with them all during the war. That's where she learned the rules she imposes.' In response to Brunetti's unspoken question, she said, 'No items of any sort from their old lives, not even underwear. Everything they wear is kept in her closet and drawers, mixed in with her things. And every time they leave the apartment, no matter for what, they have to leave their room looking as though no one uses it.'

'Just in case?' Brunetti asked.

'Just in case.'

'What happened?'

'She took as long as she could making the coffee, and all the while she could hear him moving around in the other rooms. He went into the guest room. Then he came into the kitchen, and she gave him a coffee and some biscuits, and she started talking about her grandchildren and telling him what a fine-looking young man he was, and was he married, and soon he got up and left.'

'And?'

'And we moved her to another city that night.'

'I see,' Brunetti said. 'You're very efficient.'

'We have to be. Some of these men are very clever. And all of them are violent.'

She made no gratuitous reference to her sister here, and Brunetti was glad of that.

'And Signora Altavilla?'

'A cousin of hers told her about us. She and I had a talk, and she told me she would be willing to help us. She was a widow, lived alone, had an extra room, and there were three other apartments in the building.' Seeing Brunetti's puzzled expression, she explained, 'It means people are constantly going in and out of the building.'

'How long ago was this?'

She tilted her head to the right while she searched her memory.

'Two, three years ago, I'd say. I'd have to check my records.'

'Where are your offices, if I might ask?' Brunetti said, though that would be easy enough to find out.

'Not far from here,' she said, irritating him with the unnecessary evasion.

Brunetti continued, 'Did anything similar to what happened to that old woman – a man coming to the house or suspecting that someone was staying there – ever happen to Signora Altavilla?'

She put her hands on the table and laced her fingers together. 'She never said anything.' By way of explanation, she added, 'We give clear instructions about that. The house owner has to report anything – even if it's only a suspicion – immediately.' Then she said, with a weary smile, 'Not everyone is as clever as that old woman.'

'Do you know if she was ever troubled by anything one of her guests told her?'

Her smile grew warmer. 'That's very kind of you,' she said.'

Momentarily confused, Brunetti said, 'I don't understand.'

'To call them guests.'

'It seems to me that's what they are,' he answered simply, ignoring her attempt at diversion. 'Did this ever happen, that she was troubled by something she heard?'

Signora Orsoni raised her chin and pulled in air, creating a noise Brunetti could hear from the other side of the table. 'No, not really. That is, she never told me about anything like that.' She gave him an evaluating glance, then said, 'Usually these women talk very little.' She offered no further explication, though Brunetti still felt she had something else to say.

'But?' he encouraged.

'But it came the other way,' she said, confusing him again. 'That is, a woman who was staying with her said she thought something had upset Costanza.'

'What exactly did she say?' Brunetti asked, trying to hide his rush of interest.

Orsoni rubbed her forehead, as if to show Brunetti how hard she was trying to remember. 'She said that when she went to stay with her, Costanza seemed a very calm person, but then after she had been there for a few weeks, Costanza came home one day looking troubled. She thought it would pass, but the mood she came home in seemed to linger.'

'Where had she gone? Did she know?'

'She said the only places Costanza ever went were to visit her son and to see the old people in the nursing home.'

'When did she tell you this?'

'When she was leaving – when I was going to the airport with her. It must have happened about a month ago, so perhaps Costanza's spirits improved after that.'

'Did this woman ask her about it?'

Signora Orsoni spread her palms out flat. 'You have to understand the dynamic here, Commissario. You call these women guests, but it's not like that. They're in hiding. Some of them go out to work, but most of them stay home, and the only thing they can do is worry about what's going to happen to them.'

She looked at him to be sure she had his full attention and continued. 'Bad things have happened to these women, Commissario. They've been beaten, and raped, and men have tried to kill them, so it's difficult for them to concern themselves with the problems of other people.' She paused, as if to measure the sympathy with which he greeted this, and then said, 'They find it hard even to imagine that people like the ones they stay with – who have homes, and jobs, who don't have financial problems, and who aren't at risk – it's hard for them to think that these people can have problems.' She stared across the table at him. 'So the amazing thing is not that she didn't ask what was wrong but that she even noticed that something was. Fear cripples people,' she said, and he thought of her sister.

'You say you took her to the airport?' he asked.

Displaying no surprise that her words had failed to deflect him, she said, 'She left. I told you that.'

'Why?'

'Her husband was arrested.'

'For what?'

'Murder.'

'Who?'

'His lover.'

'Ah,' escaped Brunetti, but then he asked, 'And so?'

'And so she could go back to her home.' Signora Orsoni's tone made this sound like a simple choice, even an obvious one. Perhaps it was.

'Who came then?'

He watched as she formulated an answer. 'Another young woman, but she'd left before Costanza died.'

'Tell me about her,' Brunetti said.

'There's nothing to tell, really. Only what she told me.' At Brunetti's encouraging nod, she went on. 'She's from Padova. She was in university there, studying economics.' She paused but Brunetti waited her out, and she added, 'Her family's very . . . traditional.' When Brunetti did not respond to that word, she went on. 'So when she told them she had a boyfriend,' she began, then added, 'who's from Catania . . . they told her she had to choose between him and them.' She shook her head at such things in this day and age. 'So she chose the boyfriend and went to live with him.'

'How did she get to Signora Altavilla?' he asked, if only to show her that he had not been distracted by this story of the young woman, no matter how traditional her family.

'She called our office in Treviso about three weeks ago. That was after the police said there was nothing they could do.' She looked at Brunetti, who lifted his chin in enquiry. 'The boyfriend. She said there was trouble from the start. That he was jealous. And violent: he roughed her up a few times, but she was afraid to call the police.' She sighed and raised her hands and shoulders in exasperation.

'This time she thought he was going to kill her: that's what she told them. They were in the kitchen when it happened, and to protect herself she poured the pasta water on him.' He thought she seemed unusually passive in describing this.

'And?'

'And she got out and called the police.'

'What happened then?'

'They went to the apartment to talk to him, but they didn't do anything.'

'Why?'

'Because it was his word against hers. He said she had started the argument and all he'd tried to do was defend himself.' Though she tried, she failed to disguise scorn of the police and anger at male prejudice as she recounted this. She went on, finally expressing an opinion, 'Besides, she's a

166

woman and he's a man.' Brunetti was surprised she failed to add, 'And he's a Sicilian.'

In the face of Brunetti's silence, she continued, 'They were living in Treviso and, as I said, she called our office there. They thought she'd be safe here in the city: it's far enough away.'

After considering what she had told him, Brunetti asked, 'Did the police tell you this?'

Her features appeared to contract. 'I spoke to someone in our office, and that's what they told me.'

After some time, Brunetti asked, 'Signora Altavilla helped you for several years, you said?'

It was evident that the question displeased her, but eventually she said, 'Yes.'

'Putting herself at some risk.' When he saw her begin to protest, he added, 'Theoretical risk. But she was still willing to do it.'

She nodded, looked away, then back at him.

'This woman, you say she isn't there any more,' Brunetti said. 'And there was no sign of her in the apartment.'

Again Signora Orsoni nodded.

'Could she have gone back to the apartment?'

Voice level, emotionless, she said, 'She had nothing to do with this.'

'How do I know that's true?' he asked.

'Because I'm telling you so.'

'And if I choose not to believe you?'

As he waited for her to respond Brunetti saw the moment when she decided to leave, saw it in her eyes and then heard it as she drew her feet under her chair. He raised a hand to catch her attention.

'Your organization is fairly well known, isn't it?' he asked mildly.

She smiled involuntarily at what she took to be a compliment. 'I'd like to think so,' she said.

'And I imagine the city gives you what support it can. And private donors.'

Her smile was small but gracious. 'They realize, perhaps, how much good we do.'

'Do you think bad publicity would change that?' Brunetti enquired in the same mild fashion and with every appearance of real interest.

It took a moment for her to register what he had said. 'What do you mean? What bad publicity?'

'Come now, Signora. No need to be disingenuous with me. The sort of bad publicity that would come when the papers wrote about how your society put a woman in the home of a widow – no, make that a Venetian widow – and when the Venetian woman dies in strange circumstances, the woman you put there is nowhere to be found.' He smiled and said, voice amiably conversational, 'The word "risk" can't help coming to mind, can it?'

Then, far more serious, he went on with his reconstruction of events and how they might be perceived, adding some details to strengthen his case: 'The circumstances of her death are unclear, and the police are unable to find this woman who was put there by Alba Libera.' He put his elbow on the table and propped his chin in his hand. 'That's the kind of bad publicity I'm talking about, Signora.'

She rose to her feet and Brunetti thought she was going to walk out. But she stood and stared at him for some time. Then she pulled out her *telefonino* and held up a hand for him to wait. She moved over to stand beside the door, but then looked back at Brunetti and went outside. She tapped in a number.

Brunetti called over for a glass of mineral water and, though he drank it slowly, nudging the plate containing the uneaten toast farther away from him, when he finished the water she was still holding the phone, still punching in numbers.

There was a copy of *Il Gazzettino* on the next table, but Brunetti did not want to offend her by such a blatant sign of impatience. He pulled out his notebook and wrote down a few phrases that would bring the conversation back to him. Busy with this, he did not hear her approach the table and was not aware of her return until she said, 'She isn't answering her phone.'

20

Brunetti stood to pull her chair out for her. She sat, placing her *telefonino* in front of her. 'I don't know why she doesn't answer. She can see who's calling,' she said, sounding to Brunetti forced and artificial.

He resumed his seat and reached for his glass, only to see that it was empty. He pushed it to the side and said, 'Of course.' He looked at the ugly slab of sandwich and then at Signora Orsoni.

His face was implacable; he said nothing.

'She called me,' Signora Orsoni said.

'Who?' Brunetti asked. She failed to answer, and so he asked again, 'Who called you, Signora?'

'Signora . . . Costanza. She called me.'

Brunetti weighed her weakness and asked, 'Why?'

'She told me . . . she told me she'd spoken to him.' She glanced at Brunetti, saw that he didn't follow her, and said, 'Her boyfriend.'

'The Sicilian? How did she find him?'

She put her elbows on the table and sank her head into her

hands. She shook it back and forth a few times and, looking at the surface of the table, said, 'He found her. The woman called him from the house, and then later when he called the number back Costanza answered with her name, and he asked if he could speak with her.' It took Brunetti a moment to work his way through the pronouns, but it seemed pretty clear that the woman staying with Signora Altavilla had been foolish enough to call her boyfriend from Signora Altavilla's home phone, a phone that let him read the number from which the call was coming. Easy enough then for him to call that number to see if she was living there.

'Did he threaten her?'

She moved her hands closer together, until they meshed in a shield over her forehead, covering her eyes. She shook his question away.

'What did he want?'

After a long time she said, 'He told her that all he wanted to do was talk to her. She could pick the place and he would meet her there. He told her he'd meet her at a police station or at Florian's: any public place where she'd feel safe.' She stopped talking, but she did not remove her hands from her face.

'Did she meet him?' Brunetti asked.

She said, face still hidden, 'Yes.'

Realizing that it mattered little where their meeting had taken place, Brunetti asked, 'What did he want?'

She put her hands on the table, and clenched them into fists. 'He said he wanted to warn her.'

The verb surprised Brunetti. His mind leaped ahead. Did this young man have a perverse belief in some crazy Sicilian idea of personal honour and want to warn this old woman out of the line of fire? Or did he want to invent some story about the woman in her home?

'What happened?' he asked in a voice he made as calm as if he were asking her the time.

'She said that's what he did: warned her.'

'About himself?' Brunetti interrupted to ask, running ahead with his wild scenario.

Her surprise was evident. 'No, about her.'

'The woman?' Brunetti asked. 'The one in her apartment?'

'Yes.'

Like a rugby player who dropped the ball for an instant, Brunetti picked it up, switched sides, and began to run in the opposite direction. 'What did he tell her?'

She looked away from him towards a noise that came from the door, which was just then pushed open by two men. They stood there for a moment, were joined by a third, who tossed a lighted cigarette into the street, then the three of them went to the bar and ordered coffee. The sound of their voices came across the room, the gruff friendliness of workers on their break.

'Signora?' he said, calling back her attention.

'That she was a thief and she shouldn't have her in her house.' It upset her, he could see, to repeat this. Brunetti could understand: Signora Orsoni had dedicated her energies to saving women in danger from violence. And now this.

'What happened?'

She looked trapped. At first she did not answer, but then she said, 'It was true.'

'How do you know that?'

'He had copies of newspaper articles, police reports.' Seeing his surprise, she said, 'She met him outside down in the *campo*.'

'What did the reports say?' Brunetti asked.

'That this was her tactic. She'd move to a city, start an affair with a man, either move in with him or have him come to her place. Then she'd start an argument with him, and she'd see that it got violent. And when the police came –' she drew her fists up and pushed them into her eyes, either from shame or to prevent her seeing his expression '– he said that was the most effective: when the neighbours called the police.'

Voice tight and reckless, she continued, 'She'd be the victim, and the police would get in touch with one of the groups that helps battered women, and she'd be placed in a home, and she'd stay there until she had her own key and knew what was in the house. Then she'd disappear with as much as she could carry.'

As her voice choked off in disgust, Brunetti heard the clink of cups on saucers, hearty laughter, the sound of coins dropping, and then the door opened and closed and the workmen were gone.

Her voice came back to the restored silence of the bar. 'He told Costanza this, and he showed her the reports, and begged her to believe him.'

'What about the burns?' Brunetti asked. When she seemed not to understand, he said, 'From the pasta water?'

She ran her fingernail up and down one of the deep furrows in the wood of the tabletop. 'Costanza said he still limped, but he didn't say anything about it.'

She got to her feet, then walked to the bar and came back with two glasses of water, set one in front of him, and sat down again.

'When was this, Signora?' he asked.

She drank half of the water and set the glass on the table. She gave Brunetti a long look before saying, 'The day before Costanza died.'

'How do you know about this?' he asked, ignoring the glass in front of him.

'She called me. Costanza. She called me when she went home after talking to the man, and she asked me – told me, really – to come to her place.' Her breathing grew quicker again. 'I went there, and she made me read the articles and look at the police reports.'

'Where did the man go?'

'She told me he said he just wanted to warn her and show her the danger, and once he did that he thanked her for listening to him and left. That was all. It was enough for him to see that she believed him. He said many people didn't because he's Sicilian.' She allowed, as did Brunetti, a long silence to stretch out after this until finally she said, 'She told me he seemed like a kind man.'

Her face was leaden and Brunetti had the sense not to say anything. Instead, he asked, 'What happened?'

'Costanza told me to call the woman and tell her I had to talk to her.'

'And did you?'

Her anger flashed out. 'Of course I did. I didn't have any choice, did I?' She got herself under control and continued. 'I'd got her a day job spending time with an old woman. Not doing anything, really, just preparing her lunch and being there in case anything happened.'

'I see,' Brunetti said. 'And then?'

'I asked her to come back when the old woman's daughter got home from work at four, and she said she would.'

'And?'

'When she came back, I told her we had to move her to another city.'

'Did she believe you?'

She shrugged. 'I don't know.'

'What happened?'

'She went to her room and packed.'

'Did you go with her?'

'No. We stayed in the living room. She went to her room and packed her suitcase.' She started to say something else, but whatever she read in Brunetti's face appeared to silence her.

'She didn't suspect anything?' Brunetti asked.

'I don't know. I don't care.'

'Then what happened?'

'She came in with her suitcase, said goodbye to Costanza, gave her the key, and we left the apartment.'

'Then what?'

'We took the vaporetto to the train station and went to the ticket window together, and I asked her where she wanted to go.'

'So she realized by then what had happened?'

'I suppose so,' Signora Orsoni said, and Brunetti felt a surge of irritation at her evasiveness.

'And?'

'And I got her a ticket on the last train to Rome. It leaves just before seven-thirty.'

'Did you see her get on the train?'

'Yes.'

'Did you wait until it left?'

She made no attempt to disguise her mounting anger. 'Of course I did. But she could have got off in Mestre for all I know.'

'But she'd given the key back?'

'Costanza didn't even have to ask for it,' she said, then added, almost with satisfaction, 'but she could have had a copy made.'

Brunetti said nothing about this.

'What's her name?' he asked.

He watched her hesitate, and he knew he'd take her in for questioning if she refused to answer. Before she could say anything, he added, 'And the man's. The Sicilian.'

'Gabriela Pavon and Nico Martucci.'

'Thank you,' Brunetti said and got to his feet. 'If I need any other information, I'll call you and ask you to come to the Questura.'

'And if I refuse?' she asked.

Brunetti didn't bother to answer her question.

21

Brunetti was relieved to be quit of her, accepting only then how little he had warmed to this woman. Her half-truths, delays, and attempts to manipulate him had annoyed him; worse, she seemed concerned with Signora Altavilla's death only to the degree that it was a source of guilt for herself or potential danger for her ridiculously named Alba Libera. How little they care about people, those people who wanted to help humanity.

He mulled over these things while starting on his way back to the Questura, but then, as if emerging from a dream, he suddenly noticed how much light had departed the day. He glanced at his watch and was astonished to see that it was almost five. He judged it foolish to return to the Questura but did not change the direction of his steps, seeing himself from above as he plodded along like an animal on its way back to the barn. At the Questura, he went to Signorina Elettra's office and found her at her desk, reading what appeared to be the same book he had noticed the last time. She looked up when she heard him come in and casually closed it and slid it aside. 'You have the look of someone who has brought more work,' she said, smiling.

'I just spoke to the leader of Alba Libera,' he said.

'Ah, Maddalena. What did you think of her?' she asked with complete neutrality, offering no clue to what her own opinion might be.

'That she likes helping people,' Brunetti answered with equal neutrality.

'That certainly seems a worthy desire,' Signorina Elettra allowed.

Brunetti wondered when one of them would give in and express an opinion.

'She reminds me a bit of those women in nineteenth-century novels, interested in the moral improvement of their inferiors,' she said.

For a moment, Brunetti weighed the possibility that more than a decade's exposure to his view of the world had affected hers, but then he realized how self-flattering this was: Signorina Elettra surely had her own ample reserves of scepticism.

Suddenly impatient with sparring, he said, 'One of the women she helped was staying with Signora Altavilla up until the evening before her death, but it turns out this woman has stayed in other houses, in similar circumstances . . .'

'And has made off with the silver?' Signorina Elettra joked.

'Something like that.' He watched her surprise register and liked the fact that she was surprised.

'Her name?' she enquired.

'Gabriela Pavon, though I very much doubt it's her real name. And the man from whom she was supposedly hiding is Nico Martucci, a Sicilian. That probably is his real name. Lives in Treviso.' When she began to write down the names, Brunetti said, 'Don't bother. I've got a friend in Treviso who can tell me. It'll save time.'

He turned to leave but she said, pointing to some papers on

her desk, 'I've found out a few things about Signora Sartori and the man she lived with.'

'So they aren't married?' he asked.

'Not in the records of the nursing home. Her entire pension goes directly to them, and her companion Morandi pays the rest.' Then, seeing his surprise, she added, 'He wouldn't have to pay, since they're not married. But he does.' Brunetti thought of the red-faced man he had met in Signora Sartori's room.

'What does it cost?' Brunetti asked, thinking of what he and his brother had had to pay for their mother for all those years.

'Two thousand, four hundred a month,' then, when he raised his eyebrows, she said, 'It's one of the best in the city.' She raised a hand and let it fall. 'And those are the prices.'

'How much is her pension?' he asked.

'Six hundred euros. She left four years early, so she isn't eligible for the whole pension.'

Before he tried the maths, Brunetti asked, 'And his?'

'Five hundred and twenty.' Together, their pensions covered barely half of the cost.

The man had not seemed wealthy; nor, Brunetti had to admit, had she. If he was what he seemed, a pensioner in need of paying utilities, rent, and food, where did he find the money for the nursing home?

She picked up the papers and handed them to him; he was surprised to find more than a few sheets. What could two old people like that have done in their lives?

'What's in here?' he asked, holding it up with deliberate exaggeration.

With her most sibylline look, Signorina Elettra observed, 'Their lives have not been without event.'

Brunetti allowed himself to relax into a smile for what seemed the first time that day. He waved the papers, saying, 'I'll have a look.' She nodded and turned her attention to her computer.

In his office, he first dialled his home number.

Paola answered with a 'Sì' so devoid of patience as to discourage even the most hardened telephone salesman or to frighten her children into hurrying home to clean their rooms.

'"And the voice of the turtle dove is heard in our land,"' he could not stop himself from saying.

'Guido Brunetti,' she said, voice no more friendly than it had been with that impersonal 'Sì', 'don't you start quoting the Bible at me.'

'I read the Song of Songs as literature, not as a sacred text.'

'And you use it as a provocation,' she said.

'Merely following in the tradition of two thousand years of Christian apologists.'

'You are a wicked, annoying man,' she said in a lighter voice, and he knew the danger was past.

'I am a wicked, annoying man who would like to take you to dinner.'

'And lose out on *turbanti di soglie*, eaten in peace at your own table, in the midst of the joyous harmony of your family?' she asked, leaving him uncertain whether the thought of his presence or of the meal had changed her mood.

'I'll try to be on time.'

'Good,' she said, and he thought she was about to hang up, but she added, 'I'm glad you'll be here.' Then she was gone, and Brunetti was left feeling as though the temperature of the room had just risen or the light had somehow increased. More than twenty years, and she could still do this to him, he thought; he shook his head, hunted for the number of his friend in Treviso, and called.

As he had suspected, the woman's name was not Gabriela Pavon: the Treviso police could give him six aliases used by the woman whose fingerprints were all over the apartment she had shared with her companion, but they could not supply him with her real name. The Sicilian – Brunetti told himself he had to stop calling him that and, more importantly, thinking of him as that – taught chemistry in a technical school, had no criminal record, and was, at least according to the police there, the victim of a crime. There was no trace of the woman, and his friend was resigned enough to suspect that there would be none until she committed the same crime again in some other part of the country.

Brunetti told him what the woman was probably planning to do in Venice and was asked by his weary friend to send a report, 'not that it's going to make any difference. She didn't commit a crime.'

When he hung up, Brunetti turned his attention to the papers Signorina Elettra had given him. Signora Maria Sartori had been born in Venice eighty years ago; Benito Morandi, eighty-three. The man's first name struck Brunetti: well he understood what sort of family would name their son Benito in those years. But the sight of the two names joined together prodded Brunetti's memory, as if Ginger had suddenly rediscovered her Fred. Or Bonnie her Clyde. He looked away from the papers, focusing his memory and not his eyes, and followed the meandering stream of recollection. Something about an old person, but not one of them; some other old person, and when they were not old. It was a memory from his life before work, before Paola and all that came from knowing her. His mother would remember, he caught himself thinking, his mother as she had once been.

He dialled Vianello's *telefonino* number. When the Inspector answered, Brunetti asked, 'You downstairs?'

'Yes.'

'Come up for a minute, would you?'

'I'm on my way.'

Staring helped. Brunetti went to the window, looked across the canal, letting the names rumble around in his mind, hoping that putting them together and then separating them would nudge his memory.

Vianello found him like that, hands clasped behind his back, deep in contemplation of either the façade of the church or the three-storey house for vagrant cats that had been built in front of the façade.

Rather than speak, Vianello sat in one of the chairs in front of his superior's desk. And waited.

Without turning, Brunetti said, 'Maria Sartori and Benito Morandi.'

There was silence from Vianello, the sound of his heels sliding across the floor as he stretched his legs. More time passed, and then came the long sigh of dawning memory. 'Madame Reynard,' he said and permitted himself a smile at having got there first.

Any Venetian, at least one their age, would have remembered sooner or later. Now that Vianello had given him the name, Brunetti also had the memory. Madame Marie Reynard, already a legendary beauty, had come to Venice with her husband almost – could it be? – a century before. They had had five years or so before he died a spectacular death. Brunetti couldn't recall the means: car, boat, aeroplane. The totality of her grief had cost her their unborn child, and upon her recovery she had lapsed into widowhood and seclusion in their *palazzo* on the Canal Grande.

He no longer knew when he had first heard the story, but even before Brunetti reached middle school, Madame Reynard had become legend, as is the destiny of mourning spouses, at least if they are both beautiful and rich. The mysterious French woman never left her *palazzo*, or she left it at night to walk the streets in silent tears, or she allowed only priests to enter, with whom, draped in her widow's veil, she recited endless rosaries for the repose of her husband's soul. Or she was a recluse, crucified by grief. Two elements remained constant in all variants: she was beautiful and she was rich.

And then, more than twenty years ago, aged one hundred, widowed for three-quarters of a century, she died. And her lawyer – who had nowhere appeared in any of the legends – turned out to have inherited the *palazzo* and all it contained, as well as the lands, the investments, and the patent to a process that did something to the strength of cotton fibres, making them resistant to higher temperatures. Whatever it did – and the cloth changed from cotton to silk to wool, depending on the version told – the patent ended up being immeasurably more valuable than the *palazzo* or the rest.

'Of course, of course,' Brunetti said as the tiny figures in his memory moved together and Maria found her Benito: for those were the names of the witnesses to Madame Reynard's will – Sartori and Morandi – and as such the subject of gossip and speculation that had occupied the city for months. They had worked in the hospital, had no previous knowledge of the dying woman, were certainly not named as beneficiaries of the will, and so were judged to be extraneous to the matter. Brunetti went back to his desk.

'Weren't there some French relatives?' Vianello asked.

Brunetti rummaged through the stories that had been dislodged in his memory and came up with the one he sought: 'They turned out not to be relatives but people who had read about her fortune and thought they'd have a try at it.' He let more information seep in and then added, 'But yes, they were French.'

Both sat for a while, letting their memories gather up bits and pieces. 'And wasn't there an auction?' Vianello asked.

'Yes,' Brunetti said. 'One of the last great ones. After she died. They sold everything.' Then, because it was Vianello he was talking to, and he could say such things to him, Brunetti added, 'My father-in-law said every collector in the city was there. Every collector in the Veneto, for that matter.' Brunetti knew of two drawings from that auction. 'He got two pages from a notebook of Giovannino de Grassi.'

Vianello shook his head in ignorance.

'Fourteenth century. There's a whole notebook in

Bergamo, with drawings – paintings, really – of birds and animals, and a fantasy alphabet.' His father-in-law kept his two drawings in a folder, out of the light. Brunetti held up his hands about twenty centimetres apart. 'These are only loose pages, about this big. Beautiful.'

'Valuable?' asked the far more pragmatic Vianello.

'I don't know exactly,' Brunetti said. 'But I'd guess so. In fact, my father-in-law said that most collectors went because of her husband's collection of drawings – it wasn't like today, when you could check everything that was in the auction by going online. He said there were always surprises. But this time, the surprise was that there were so few drawings. Still he managed to get those two.'

'Pity about Cuccetti, isn't it?' Vianello asked, surprising Brunetti by remembering the name of the lawyer who had swept the board.

'What, that he died so soon after? What was it, two years?'

'I think so. And with his son. The son was driving, wasn't he?'

'Yes, and drunk. But it was all hushed up.' Both of them knew a fair bit about this sort of thing. 'Cuccetti had a lot of important friends,' Brunetti added.

As if Brunetti's statement were the night, and his question the day, Vianello asked, 'The will was never contested, was it?'

'Only by those French people, and that didn't last a day.' Leaning across his desk Brunetti retrieved the papers Signorina Elettra had given him and said, 'This is what she found.' He read the first sheet and passed it to Vianello. In amiable silence, neither thinking it necessary to comment, they read through the papers.

Maria Sartori had been a practical nurse, first at the Ospedale al Lido, and then at the Ospedale Civile, from which she had retired more than fifteen years before. Never married, she had lived at the same address as Benito Morandi for most of their adult lives. She had kept an account at the same bank during her working life, into which modest sums were deposited and then withdrawn. She had never been in hospital, nor had she ever come to the attention of the police. And that was all: no mention of joy or sorrow, dreams or disappointments. Decades of work, retirement and a pension, and now a room in a private *casa di cura*, paid for by her pension and the contribution of her companion.

Attached was a photocopy of her *carta d'identità*; Brunetti barely recognized the soft-featured woman who gazed out at the world from the photo: surely she could not be the ancestor of the woman with the deeply lined face he had seen. He fought off the temptation to whisper to the younger face how right she had been: trouble comes.

As he handed the second sheet to Vianello, Brunetti turned his attention to her companion. Morandi had served in the Second World War. Brunetti's first thought was that Morandi must have lied about that, but then he did the numbers and saw that it was just barely possible.

Brunetti's father had often referred to the chaos that had prevailed during those dreadful years, so he believed that a boy in his early teens might have been allowed to enlist at the very end. But then Brunetti read Morandi's service record, stating that he had seen service in Abyssinia, Albania, and Greece, where he had been wounded, sent home, and discharged back into civilian life.

'*No, eh?*' Brunetti heard himself say aloud, startling Vianello, who turned to look at him. If the date of birth in this file was true, then Morandi would have gone off to Greece when he was as young as twelve, and he would have been only sixteen when Italy surrendered to the Allies. No matter how eager to name their son 'Benito' his family might have been, few families would have allowed their adolescent son to follow the other Benito off to war.

A few years after Morandi's return – or at least after

documentary evidence of his war service had entered the record – he took a job at the port of Venice and remained there for more than a decade, though no more precise job description than 'manual labourer' was provided. Brunetti learned that he had been dismissed from this job without explanation.

Some years later, he began working as a cleaner at the Ospedale Civile. Brunetti leaned aside and picked up the papers Vianello had set on his desk; Signora Sartori was already working at the Ospedale by then.

Morandi had worked as a *portiere* and cleaner for more than two decades and had retired about twenty years before, entitled to a minimal pension.

Brunetti recognized the seal of the Ministry of Justice on the next three sheets of paper, which catalogued Morandi's relationship with the forces of order, to which he was no stranger. He had first been arrested when he was in his early thirties, charged with selling smuggled cigarettes to tobacco shops on the mainland. Five years later, he was arrested for selling items stolen from ships being unloaded at the port and was given a one-year suspended sentence. Seven years after that he was arrested for having assaulted and seriously injured a colleague at work. When the man failed to testify against him, the charges were dropped. He had also been arrested for resisting arrest and for passing stolen goods to a fence in Mestre. There was some sort of clerical error in the processing of evidence in that case, and after five years it was abandoned, though by then Signor Morandi seemed to have passed to the side of the angels, for he had not been arrested since the time he had begun work at the hospital.

The last sheets of paper concerned Signor Morandi's life as a fiscal being. About the time of his retirement, Morandi bought an apartment in San Marco without taking out a mortgage to do so. A note in Signorina Elettra's handwriting informed Brunetti that he and Signora Sartori had moved into that apartment soon thereafter, for both of them had changed residence to that address within months of the purchase.

His bank account, completely undisturbed by the purchase of the apartment, showed much the same routine seen in Signora Sartori's: modest deposits and withdrawals, and, since the purchase of the apartment, the monthly payment of a condominium fee. This fee had risen during the years and was now more than four hundred euros a month and thus could no longer easily be offset by his modest pension.

From the time Signora Sartori had entered the nursing home Signor Morandi's banking habits had changed. A month before her first bill was due, his account had been credited with a deposit of almost four thousand euros. Since then, every three or four months, a deposit of between four and five thousand euros was made, and each month more than twelve hundred euros was routinely transferred from his account to that of the nursing home.

That seemed to be that. Brunetti leafed back through the papers to check the dates and saw that, though the apartment had been purchased after Morandi's retirement, Signora Sartori continued working at the hospital. It was unlikely that people holding such jobs could have managed, even jointly, to save enough to buy an apartment: given the absence of a mortgage and the low salary of the one still working, it became almost impossible. Neither Brunetti's brief meeting with Morandi nor the contents of these papers suggested a man whose behaviour would be characterized by fiscal prudence.

Brunetti got to his feet and went over to the window, resuming his study of the two façades on view. He returned his attention to the wall, considering the report and wondering why it had caught Signorina Elettra's attention. He knew her well enough to know that all of the information she had acquired would be in these papers: not to provide it would be – he was struck by the word that came to mind – to cheat. He waited for Vianello to conclude his contemplation and pass some observation on the papers.

While he waited, Brunetti considered the phenomenon of retirement. People in other countries, he had been told, dreamed of retirement as a chance to move to a warmer climate and start a whole new chapter: learn a language, buy a scuba outfit, take up taxidermy. How utterly alien that desire was to his own culture. The people he knew and those he had been observing all his life wanted nothing more, upon retirement, than to settle more deeply into their homes and the routines they had constructed over decades, making no change to their lives other than to excise from them the necessity of going to work each morning and perhaps to add the possibility of travelling a bit, but not often, and not too far. He knew no one who had bought a new home upon retirement or who had considered changing address.

What, then, would explain the sudden acquisition, at the conclusion of his working life, of a new apartment by Signor Morandi? Could there be some other Morandi? Was this an error on Signorina Elettra's part. Error? What was he thinking? Brunetti put his fingers to his mouth, as if to stifle that rash word.

'Why did he buy an apartment?' Vianello asked from his side of the room.

'What did he buy it with?' Brunetti asked. 'There's no mention of a mortgage.'

Vianello returned to his chair, leaned forward to place his palm on the papers, saying, 'Nothing in here suggests a man who saved all his life to buy a home.'

Brunetti dialled Signorina Elettra's number.

'Sì, Commissario?' she answered.

'The Inspector and I are curious about how Signor Morandi managed to buy his apartment,' he said.

She allowed a moment to pass and then asked, 'Did you see the date of purchase?'

Brunetti raised his shoulder and propped the phone against his ear then used both hands to leaf through the papers. He found the date and said, 'It's three months after he retired. But I don't see why it's significant.'

'Perhaps if you looked at the date of Madame Reynard's death,' she suggested.

He found the copy of her death certificate and saw that Morandi had bought the apartment exactly one month after her death. He made a noise.

When no comment or question followed, she asked, 'Did you see the name of the person selling the apartment?'

He looked. He said, 'Matilda Querini.' He caught Vianello's confused glance and switched on the speaker, then replaced the receiver.

Again, he did not comment. 'You and the Inspector don't remember the case, then?' she asked.

'I remember that those people witnessed it and that Cuccetti inherited the lot.'

'Ah,' she said, drawing the syllable out and letting it end on a dying fall.

'Tell me,' Brunetti said.

'Matilda Querini was his wife.'

'Ah, his wife,' Brunetti let himself say in conscious imitation. Then, a few heartbeats later, he asked, 'Is she still alive?'

'No. She died six years ago.'

'Wealthy?'

'Money without limit.'

'And where did it go? The son was the only child, wasn't he?'

'Rumour has it that she left it to the Church.'

'Only rumour, Signorina?'

'All right,' she said. 'Fact. She left it to the Church.' Before he could ask, she explained, 'I have a friend who works in the Patriarch's office. I called and asked him, and he told me it was the biggest sum they've ever been left.'

'Did he say how much?'

'I thought it impolite to ask.' Vianello made a small moaning noise.

'So?' he asked, knowing she'd be unable to leave something like that alone.

'So I asked my father. Her money wasn't at his bank, but he knows the director of the one where it was, and he asked him.'

'Do I want to know?'

'Seven million euros, give or take a few hundred thousand. And the patent for that process, and at least eight apartments.'

'To the Church?' Brunetti asked, at the sound of which question Vianello put his head, rather melodramatically, in his hands and shook it violently from side to side.

'Yes,' she answered.

An idea came to him and he asked, 'Have you looked at Cuccetti and his wife's bank accounts?' For her to do so was for her to break the law. For him to know that she had done so and then do nothing was for him to break the law.

'Of course,' she answered.

'Let me guess,' Brunetti said, unable to resist the temptation to show off a little, 'there was no money put into either account after the sale?'

'Nothing,' she answered. 'Of course, she may have given Morandi the apartment from the goodness of her heart,' she said, her tone excluding this possibility *a priori*.

'Cuccetti's reputation makes that unlikely, wouldn't you say?' Brunetti asked.

'Yes,' she agreed, then added, 'But it also makes his wife's decision to leave it all to the Church . . .' she began and then paused to search for the suitable word.

'Grotesque?' Brunetti suggested.

'Ah,' she said in appreciation of the justness of his choice.

22

Brunetti filled Vianello in on the missing half of his conversation with Signorina Elettra. 'I shouldn't laugh, I know,' Vianello said, sober-faced, 'but the thought that everything that greedy old bastard Cuccetti stole during his miserable life ended up in the pockets of the Church is . . .' He gave a resigned nod, either in admiration or astonishment, and said, 'Like them or not, you have to admit they're the best.'

'The priests?'

'Priests. Nuns. Monks. Bishops. You name them. They'll have their snouts in the soup before you set the plate on the table. They got to her in the end, and they sucked it all up. My compliments to them,' he said, shaking his head in what Brunetti took to be real – however grudging – admiration.

Deciding he had nothing to oppose that sentiment, Brunetti suggested they would both be better off at home with their families, an opinion in which Vianello joined him. They left the Questura together, going their separate ways just outside the front door.

Brunetti decided to walk, needing the sense of motion and freedom that came from moving through the city without having to give conscious thought to where he was going. Memory and imagination, tranquillized by walking, floated back to consider the names Cuccetti and Reynard. The first brought only a sense of vague distaste, while the second brought pathos and loss.

He paused at the bottom of the Rialto and reeled in his thoughts. The prospect of walking home along the less crowded *riva* appealed to him, but he decided to go down to Biancat and get Paola some flowers: it had been an age since he had. He found the florist closed. Having got the idea of flowers in his head, he was irritated – more than that – not to be able to take them to Paola. He stood in front of the window and looked at the irises he wanted, a white plastic cylinder of them visible behind the humidity-clouded window, beautiful and all the more desirable because he could not have them. 'How like a man,' he muttered to himself and turned away and down his own *calle*. He was on time; that would have to take the place of flowers.

Brunetti was not a man of faith, at least not in a way that posited a supreme being that concerned itself with the doings of men: as a policeman, Brunetti knew enough about the doings of men to make him hope the deity would be warned away from them in search of some more rewarding species. But at odd times during his life he found himself racked with a sense of limitless gratitude: it could come upon him at any time, and it always leaped upon him with maximum surprise. This evening it hit him as he turned into the last flight of steps leading to the apartment. He was healthy, he didn't think he was crazy or violent, he had a wife he loved to the point of folly, two children in whom he had invested every hope of happiness on this earth. And, to date, misery and pain and privation and sickness had stayed outside the ring of fire he liked to think encircled them. What he thought of as primitive superstition kept him wary of daring to make any conscious expression of gratitude: to do so was to invite disaster. And to think like this, he knew, was to be a primitive fool.

He let himself in, hung his jacket to the left of the door, and went towards the kitchen. Indeed, *turbanti di soglie*, or else both Paola and his nose were liars. She was in the kitchen, standing at the table, palms splayed on either side of an open newspaper, head bent as she read.

He came up behind her and kissed the back of her neck. She ignored him. He opened the cabinet to her right and pulled down a glass, then another one. He opened the fridge and removed another bottle of the Moët from the vegetable drawer, thinking how lucky he was to be married to a woman who would be offered such a tasteful bribe. He stripped off the foil, put his thumbs under the cork, and shot it across the room. Not even the explosive sound stirred her to action or comment.

He poured carefully into both glasses, allowed the bubbles to subside, added, waited, added, then put a stopper in the bottle and put it back in the door of the fridge. He slid one glass towards her until it touched the edge of the page, then picked up his glass and tapped it against hers. '*Cin cin*,' he said in his gruff, hearty voice.

She ignored him and turned a page. He put a hand out to steady her glass, nudged to one side by the turning page of the newspaper. 'It does a man's heart good to come into the bosom of his family and be welcomed with the affection he is accustomed to,' he said and sipped at his wine. 'Ah, that effusive warmth, that sense of familial intimacy and well-being to be had only in a man's home, surrounded and revered by the people he most cherishes.'

She reached aside, picked up her glass, and took a sip. What she tasted caused her to look aside at him. 'Is this more of the Moët?' she asked.

'The woman wins a prize,' he said, toasted her, and took another sip.

'I thought we were going to save it for something special?' she asked, sounding surprised but not at all displeased.

'And what is more special than that I return to my lady wife and she greets me with the loving kindness – beneath which glow the embers of raging passion – that has characterized our union for these two decades and more?' He tried to make his smile as idiotic as possible.

She set her glass on top of the newspaper – in fact, right on the face of the man who had that day declared his candidacy for mayor – and said, 'If you've stopped for a few *ombre* on the way home, Guido, then I think we might be wasting this champagne.'

'No, my sweet. I was borne home on the wings of love and was so driven to be united with your sweet self that I had no time to think of stopping.'

She picked up her glass took another sip, then tipped the base of the glass to point at the photo. 'Can you believe this? He's going to remain a cabinet minister and at the same time be mayor.'

'Which days do we get?' Brunetti asked. 'Monday, Wednesday, and Friday? And the government in Rome gets Tuesday, Thursday, and Saturday?' He took a sip and said, 'Any sane person would think this an insult, both to the nation and to the city.'

She shrugged. 'Didn't the last one keep his job in Brussels and his university teaching job?' she asked.

'We are ruled by a race of heroes,' Brunetti declared, reaching to open the refrigerator.

'Do you think drinking the whole bottle quickly will make them all go away?' she asked, emptying her glass and holding it out.

He poured, waited, poured, then said, 'Only for a while, and then they'll all come back, like cockroaches, but we'll at least be able to look at them through the bubbles of champagne.'

In quite a conversational voice, she asked, 'Do you think there are any people on earth who despise their politicians as much as we do?'

He filled his own glass before he said, 'Oh, I'm sure that, except for places like Scandinavia and Switzerland, most people do.'

She heard the teasing end of that sentence and asked, 'But?'

Brunetti studied the photo in the newspaper. 'But we have more cause than most, I think.' He took a long drink.

'I often wonder what planet they think they're living on,' Paola said, folding the paper closed and shifting it to one side. 'They speak no language known to man, they know no passions other than greed and—'

'If you're listing their passions, don't forget to include the current one for transsexuals,' he said, aiming for precision and hoping to lighten her mood, though he was not quite sure how the subject of transsexuals was meant to do that.

'Their sense of ethics would make that dead transsexual – I can't even remember her name any more, poor girl – look like the late Mother Teresa.'

'That is a comparison which many religious people would find offensive,' he said.

She gave this the consideration it deserved and said, 'You're right. Even I find it offensive. But I get carried away by these things.'

He leaned over and kissed her on the lips. 'I know, my dear, and that's one of the reasons you have captured my heart.'

'Oh, stop it, Guido,' she said, holding out her glass. 'Pour me some more and I'll put the water on for the pasta.'

He did as she requested, then helped her set the table, pleased to learn that the kids were both to be there. How life plays tricks with us, he thought, as he folded the napkins and set them beside the plates. When Raffi was just starting to sit at the table and eat with them, dropping as much on the table or the floor as he got into his mouth, sipping and spilling and never quite sure what to do with his fork, Brunetti had viewed his behaviour not as charming, but as a continual distraction from his own meal. Yet here he was, years later, hoping that boy – now fully competent in the use of his fork – would find the time to eat with them and not take himself off to a friend's house. It had nothing whatsoever to do with his son's conversation, nor his wit nor his grasp of ideas, Brunetti realized. It simply filled Brunetti's heart to have them there and to be able to see and hear them, knowing they were safe and warm and well fed.

'What's wrong?' Paola asked from behind him.

'Hmmm?' Brunetti asked, turning to face her.

'You were standing there, staring at the table, and I wondered if something were wrong,' she said, puzzled.

'No. Nothing. I was thinking.'

'Ah,' she said in the voice of someone who had heard that one before. Then, 'Shall we have another whack at that bottle before the kids get here?'

With Pavlovian rapidity, Brunetti turned to the refrigerator. 'The elegance of your thinking is matched only by that of your language,' he said.

She smiled and held her empty glass towards him. 'It's the fate of the person who lives with two teenagers.'

There remained sufficient champagne for each of the children to find a glass in front of them as they sat down to dinner.

'What are we celebrating?' Raffi asked as he picked up his glass.

'You don't have to have something to celebrate to drink champagne,' Chiara said, trying to sound like the sort of person who has left a trail of empty jeroboams behind her. She lifted her glass and clicked it against Raffi's, then took a sip.

Raffi, looking at his glass but making no attempt to drink from it, said, 'I don't get it about champagne.'

Paola placed a plate of *turbanti* in front of him and one in front of Chiara, then went to fill two for Brunetti and herself. She set them down and took her place. 'What don't you understand?' she asked, though not before she had taken a sip, as if to re-test the evidence.

'Why people go crazy about it or think it's so good,' Raffi said, sliding his glass to the side of his plate and picking up his fork.

'Snobbery,' Chiara said through a mouthful of fish.

'Chiara,' Paola said in a warning voice, and Chiara nodded and put her hand to her mouth in acknowledgement of the reprimand. She poured some mineral water and took a sip, set her fork down and repeated, 'Snobbery.' Brunetti, studying her face, saw that some of the plumpness of adolescence had given way to the angles of maturity, making her resemblance to her mother even stronger.

'Which means what?' Raffi said, turning his attention to his dinner.

'To impress people,' Chiara said. 'With how sophisticated they are and how good their taste is.' Before Raffi could say anything, she added, 'People do it all the time, with everything. Cars, what they wear, what they say they like.'

'Why say you like something when you don't?' Raffi asked with what sounded to Brunetti like honest confusion, forcing him to wonder if, unbeknownst to either him or Paola, their son had been spending his free time on some other planet for the last few years.

Chiara set her fork down, rested her chin on one hand, and stared across the table at her brother. He ignored her. Finally she said, 'It's why you want a pair of Tod's and not a plain old pair of shoes.'

Raffi ignored her and continued to eat.

'Or why my friends' parents all think they have to go to

the Maldives or the Seychelles for vacation,' she persisted.

Raffi poured himself a glass of water, ignoring the champagne. He drank the water and set the glass on the table, then pushed his chair back and turned to face his sister. He held up one foot and extended it in her direction. 'Bought at the Lignano market this summer for nineteen euros,' he said proudly, waving his foot in a circle, the better to display his shoe. 'No Tod's, no label.' He lowered his foot and turned his chair, pulling himself back into place at the table. He picked up his fork and resumed eating.

Crestfallen, Chiara looked at her mother and then at her father. Had she been a boy, she and Raffi would probably have got into a scuffle of some sort, and Brunetti suspected he would have broken it up to protect the smaller child. Why was it, then, that when the combatant used only words, she had to be left alone to protect herself?

Brunetti had been in what he assumed was the normal number of fights when he was growing up: nothing had ever passed beyond a few punches and a good deal of shoving. He could not remember ever having been hurt, nor indeed hurting anyone, and none of the fights had left any clear memory. But he still remembered an afternoon when Geraldo Barasciutti, who sat next to him in mathematics class, had laughed when Brunetti made a grammatical error, mixing Veneziano with Italian.

'What's the matter with you? Does your father unload ships for a living?' Geraldo had asked, poking him in the ribs as he said it.

He had meant it as a joke: it was common enough for kids to confound the two languages. But the truth had sliced into Brunetti's sense of self – a sense made delicate by having to wear his brother's cast-off shoes and jackets – for his father had indeed once worked at the docks, unloading ships for a living. It was that day and that remark that Brunetti remembered as the worst thing that had happened to him as a child.

His university education, his position as a commissario of police, the stature and wealth of his wife's family: all of these things could be called into question by the memory of those words and the pain caused by their unintentional truth.

'The strange thing,' Brunetti said, holding up his glass to Raffi though speaking in defence of Chiara's position, 'is that I probably couldn't tell the difference between this, and the prosecco we drink every day.'

'*Every* day?' Paola asked, though not before Brunetti had exchanged a smile with his daughter.

'The prosecco we normally drink,' he said, correcting the ambiguity. He finished his champagne, picked up the empty bottle, and went to the refrigerator in search of a second. He settled for their everyday prosecco and took it back to the table.

'What your father is doing,' Paola said to the children as Brunetti unpeeled the foil wrapping, 'is giving an example of the scientific method. He is not prepared,' she continued, 'to allow his remark to go untested.'

'Which one?' Raffi asked. 'About the difference between champagne and prosecco or that you drink it every day?'

'Two pigeons with one bean,' Brunetti said, a remark that was followed by a very loud 'Pop.'

23

The following morning, Brunetti woke early and went to make himself coffee. While he was waiting for the coffee to boil, he went to the back window, hoping the mountains would be visible, but they were not. He stared at the distant haze while he considered the strange case of Madame Reynard. There was no way of knowing, short of asking them directly, how Sartori and Morandi had come to sign the will. And why had a woman of Madame Reynard's age – to make no mention of her wealth – been in the Ospedale Civile and not a private clinic?

The spluttering of the coffee distracted him. He poured it out, stirred in some sugar, and added cold milk, though he would have preferred it to be heated. He returned to his thoughts. In what conjunction had the orbits of those four people intersected in a hospital room: a dying heiress and the lawyer who became her heir; the witnesses to the handwritten will that named him as such? As if fallen from the heavens, a practical nurse and a man with a criminal record had witnessed the will that saw to the transfer of millions. An odd constellation, and how large was the apartment which one of the witnesses bought soon thereafter?

His thoughts turned to the woman who had been living with Signora Altavilla. Brunetti recalled with some uneasiness his initial willingness to suspect, not her, but her lover, the chemistry teacher with the courage to come and warn Signora Altavilla of the cuckoo in her nest. The southerner.

He stared at the painting on the kitchen wall, of the Grand Canal as it had appeared centuries before, then he pictured Signora Altavilla's apartment as they had found it. He looked again at their painting, and the sight conjured up the memory of the lonely nails on Signora Altavilla's walls. He retrieved his *telefonino* from his jacket pocket and dialled Niccolini's number.

As soon as the doctor heard his name, he said, 'Commissario, I was going to call you today.'

'About what, Dottore?' Brunetti asked, relieved that he was being spared an exchange of pleasantries, though there was nothing pleasant either man had to say to the other.

'My mother's apartment. Some things are missing,' Niccolini said, sounding troubled, not angry.

'How do you know this, Dottore?'

'I went there yesterday. With a friend. Just to see. He came with me to . . .' His voice faded, but Brunetti, at the memory of what there was to see in that apartment, decided it would be kinder to let him find his voice.

'To help.'

Brunetti certainly understood that.

'Could you tell me what's missing?' Brunetti prodded.

'Three drawings,' the doctor answered. 'They were all quite small.'

'Is that all?'

'I think so. So far, that is.'

'Missing from where?

'One was in the guest room. And two were in the hallway just outside it.'

Brunetti remembered the ghost shadows under the nails in the guest room, was vaguely conscious of two in the hallway. He did not remember seeing any others. But surely, if Gabriela Pavon had decided to add them to her last-minute packing, then those were the easiest to grab. What nerve she must have had, to take them while the other two women were just down the corridor.

'What were they, the drawings?'

'One was a Corot. The other two were by Salvator Rosa. Small, but good quality.'

The doctor remained silent for a long time, and then he said, sounding weak and hesitant, 'I thought I should tell you. It might mean something.' Brunetti thanked the doctor and hung up.

He sat and looked at the painting for some time, and then he finished his coffee, set the cup in the sink, and went to take a shower.

Forty minutes later, he emerged on to the embankment of San Lorenzo. He rested his elbows on the railing and watched the boats pass by, trying to think of how he might convince Patta to pursue more actively an official investigation into the death of Signora Altavilla. He imagined the statue of blindfolded Justice, in her hand the scales of her trade. On one side he put the words 'only a possibility' and on the other the publicity sure to accrue at the news that a woman had been killed in her home. After all these years, he was well aware of the workings of his superior's mind and knew that the first obstacle would be the damage to the image of the city, second the damage to tourism.

'And the effect on tourism?' an outraged Patta demanded of him half an hour later, reversing the order of his concerns but still not managing to surprise Brunetti. The Vice-Questore had, by evident force of will, contained himself until he finished listening to these latest ravings from his ever-insubordinate subordinate. 'What are we supposed to tell these people? That they aren't safe in their homes, but to have a good time anyway?'

Brunetti, well schooled in the rhetorical excesses and inconsistencies of his superior, forbore to point out that tourists, at least when they were in Venice, were not in their homes, however safe or unsafe they might be therein. He nodded in a manner he hoped would be considered sage.

Brunetti concentrated on meeting his superior's gaze – Patta hated to have anyone's attention stray from him, surely the first step on the road to disobedience – and gave every appearance that he was dealing with rational opposition. 'Yes, I see your point, Vice-Questore,' Brunetti said. 'I just hope that Dottor Niccolini . . .' he allowed his voice to trail away, as if his thoughts had been written on a blackboard and he was wiping them out.

'What about him?' Patta asked, eyes alert to everything he considered a nuance.

'Nothing, sir,' Brunetti said evasively, uncertain whether he should be bored or mortified by his own behaviour.

'What about Dottor Niccolini?' Patta said in a cold voice, exactly the one Brunetti had tried to provoke.

'That's just it, sir: he's a doctor. That's how he introduced himself at the hospital, and that's how Rizzardi addressed him.' This was pure fantasy on Brunetti's part. But it might have been true, which sufficed.

'And so?'

'They asked him to identify his mother's body,' Brunetti added, trying to make it sound as if he were suggesting something to Patta that delicacy made difficult to say.

'People just see the face,' Patta asserted, but an instant later he compromised his certainty by asking, 'don't they?'

Brunetti nodded and said, 'Of course,' as though that were the end of it.

'What does that mean?' Patta demanded in a voice intended to be menacing but which Brunetti, familiar with the beast these many years, recognized as the voice of uncertainty.

Brunetti forced himself to look at his hands, carefully folded in his lap, and then directly into Patta's eyes, always the best tactic for lying. 'He would have been shown the marks, Vice-Questore,' he said; then, before Patta could ask about that, he continued, 'And because they thought he was a doctor, they would have explained them to him. Well, explained what they might be.'

Patta considered this. 'You think Rizzardi would actually do that?' he asked, unable to disguise his dissatisfaction that the *medico legale* might have told someone the truth.

'He'd think it was correct because he was speaking to a colleague,' Brunetti said.

'But he's only a veterinarian,' Patta raged, speaking the noun with contempt and apparently forgetting not only his son's relationship with his husky but the many times he had expressed his belief that vets' professional skill exceeded that of the doctors at the Ospedale Civile.

Brunetti nodded but chose to say nothing. Instead, he sat quietly and observed Patta's face as the consciousness behind it measured the odds and considered the possibilities. Niccolini was an unknown player: he worked outside the province of Venice, so he could have some political weight unknown to Patta. Veterinarians worked with farmers, and farmers were close to the Lega, and the Lega was a growing political force. Beyond this, for lack of fantasy, Brunetti's imagination could not go in pursuit of Patta's.

Finally Patta said, sounding not at all happy about the fact, 'I'll have to ask a magistrate to authorize something.' A sudden thought crossed his handsome face; did the Vice-Questore actually pause to adjust his tie? 'Yes, we've got to get to the bottom of this. Tell Signorina Elettra what you want me to ask him for. And I'll see to it.'

It had been so flawless that Brunetti had not seen the change take place. He recalled the passage – he thought it was in the Twenty-Fifth Canto – where Dante sees the thieves transformed into lizards, lizards into thieves, the moment of transformation invisible until complete. One instant one thing, the next another. So too had Patta passed from the sustainer of peace at any compromise to the relentless seeker after justice, ready to mobilize the forces of order in the pursuit of truth. Like Dante's sinners, he fell back to earth already in the guise of his opposite, then rose and walked away with nothing more than a glance over his shoulder.

'I'll go and speak to her about it now, shall I, sir?' Brunetti suggested.

'Yes,' Patta encouraged. 'She'll know which magistrate is best. One of the young ones, I think.'

Brunetti got to his feet and wished his superior good morning.

Signorina Elettra appeared neither surprised nor pleased at her superior's change of course. 'There's a nice young magistrate I can ask,' she said with the calculating smile she might use when asking the butcher for a plump young chicken. 'He hasn't had much experience, so he's likely to be open to . . . suggestion.' This, Brunetti thought, was probably much the way the Old Man of the Mountain spoke of his apprentice assassins as he sent them about their tasks.

'How old is he?' Brunetti asked.

'He can't be thirty,' she said, as though that number were a word she had heard in some other language and perhaps knew the meaning of. Then, in a far more serious voice, she asked, 'What do you want him to ask for?'

'Access to the records of the Ospedale Civile for the time Madame Reynard was a patient there; employee records for the same period, if such things exist; authorization to speak to Morandi and Signora Sartori; tax records for both of them and all documents regarding the sale of Cuccetti's wife's house to Morandi; Reynard's death certificate, and a look at the will to see how much she left him, as well as any other bequests.' That sounded, to Brunetti, like more than enough to be getting on with.

She had been taking note of his requests, and when he finished, she looked at him and said, 'I have some of this information already, but I can change the dates and make it look as if the request wasn't made until the magistrate authorized it.' She glanced at her notes and said, tapping at the list with the end of her pencil, 'He probably doesn't know yet how to ask for all of this, but I suspect I could make a few suggestions that might help him.'

'Suggestions,' Brunetti said in a dead level voice.

The look she gave him would have brought a lesser man to his knees. 'Please, Commissario,' was all she said, and then she picked up the phone.

Within minutes it was done, and the magistrate's secretary, with whom Signorina Elettra spoke with easy familiarity, said the warrants would be delivered the next morning. Brunetti restrained himself from asking the name of the magistrate, certain that he would learn it from the signature when he saw the papers the next day. Well, he told himself as he considered the speed and efficiency with which her request had been granted: why should the judiciary be any different from any other public or private institution? Favours were granted to the person whose request was accompanied by a *raccomandazione*, and the more powerful the person who made the *raccomandazione*, or the closer the friendship between the assistants who saw to the details, the more quickly the request was granted. Need a hospital bed? Best to have a cousin who is a doctor in that hospital, or is married to one. A permit to restore a hotel? Problems with the Fine Arts Commission about a painting you want to move to your apartment in London? The right person had but to speak the word to the right official or to someone to whom the official owed a favour, and all paths were made smooth.

Brunetti found himself, not for the first time, trapped in ambivalence. In this case, it worked to his advantage – and, he told himself, to the civic good – that Signorina Elettra had turned the judicial system of the city into her fief. But in places where persons of lesser . . . lesser probity . . . were in charge, the results might not be as salutary.

He left these thoughts, thanked her for her help, and went back to his office.

It was there, after an hour during which he read and initialled various documents and reports, that Signorina Elettra came to speak to him. 'I've found the man of my dreams,' she said as she came in, and said it in such a way as to lead Brunetti to understand that the man was the young magistrate.

'I take it he availed himself of your experience with the peculiarities of the city.'

Her smile was calm, her nod an exercise in graciousness. 'His secretary said a few kind words about me before she put me through to him.'

'After which you induced him to overlook the dubious legality of some of the things you asked him to authorize?'

The phrase appeared to wound her; if nothing else, it spurred her into saying, 'I'm not sure there any longer exists a legality in this country that is not dubious.'

'Be that as it may, Signorina,' Brunetti said, 'I'm curious to know what you persuaded him to authorize.'

'Everything,' she said with unconcealed delight. 'I think this young man might prove a gold mine for us.'

Brunetti thought of the warning written above the Gates of Hell and was for a moment tempted to dissociate himself from her further progress into a land, not of dubious, but of absent, legality, but hypocrisy was not among his vices. Also, he appreciated the fact that she had used the plural, and so he smiled and said, 'I tremble at the thought of what you might ask him to authorize.'

Failing to disguise her disappointment, she said, 'I'd never compromise you in any of this, Dottore.'

'Just yourself?' he enquired, knowing the impossibility of this.

Her failure to answer forced him, finally, to confront the fact that she had for years been making requests that lay far beyond her mandate. But how to ask the question without making it sound like an accusation?

'To whom will the responses to these requests be sent?'

'To the Vice-Questore, of course,' she said simply, and for a moment Brunetti had a vision of her as she would appear when saying this to a judge, saw her hair pulled tightly back, face completely unadorned by makeup, jewellery forgone; the modest way she was dressed, perhaps in a dark blue suit with a skirt of an unfashionable cut and length, sensible shoes. Would she risk wearing a pair of glasses? Her eyes would be modestly turned down in the face of the majesty of the law; her speech modest; no jokes, no sparring, no wit. He wondered, for the first time, if she had some sort of dreary second name she would pull out for an occasion like this: Clotilde, Olga, Luigia. And Patta – Brunetti had no choice but to use the American phrase – would take the fall.

'You'd do that to him?' Brunetti asked.

'Please, Dottore,' she said in an offended voice, 'you must give me some credit for human affection, or weakness.'

As a matter of fact, Brunetti had reason to give her more than some credit for those things, and so he asked, deciding to speak bluntly, 'But if anything went wrong, you'd let Patta hang for this?'

She managed to look genuinely shocked at his question, shocked and then disappointed that he could think of asking such a thing. 'Ah,' she said, letting the syllable run on for a long time, 'I could never live with myself if I did that. Besides, you have no idea of how long it would take me to train whoever was sent to replace him.' At least, Brunetti thought, there was something other than rank hypocrisy on offer here.

With grudging voice, she said, 'And I must confess that, over the years, I've become almost fond of him.' Hearing her say it like this surprised Brunetti into accepting that he probably shared her feelings.

After leaving him with enough time to consider everything she had said, she added, with an easy smile, 'Besides, all of the requests are sent in Lieutenant Scarpa's name.' Her use of the passive voice did not go unremarked by Brunetti.

It took him but a moment to realize the genius of it. 'So it appears that the Lieutenant has been exceeding his professional powers all these years? Asking for information without an order from a magistrate,' he mused, not thinking it necessary to comment on the trail of cyber-proof that was sure to have been left behind him.

'He's also been breaking into bank codes, pilfering information from Telecom, rifling through the classified files held on citizens in state offices, and stealing copies of people's credit card statements,' she said, scandalized by the magnitude of the Lieutenant's perfidy.

'I'm shocked,' Brunetti said. And he was: what kind of mind could set up such an elaborate trap for the Lieutenant? 'And all of these requests came directly from his email?' he asked, wondering what labyrinth she had created to deal with the responses.

Her hesitation was minimal, her answer a smile as she said, 'The Lieutenant believes he is the only person who has the password to his account.' Her voice softened, but her look did not. 'I didn't want him to be troubled reading any replies, so they're transferred automatically to one of the Vice-Questore's accounts.' The name 'Giorgio' slithered into Brunetti's ear, Signorina Elettra's frequently named friend, the cyber-genius of all cyber-geniuses, but discretion stood on Brunetti's tongue and he did not speak the name aloud, nor did he ask if the Vice-Questore knew of the existence of his account.

'Remarkable, that the Lieutenant would be so rash as to use his own address to get this information,' Brunetti said, his thoughts turning to Riverre and Alvise and how very safe this information would make them.

'He probably thinks he's too clever to be caught,' she suggested.

'How very foolish of him,' Brunetti said, recalling how often the Lieutenant had made a point of attempting to prove to Signorina Elettra his own superior cleverness. 'He should have realized how dangerous it was,' Brunetti began and, seeing her smile at the breadth of his understanding, added, 'to have thought he could get away with anything.'

'The Lieutenant does at times try my patience,' she said. The coolness of her smile warmed his heart.

24

As though given wings by the novel experience of working within the limits of the law, Signorina Elettra obtained the missing information by noon the following day, when she came into his office. Though she perhaps attempted to imitate the bland expression of blindfolded Justice as she placed the papers on his desk, she failed to disguise her satisfaction at having so quickly succeeded in her task.

'It's so easy, it's enough to make me think of changing my ways,' she said, though Brunetti was quick to hear the lie.

'I shall live in that single hope,' he said mildly as he looked at the first paper, which was a copy of a document written in a spidery hand, signed with an indecipherable scribble at the bottom. Two other signatures stood below it.

'You might want to look at the second paper, sir,' she suggested. He did so and saw that it was the death certificate of Marie Reynard.

In all these years, Brunetti had never decided whether Signorina Elettra preferred to explain things to him or have him discover them himself. To save time, he asked, 'And I am looking for?'

'The dates, sir.'

He glanced back at the first sheet and saw that its date was four days before that on the death certificate. Pointing to it, he said, 'So this is the famous will?' No wonder it had caused so much trouble: only an expert could make out this script.

'The third sheet is a transcript, sir. It was done by three different people, and they all produced roughly the same text.'

'Roughly?'

'Nothing that mattered. Or so the accompanying papers state.'

He turned to the third page and read that, being of sound mind, Marie Reynard left her entire estate, comprising bank accounts, investment accounts, houses and their attached estates, apartments, patents, and all moveable property to Avvocato Benevento Cuccetti, and that this will precluded and superseded all previous wills and was an expression of her total desire and irrevocable decision.

'Nice mixture of the poetic and the legal: "total desire and irrevocable decision",' Brunetti observed.

'Nice mixture of fixed and moveable property, as well,' Signorina Elettra added, nodding to the papers in his hand. Brunetti turned over the transcript and found a list of bank accounts, properties, and other possessions.

'What else did you learn?' he asked.

'The apartment that was sold to Morandi is behind the Basilica, top floor, one hundred and eighty metres.'

'If the owner was Cuccetti's wife, then it can't have been part of the Reynard estate.'

'No, she'd owned it for more than ten years before she sold it to him.'

'The declared price?'

'One hundred and fifty thousand euros,' she answered.

Then before he could say anything, she added, 'It's probably worth more than ten times that today.'

'And was worth at least three times that when he bought it,' Brunetti commented neutrally. Then, more to the point, 'It's interesting that no one in the tax office questioned that price: it's so obviously false.'

She shrugged this away. A man as powerful and rich as Cuccetti had probably got away with much worse things during his life, and to whom should the tax office do a favour if not to Avvocato Cuccetti?

Vianello appeared at the door. 'Signorina, the Vice-Questore would like to speak to you.'

None of the three of them wondered why Patta had not simply used the telephone. This way, all of them would take note, the Vice-Questore could send Vianello on an errand upstairs, force Signorina Elettra to stop whatever she was doing and come to his office, and make clear to Brunetti who it was she worked for, and to whom her loyalty was meant to be given.

She left and Vianello, unasked, came and sat in front of Brunetti's desk.

'I've had a look in the law books,' Brunetti said, using his thumb to point to the bookcase behind him, which held volumes of both civil and criminal law. 'And the statute of limitations expired years ago.'

'For what?'

'Falsification of an official document. In this case, a will.'

'I didn't know that,' Vianello said with heavy emphasis on the first word.

'Meaning?'

'That if I didn't know it, then it's unlikely that someone like Morandi would know it, don't you think?'

'And that means?'

Vianello crossed his legs and folded his arms, slumped down in the chair, and said, speaking so slowly that Brunetti could almost hear the Inspector fitting the pieces together as he spoke, 'And that means that one way to put these things together is to assume that Signora Sartori said something to Signora Altavilla about whatever it was she and Morandi did. About the will, that is.'

Brunetti interrupted him to ask, 'That they knew it was false when they witnessed it?'

'Perhaps,' Vianello said.

'Madre Rosa referred to her "terrible honesty". Something like that,' Brunetti said, failing to recall the precise phrase, though its strangeness had struck him when she said it. 'So if Signora Altavilla learned something from Signora Sartori, she might have been capable of confronting Morandi with it.'

'Because she'd want him to confess?' Vianello asked.

Brunetti considered this for some time before he answered. 'I thought about that. But to what purpose? The old woman's dead, Cuccetti and his wife and son are dead. The estate's disappeared: the Church has whatever was left.' Then he added, with a shrug of incomprehension, 'Maybe she believed it would save his reputation, or his conscience.' After a moment, he added, 'Or save his soul.' Who knew, people believed even stranger things.

'Morandi's not the sort of man who'd worry about his conscience,' Vianello said abruptly. 'Or his reputation.' The Inspector chose not to comment on the third.

'You'd be surprised.'

'At what?'

'At how important their reputation can be to the people we'd least expect to give it a thought.'

'But he's a man with no education, with a long criminal record, a known thief,' Vianello said, making no attempt to disguise his astonishment.

'You could be describing many of the men in Parliament,' Brunetti said in return, intending it as a joke but then suddenly oppressed by the truth of it. But beyond the joke,

Brunetti had struck on a truth, and he knew it: even the worst men wanted to be perceived as better than they were. How else could hypocrisy have risen to such delirious levels?

He thought back to his meeting with Morandi. The old man had been surprised to find him there and had reacted instinctively. But as soon as he realized that Brunetti was a representative of the state, there in performance of his duty – which duty he believed was to help Signora Sartori – his manner had softened. Brunetti thought of his own violent father: even at his worst, he had always remained deferential to authority and to those whose good opinion he valued. And he had always treated his wife with respect and strived to have hers. How slowly these old forms disappeared.

Vianello pulled him back from these thoughts by saying, though he said it grudgingly, 'Maybe you're right.'

'About?'

'That people's good opinion would be important to him. You said he was protective of the woman?'

'It seemed so.'

'Protective because he didn't want her to talk to you or because he didn't want you to trouble her?'

Brunetti had to think about this for a moment before he answered, 'I'd say a bit of both, but more the second than the first.'

'Why would that be?'

'Because he loves her,' Brunetti said, remembering the way the old man looked at her. 'That would be the obvious reason.' Before Vianello could comment or object, Brunetti said, 'One of the things Paola once told me is how prone we are to scorn the emotions of simple people. As if ours were better somehow.'

'And love is love?' Vianello enquired.

'I think so, yes.' Brunetti had still to fight against his reluctance to believe this wholeheartedly, as Paola seemed to do. He thought of it as one of his essential failures of humanity.

Then, changing tack entirely, Brunetti asked, 'So where's the money coming from?' Seeing Vianello's surprise, he said, 'The money that's going into the account.'

'Beats me. It's unlikely he's selling drugs,' Vianello said, meaning it as a joke.

'But at more than eighty, it's got to be that he's selling something; he's certainly not going around breaking into houses, and he's too old to work,' Brunetti said. In response to Vianello's glance, he said, 'And since Cuccetti's dead, and all his family, and everything's gone to the Church, there's no one he can be blackmailing.'

Vianello smiled and could not resist saying, 'I'm always cheered by your uplifting view of human nature, Guido.'

Was rhetorical style contagious? Brunetti wondered. A decade ago, Vianello would not have been capable of a verbal flourish such as this. Brunetti was pleased at the thought.

'So he's selling something,' Brunetti went on as though the Ispettore had not spoken. 'And if that's so, and if he's not stealing things from the docks any more, then it might be something they gave him when they signed the will or when he got the apartment from them.'

'Or something he stole,' Vianello added, as though he too had something to contribute to the view of human nature.

This possibility left Brunetti uncomfortable. 'He met her when he went to work at the hospital, and he had no more trouble with us after that.'

'Or he didn't get caught.'

'He's not very bright, so he would have been caught,' Brunetti insisted. 'Look how many times he was arrested before that.'

'But he always got out of it. He could have threatened his way out.'

'If he was really violent, or dangerous, it would be in the files,' Brunetti said. 'We'd know.'

Vianello considered this and finally nodded in agreement.

'It's possible. I've known love to do stranger things to people than to make them careful.'

'Or make them better,' Brunetti amended.

'You make him sound like Saint Paul,' Vianello said, sounding amused at the unlikelihood. 'He's riding along on his way to steal an X-ray machine from the hospital, sees Signorina Sartori in her white nurse's uniform; he falls to the ground at the sight of her, and when he gets to his feet, he's a man transformed?'

Perhaps he had had enough of Vianello's rhetorical flights. 'Are you a better man since you married Nadia?' he surprised Vianello by asking.

Vianello uncrossed his legs, then crossed them the other way. He looked so uncomfortable that Brunetti almost expected him to cry 'foul' and refuse to answer. Instead, the Inspector nodded, smiled, and said, 'I see your point.' Then, after another moment of consideration, he said, 'It's possible.'

'Maybe the request that they witness the will was too big a temptation to resist,' Brunetti suggested. 'A house in exchange for two signatures.' It occurred to Brunetti to add that Paris was worth a Mass, but he feared that Vianello might not understand and so he said nothing further.

Vianello smiled and added, 'Who was that saint who said, "Make me chaste, but not yet."?'

'Augustine, I think.'

Vianello smiled.

'But it doesn't tell us where the money's still coming from, does it?' Brunetti asked.

They tossed the subject back and forth for some time, trying to find an explanation for the recurring deposits. 'And why put the money in the bank?' Vianello asked. 'Only a fool would leave traces like that.'

'Or a person with no idea of how easy it is to check on a money trail.' Hearing himself speak, Brunetti decided to take another look at the list of deposits. He pulled the folder with

Morandi's bank records from his drawer and found the statements. Running his finger down the column of deposits, he found that the first two had been paid by cheque.

He dialled Signorina Elettra's number and while he waited for her to answer, he heard Vianello muttering to himself, 'No one could be this stupid.'

He explained what it was he wanted her to find, to which she answered, 'Oh, wonderful, and I can do it legally this time,' as delighted as if he had told her to take the rest of the day off and go home.

Uncertain how much she was baiting him, he said, 'It's always helpful for us to have new experiences,' and hung up.

25

Though Signorina Elettra managed to find the complete records of all of Morandi's bank transactions in less than twenty minutes, Brunetti did not for an instant believe that the ease with which she managed it would in any way convert her to the paths of legality.

The deposits, the first for four thousand euros, the second for three, had been made by cheques written by Nicola Turchetti, a name which resounded in Brunetti's memory. Vianello had gone back to the squad room, so Brunetti was left to search for the name on his own. After some time, having found no resonant chord, he pulled the phone book from his bottom drawer and opened it to the Ts.

For some reason, seeing the name in print was enough to nudge Brunetti's memory. Turchetti, the art dealer, was a man with a Janus-like reputation: his expertise was never questioned; the probity of his dealings sometimes was. To the best of Brunetti's knowledge, no charges had ever been brought against the man. His name, however, was often mentioned when sharp business practices were discussed:

positively by those who found rarities in his shop; negatively by those who speculated about the sources of some of his acquisitions. Brunetti's father-in-law, ignoring both opinions, remained a client of Turchetti's and had, over the years, acquired from him many paintings and drawings.

Drawings. Brunetti's thoughts flew to the legendary Reynard auction and the drawings that had not appeared on the block, thus disappointing so many collectors of the chance to add to their collections. Had no one done an inventory? Or, as was most likely, had the inventory been overseen by Avvocato Cuccetti? The Reynard *palazzo* was now a hotel, Brunetti knew, and the objects that had once filled it had long since been consigned to the hands of eager buyers. Avvocato Cuccetti was wherever Madame Reynard had preceded him, neither of them having been able to take anything with them.

Because the phone book was open in front of him, Brunetti dialled the number. His call was answered by a female secretary with the sloppy sort of Roman accent that irritated Brunetti. Brunetti gave his name, not his rank, and when the woman explained that Signor Turchetti was busy, he added his father-in-law's name, and his title, whereupon the waters parted and the call was transferred immediately to Dottor Turchetti.

'Ah, Dottor Brunetti,' a deep voice intoned, 'Conte Orazio has spoken of you often.'

'And of you, Dottore,' Brunetti answered with oleaginous civility.

'In what way may I be of service to you?' Turchetti asked after a moment's hesitation.

'I wonder if you'd have time to speak to me about one of your clients.'

'Of course,' he said easily. 'Which one?'

'I'll come over and tell you, shall I?' Brunetti asked and, without waiting for an answer, replaced the phone and left his office.

Brunetti took the Number One and got off at Accademia, turned left and started back in the direction of the Guggenheim. Before the first bridge, he found the gallery, paused to study the paintings in the window, and then entered. The space was large and low-ceilinged, though the effect was counteracted by the lighting, which angled up from the walls and thus effectively disguised the lowness. More light reflected from the canal in front, augmenting the sense of space.

A man Brunetti recognized from having seen him on the street more than a few times rose to greet him from a catalogue-covered desk at the back of the gallery. There was no trace of the woman who had answered the phone.

'Ah, Dottor Brunetti,' Turchetti said as he approached, hand extended. He was a man best described as '*robusto*', not particularly tall and thus seeming thicker because of that. Had he been a taller man, the brisk energy of his movements would have been imposing; because he was not, there remained something faintly pugnacious about him, as though all that energy stuffed into such a low space would be forced to find some other means of escape. He had dark eyes set in a very broad face and a nose that veered to the left, as if to give further suggestion of something that might turn into belligerence.

His smile was pleasant and inviting, evident in both his eyes and mouth, but Brunetti could not help seeing it as a salesman's smile. His grip was strong but completely uncompetitive. His lapels were hand-stitched. 'How may I be of help, Dottore?' he asked, surprising Brunetti by making it sound like a real question.

Before he answered, Brunetti cast his eyes around the gallery. On the wall to his left was a small portrait of Santa Caterina of Alexandria, her head turned to her left, glancing off towards martyrdom and beatification, one traitor hand placed protectively on her single string of pearls. She already wore her martyr's crown, but that too was compromised by a row of inset pearls. Her right hand was placed negligently on her martyr's wheel, the palm frond about to drop from her fingers. Which is it to be, girl? Earth or heaven? Pleasure or salvation? Poised in a moment of perfect indecision, she stared at a ray of light in the top corner of the painting, uncertainty evident in her every feature.

'She's lovely, isn't she?' Turchetti asked. He stepped aside to look square at the painting. 'I'll hate to see her leave,' he said, just as though the woman in the painting were capable of making the decision about when to pick up her skirts and walk out of the gallery.

Then, turning away from the painting, the dealer faced Brunetti and said, 'You were interested in one of my clients?'

'Yes. Benito Morandi.'

The name registered in Turchetti's eyes and his mouth contracted a bit at the corners, as if he had been reminded of an unpleasant taste. 'Ah,' he sighed, a noise that could register confusion as easily as recognition but, in either case, would give him time to consider his response. Brunetti, familiar with the tactic, stood and waited, saying nothing and offering only his impassive face.

'Why don't we go and sit down?' Turchetti suggested, turning back towards his desk. Brunetti followed him, sat in one of the chairs placed on the client side and glanced around the gallery, taking in the paintings and drawings but seeing nothing as inviting as the martyr. At first Turchetti leaned back against the desk and folded his arms, but then, as if suddenly conscious of how this placed him so much higher than his guest, sat in a chair facing Brunetti. 'Your father-in-law,' Turchetti began, 'has told me the work you do.'

Brunetti had to admire the exquisite sensibility that could not bring itself to pronounce the word, 'policeman'. He nodded.

'And that you are a man with a certain . . . how shall I put it?' Turchetti said, pausing as if in search of the most flattering term. Brunetti, for his part, sat, resisting the impulse to tell the other man he didn't much care what he called anything, so long as he told him about Benito Morandi. Instead, he tilted his head rather in the manner of Santa Caterina but in a fashion he hoped would suggest mild curiosity rather than angelic rapture.

'. . . sense of justice? Is that the term I'm searching for?'

Brunetti thought it probably was and so nodded.

Turchetti renewed his smile. 'Good, then.' He sat back and crossed his legs, suggesting that, now that the preliminaries were established, they could start talking. 'Morandi is a client of mine in that he has occasionally sold me things.'

Brunetti smiled as at the hearing of truth, already known, universally acknowledged. So Turchetti must remember, perhaps regret, writing those cheques to Morandi. Had he been short of cash? Had he needed to delay payment? Or had he paid with cheques so as to allow time to have whatever he bought authenticated? Or to verify the provenance?

'What things?' Brunetti asked.

'Oh, this and that,' Turchetti said with an easy smile and an airy wave of his hand.

'What things?'

Displaying no surprise whatsoever at Brunetti's tone, he said, 'Oh, the occasional drawing.'

'What drawings?'

While Turchetti thought about how to answer this, Brunetti reached into his pocket and pulled out his notebook. He opened it to the page that had the name of Chiara's teachers and looked down the list.

Before he could repeat his question, Turchetti said, 'Oh, minor artists, no one you've ever heard of, I'd guess.'

Brunetti took a pen from his inside pocket, opened it, gave Turchetti a neutral glance, and said, 'Try me.'

Turchetti's smile was gracious. 'Johann von Dillis and

Friedrich Salathé,' he said, pronouncing the first name of the second painter as though he were a man nursed on Goethe and Heine.

Brunetti had heard of the first, but he nodded as though both names were familiar to him and wrote them down. Though he had never heard his father-in-law mention either name, the Count was a collector and spent a lot of time in galleries, and so he might have seen them, had Turchetti shown them in his gallery, and thus Brunetti might learn their resale price.

'And the others?' Brunetti asked.

Turchetti smiled. 'I'd have to check my records. It was so long ago.'

'But the last sale was only . . .' Brunetti said, trying to recall the papers Signorina Elettra had given him as he turned a page of his notebook, 'about three months ago.'

Had Turchetti been a fish, Brunetti would have seen him squirming around as he tried to free himself from the hook in such a manner as to do himself as little harm as possible. Turchetti did not gasp, at least not in the way of a fish: he drew in two long breaths and finally said, 'Shall we save time, Commissario, and you tell me what it is you want?'

'I want to know what he sold you and how much they were worth.'

With a smile that would have been flirtatious, had it been directed at a woman, the dealer asked, 'You don't want to know what I paid him?'

Brunetti felt the urge to swipe him aside, but Turchetti did not know that since Morandi had so conscientiously deposited the money into his account Brunetti already knew what he had been paid. It was probably impossible for an art dealer to conceive of a person who would sell something and deposit that amount in the bank.

'No, Signore,' Brunetti said, removing Turchetti's title, 'only what they were worth.'

'May I estimate?' Turchetti asked directly, as if he had tired of the game. He no longer bothered talking about his 'records'. Brunetti had grown up hearing priests speak of indulgences, so he well knew how malleable was the interpretation of value.

'Feel free,' Brunetti told him.

'The Dillis was worth about forty thousand; the Salathé a bit less.'

'And the others?' Brunetti said, glancing down at the names of Chiara's history and geometry teachers.

'There were some prints: Tiepolo, not worth more than ten or twelve. I think there were six or seven of them.'

'You didn't offer him a price for the lot?'

'No,' Turchetti said, unable to disguise his irritation. 'He insisted on bringing them in one at a time.' Then, unable to disguise his satisfaction at a job well done, he added, 'He thought he'd get more for them that way.' So much, his tone stated, for *that* possibility.

Brunetti refused to give him the satisfaction of a response and asked, 'What else?'

'You want to know everything?' Turchetti asked with carefully orchestrated surprise and another flirtatious smile.

With careful slowness, Brunetti clipped his pen to the inside of the notebook and closed it. He looked across at Turchetti and said, 'Perhaps I'm not making myself clear enough, Signore.' He moved his lips in something that was not meant to be a smile. 'I have a list, with amounts and dates, and I want to know what he gave in exchange for the money he received.'

'And I assume you have the authorization to ask for such information?' Turchetti asked. All smiles stopped together.

'Not only can I have it if I ask for it,' Brunetti said, 'but I also have the attention of my father-in-law.'

Turchetti could not hide his surprise, nor could he disguise his uneasiness. 'What does that mean?'

'That I have only to suggest to him that the provenance given to some of the objects in this gallery is questionable, and I'm sure he'd call around to his friends to ask if they've heard the same thing.' He waited for a moment, and then added, 'And I suppose they'd call their friends. And so it would go.' Brunetti returned to smiling and reopened his notebook. He bent over it and said, 'What else?'

Turchetti, with a precision that Brunetti found exemplary, gave him a list of drawings and prints, approximate dates, and values. Brunetti made a note of them, using the space to the right of the names of Chiara's teachers and then turning to a blank page to finish the list. When Turchetti finished, Brunetti did not bother to ask him if he had mentioned everything.

He closed the notebook and put it and his pen back in his pocket, then got to his feet. 'Have you sold them all?' he asked, though the question was not necessary. They belonged to whoever had them, and even if the law could get them back, to whom did they now belong?

'No. There are two left.' Brunetti saw Turchetti start to say something, force himself to stop, and then give in to the impulse. 'Why? Do I have to give you one?'

Brunetti turned and left the gallery.

26

Well, well, well. Brunetti walked back towards the bridge. The Dillis was worth forty thousand and poor silly Morandi got four, and why was he thinking of Morandi as poor, or silly? Because the Salathé was worth almost as much and he let Turchetti pay him three?

Brunetti was aware that, no matter how right his own ethical system might feel to him, he still found it difficult to explain, even to himself. He had read the Greeks and Romans and knew what they thought of justice and right and wrong and the common good and the personal good, and he had read the Fathers of the Church and knew what they said. He knew the rules, but he found himself, in every particular situation, bogged down in the specifics of what happened to people, found himself siding with or against them because of what they thought or felt and not necessarily in accord with the rules that were meant to govern things.

Morandi had once been a thug, but Brunetti had seen his protective look at that solitary woman across the room, and so he could not believe Morandi had wanted to keep her from talking to him so much as he wanted to keep anyone from disturbing whatever peace remained to her.

He waited for the Number Two, watching the people cross the bridge. Boats passed in both directions, one of them filled to the gunwales with the possessions, and perhaps the hopes, of an entire family that was moving house. Down to Castello? Or turn in to the left and back into San Marco? A shaggy black dog stood on a table precariously balanced on a pile of cardboard boxes at the prow of the boat, its nose pointing forward as bravely as that of any figurehead. How dogs loved boats. Was it the open air and the richness of scents passing by? He couldn't remember whether dogs saw at long distance or only very close, or perhaps it differed according to what breed they were. Well, there'd be no determining breed with this one: he was as much Bergamasco as Labrador, as much spaniel as hound. He was happy, that was evident, and perhaps that's all a dog needed to be and all Brunetti needed to know about a dog.

The arrival of the vaporetto cut off his reflections but did not remove Morandi from his mind. 'People don't change.' How many times had he heard his mother say that? She had never studied psychology, his mother. In fact, she had never studied much at all, but that did not prevent her from having a logical mind, even a subtle one. Presented with an example of uncharacteristic behaviour, she would often point out that it was merely a manifestation of the person's real character, and when she reminded people of events from the past, she was often proven right.

Usually people surprised us, he reflected, with the bad they did, when some dark impulse slipped the leash and brought them, and others, to ruin. And then how easy it became to find in the past the undetected symptoms of their malice. How, then, find the undetected symptoms of goodness?

When he got to his office, he tried the phone book again and found that Morandi was listed, but the phone rang unanswered until the eighth ring, when a man's voice said he was not at home but could be reached on his *telefonino*. Brunetti copied the number and dialled it immediately.

'*Sì*,' a man's voice answered.

'Signor Morandi?'

'*Sì. Chi è?*'

'Good day, Signor Morandi. This is Guido Brunetti. We spoke two days ago in the room of Signora Sartori.'

'You're the pension man?' Morandi asked, and Brunetti thought he heard rekindled hope, knew he heard civility, in his voice.

Without answering the question, Brunetti said, 'I'd like to speak to you again, Signor Morandi.'

'About Maria's pension?'

'Among other things,' Brunetti answered blandly. He waited for the question, the suspicion about what those other things could be. But they did not come.

Instead, Morandi asked, 'When can we talk? Do you want me to come to your office?'

'No, Signor Morandi; I don't want you to trouble yourself. Perhaps we could meet somewhere nearer to you.'

'I live behind San Marco,' he said, unaware that Brunetti knew much more about his house than its location. 'But I have to be at the *casa di cura* at five-thirty; perhaps we could meet near there?'

'In the *campo*?' Brunetti suggested.

'Good. Thank you, Signore,' the old man said. 'Fifteen minutes?'

'Good,' Brunetti said and hung up. There was enough time, so he first went down to the evidence room and then started towards the *campo*. The late autumn sun smacked him in the back of the head but cheered him by doing so.

The old man sat on one of the benches in front of the the *casa di cura*, bent forward from the waist, tossing something to a mini-flock of sparrows dancing around his feet. Oh God, was Brunetti to find himself seduced by a few breadcrumbs tossed to hungry birds? He steeled himself and approached the older man.

Morandi heard him coming, tossed the rest of whatever he had in his hands to the birds, and pushed himself to his feet. He smiled, all memory of their first meeting erased or ignored, and put out his hand; Brunetti took it and was surprised at how weak the other man's grasp was. This close, he was much taller than the old man. Looking down, Brunetti could see the pink skin of his head shining through the strands of dark hair pasted across it. 'Shall we sit down?' Brunetti asked.

The old man bent, bracing himself with one hand, and lowered himself slowly on to the bench. Brunetti left a space between them and sat, and the birds scuttled up to Morandi's feet. Automatically, he reached into the pocket of his jacket and pulled out some pieces of grain, which he tossed far out into the *campo*. Startled by the motion of his arm, some of the birds took flight, only to land amidst the grains just as the ones that had decided to run arrived. They did not squabble or dispute but all set to picking up as much as they could.

Morandi glanced at Brunetti and said, 'I come here most days, so they know me by now.' As he spoke, the birds began to approach, but he sat back and folded his arms across his chest. 'No more. I have to talk to this gentleman now.' The birds peeped their protest, waited a moment, then abandoned him in a group on the arrival of a white-haired woman on the other side of the *campo*.

'I think I should tell you, Signor Morandi,' Brunetti began, believing it best to clear his conscience, 'I wasn't there about the pension.'

'You mean she's not going to get an increase?' he asked, leaning forward and turning to Brunetti.

'There was no mistake: she's already getting her pension for those years,' Brunetti said.

'So there won't be an increase?' Morandi asked again, unwilling to believe what he heard.

Brunetti shook his head. 'I'm afraid not, Signore.'

Morandi's shoulders sank, then he pushed himself upright against the back of the bench. He looked across the *campo*, dappled in the afternoon sun, but to Brunetti it seemed as though the old man was looking across a wasteland, a desert.

'I'm sorry to have got your hopes up,' Brunetti said.

The old man leaned aside and placed a hand on Brunetti's arm. He gave it a weak squeeze and said, 'That's all right, son. It's never been right since she first started to get it, but at least this time we were able to hope a little bit.' He looked at Brunetti and tried to smile. There were the same broken veins, the same battered nose and ridiculous hair, but Brunetti wondered where the man he had seen in the *casa di cura* had gone, for surely this was not the same one.

The anger or fear or whatever it was had disappeared. Here in the sunlight, Morandi was a quiet old man on a park bench. Perhaps, in the manner of a bodyguard, Morandi reacted only in defence of whom he was sent to guard and for the rest was content to sit and toss seeds to the little birds.

What then to make of his criminal record? After how many years did a record cease to matter?

'Are you a policeman?' Morandi surprised him by asking.

'Yes,' Brunetti said. 'How did you know?'

Morandi shrugged. 'When I saw you there in the room, that was the first thing I thought, and now that you tell me you weren't there for the pension, that's what I go back to thinking.'

'Why did you think I was a policeman?' Brunetti wanted to know.

The old man glanced at him. 'I thought you'd come. Sooner or later,' he said, speaking in the plural. He shrugged, placed his palms on his thighs, and said, 'I didn't think it would take you this long, though.'

'Why? How long has it been?' Brunetti asked.

'Since she died,' Morandi answered.

'And why did you think we'd come?'

Morandi looked at the backs of his fingers, at Brunetti, and then again at his hands. In a much softer voice, he said, 'Because of what I did.' That said, he stiffened his elbows and leaned forward, arms braced on his thighs. He wasn't getting ready to get to his feet, Brunetti could see: he looked at the ground. Suddenly the birds were back, looking up at him and peeping insistently. Brunetti thought he didn't see them.

The old man, with visible effort, pulled himself up and leaned against the back of the bench once again. He looked at his watch and abruptly got to his feet. Brunetti stood. 'It's time. I have to go and see her,' Morandi said. 'Her doctor came at five, and the sisters said I could see her after he spoke to her. But only for a few minutes. So she doesn't have to worry about anything he said.'

He turned and walked in the direction of the *casa di cura*, just on the other side of the *campo*. The building had only the front door, so Brunetti could easily have waited in the *campo*, but he fell into step with Morandi, who seemed not to notice or, if he did, to mind.

This time, in deference to the other man's age, Brunetti took the elevator, though he hated them and felt trapped inside. The Toltec waited in front of the elevator, smiled at Morandi, nodded to Brunetti, and took the old man's arm to lead him through the door of the nursing home and down the corridor.

Left alone, Brunetti went into a small sitting room that had a view of the front door. He sat on a precarious chair and picked up the single magazine – *Famiglia cristiana* – that lay on a table. At a certain point, he found himself confronted with the need to choose between reading the Pope's catechism lesson for the week or the recipe for a cheese and ham pie. The ingredients were just being slipped into the oven when he heard footsteps coming into the room.

One strand of Morandi's hair had come loose and snaked down on to the shoulder of his jacket. He looked at Brunetti with stunned eyes. 'Why do they have to tell the truth?' he asked as he came in, voice harsh and desolate. Brunetti got quickly to his feet and took the man under the arm, holding him up and leading him to the overstuffed sofa.

Morandi sat in the centre, made his right hand into a fist, and pounded it a few times into the seat next to him. 'Doctors. To hell with them all. Sons of bitches, all of them.' With each phrase, his face grew more mottled as his fist came crashing down on to the cushion, and with each phrase he came more to resemble the man Brunetti had seen in Signora Sartori's room.

Finally spent, he fell against the back of the sofa and closed his eyes. Brunetti returned to his chair, closed the magazine and put it back on the table. He waited, wondering which Morandi would open his eyes, the soft-hearted San Francesco or the enraged enemy of doctors and bureaucrats?

Time passed, and Brunetti used it to construct a scenario. Morandi expected the police to come and find him after Signora Altavilla's death: and for what reason other than guilt? At the memory of those bruises, Brunetti turned his eyes to Morandi's hands: broad and thick, the hands of a worker. If the sight of a stranger in Signora Sartori's room or the thought that a doctor would tell the truth could catapult him into such anger, how was he likely to respond to . . . to what, exactly? What form had Signora Altavilla's dangerous honesty taken? Had she encouraged him to confess their help in the deceit of Madame Reynard without considering its effect on Signora Sartori?

Brunetti's mind ran into a wall. *Oddio*, what if Madame Reynard's will had not been falsified? What if the hand-writing had indeed been hers, and she had really wanted her lawyer – who certainly would have been as courteous and helpful as Lucifer himself – to have it all? The fact that Cuccetti was a liar and a thief in the eyes of half of Venice meant nothing if the old woman had sincerely wanted him to inherit her estate. Must only the good be rewarded?

Why, then, the apartment, and whence the Dillis and the Tiepolos and the Salanthé? Brunetti looked at the old man, who appeared to have fallen asleep, and the desire swept over him to grab him by the shoulders and shake him until he told the truth.

27

Silently, so as not to disturb the sleeping man, Brunetti pulled from his pocket Signora Altavilla's key ring, which he had taken from the evidence room before leaving the Questura. He trapped it between his palms and used his thumbnail to prise open the metal ring, then slid the third key – the one that fitted neither door – towards the narrow opening. He slipped it along and slowly, slowly, urged it until it came free in his hand. Leaning forward, he laid the key on Morandi's right thigh, then returned the key ring to his pocket, folded his arms, and pushed himself back in his chair.

He thought it invasive to look at the sleeping man, so he turned his eyes to the window and the wall on the opposite side of the canal while he thought about monkeys. He had recently read an article that explained experiments devised to test the inherent sense of justice in a species of monkey, Brunetti could not remember which. Once each member of the group was accustomed to receiving the same reward for the same action, they grew angry if one of their band received a greater reward than his peers. Though the cause of their agitation was nothing more than the difference between a piece of cucumber and a grape, it seemed to Brunetti that they were reacting in a very human way: unmerited reward was offensive even to those who lost nothing by it. Add to this the presumption of deceit or theft on the part of the winner of the grape, and the sense of outrage became stronger. In the case of Avvocato Cuccetti, all that had ever existed was the presumption of theft, nothing more, though he had been rewarded with considerably more than a grape. Enough time had passed, however, for there to be no legal consequences even if the presumption were confirmed. Even if he could be proven to have stolen the grape, there was to be no giving it back.

Morandi had not been surprised at the arrival of a policeman: he thought the police were bound to come because of what he had done. Because of Madame Reynard's will? Because he went to see Signora Altavilla? Because he tried to reason against her terrible honesty? Or because he put his hands on her shoulders and tried to shake some sense into her? Or pushed her to the ground, having seen or not seen the radiator?

People occasionally rang the bell, and the Toltec went to open the door for them, but they were all preoccupied with other things and did not bother to look into the room. Had they done so, what would they have seen? Another of the residents of the home, fallen away from the worries of the day – and was that his son sitting with him?

'What do you want?' the old man asked in a dead level voice.

Brunetti looked at Morandi and saw that he was fully awake and held the key in one hand. He rubbed it between his thumb and index finger, as though it were a coin and he was testing to see if it were counterfeit or not.

'I'd like to know about the key,' Brunetti said.

'So she did have it,' Morandi said with quiet resignation.

'Yes.'

The old man shook his head in evident regret. 'I was sure she did, but she told me it wasn't there.'

'It wasn't,' Brunetti told him.

'What?'

'She'd given it to someone else.'

'Her son?'

'A friend.'

'Oh,' Morandi said, resigned, then added, 'she should have given it to me.'

'Did you ask her for it?

'Of course,' Morandi said. 'That's why I went there; to get it back.'

'But?'

'But she wouldn't give it to me. She said she knew what it was and that it wasn't right for me to have it, or to have them.'

'I see,' Brunetti said. 'Did Signora Sartori tell her?'

The old man gave himself a shake, the way Brunetti had seen dogs do. It started with his head and gradually enveloped his shoulders and part of his arms. Two more strands of hair broke free of his scalp and draped themselves across the lapel of his jacket. Brunetti did not know if he was trying to shake away Brunetti's question or the answer it required. After he stopped moving, the old man still did not speak.

'I suppose Signora Sartori must have told her,' Brunetti said resignedly, as though he had just followed a very complicated train of thought, and this was the only place it could lead.

'Told her what?' the old man asked, but his voice was slowed by tiredness, not by suspicion.

'About what you and Signora Sartori did,' Brunetti answered.

As if suddenly aware of the disorder of his hair, Morandi raised a hand and delicately replaced the wanton strands, draping them one after the other across the pink dome of his head. He patted them into place, then kept his hand on them as if waiting for some signal that they had adhered to the surface.

He lowered his hand and said, not looking at Brunetti when he spoke, 'She shouldn't have told her. Maria, that is. But ever since she . . . since this happened to her, she hasn't been careful about what she says, and she . . .' He trailed off, patted his hair into place again, though it was not necessary, and looked across at Brunetti, as though he expected some response to what he had said. 'She drifts,' he finally said.

'What do the doctors say?' Brunetti asked.

'Oh, doctors,' Morandi answered angrily, waving his hand at some place behind him, as if the doctors were lined up there and, hearing him, should be embarrassed. 'One of them said it was a small stroke, but another says it might be the beginning of Al . . . of something else.' When Brunetti said nothing and the invisible doctors did not contest his remarks, Morandi went on. 'It's just old age. And worry.'

'I'm sorry she's worried,' Brunetti said. 'She deserves peace and quiet.'

Morandi smiled, bowed his head as at a compliment he did not deserve, and said, 'Yes, she does. She's the most wonderful woman in the world.' Brunetti heard the real tremor in his voice. He waited, and Morandi added, 'I've never known anyone like her.'

'You must know her very well to be this devoted to her, Signore,' Brunetti said.

Because Morandi had again lowered his head, Brunetti could see only his pink scalp and the dark strands of hair that transected it. But as he watched, the pink grew darker and Morandi said, 'She's everything.'

Brunetti let some time pass before he said, 'You're lucky.'

'I know that,' Morandi said, and again Brunetti heard the tremor.

'How long have you known her?'

'Since the sixteenth of July, nineteen fifty-nine.'

'I was still a child,' Brunetti said.

'Well, I was a man by then,' Morandi said, then added in a softer voice, 'but not a very good one and not a very nice one.'

'But then you met her?' Brunetti encouraged him.

Morandi looked up then, and Brunetti saw that same smile, strangely childlike. 'Yes.' Then, as an afterthought, 'At three-thirty in the afternoon.'

'You're lucky to remember the day so clearly,' Brunetti said, surprised that he could no longer remember the date he met Paola. He knew the year, certainly, and remembered why he was in the library, the subject of the essay he had to write, so if he checked his university records for when he took that class, he could probably work out at least the month, but the date was gone. He would be embarrassed to ask Paola because, if she knew it off by heart, he'd feel a cad for not remembering it. But she might just as easily say he was a sentimental fool for wanting to remember something like that, which was probably true. Which made Morandi a sentimental fool, he supposed.

'How did you meet her?' Brunetti asked.

Morandi smiled at the question and at the memory. 'I was working as a porter at the hospital and I had to go into a room to help lift one of the patients on to a stretcher so they could take him down for tests, and Maria was there already, helping the nurse.' He looked at the wall to the left of Brunetti, perhaps seeing the hospital room. 'But they were both very small women and couldn't do it, so I asked them to get out of my way, and I lifted the man onto the stretcher, and when they thanked me, Maria smiled, and . . . well, I suppose . . .' His voice trailed off but his smile remained.

'I knew right then, you know,' he said to Brunetti, man to man, though Brunetti thought more women than men would understand this, 'that she was the one. And nothing in all these years has changed that.'

'You're a lucky man,' Brunetti repeated, thinking that any

man, or any woman, who spent decades wrapped in this feeling was a lucky person. Why, then, had they never married? He recalled the thuggish first impression Morandi had made and wondered if perhaps he had an inconvenient family lodged somewhere. Paola often referred to men who had a Mrs Rochester in the attic: did Morandi have one?

'I think so,' Morandi said, the key still in his hand.

'How long has Signora Sartori been here?' Brunetti asked, waving his hand to take in all that stood around them, as innocently as if copies of all of the payments for her care from the day she entered were not sitting on his desk to be checked at a glance.

'Three years now,' he said, a time that began, as Brunetti knew, with the deposit of the first of Turchetti's cheques.

'It's a very good place. She's very lucky to be here,' Brunetti said. He would not allow himself to mention his mother's experience, and so he said only, 'I know that some of the other places in the city don't take as good care as the sisters here do.' When Morandi failed to answer, Brunetti said, 'I've heard stories about the public places.'

'We were very lucky,' Morandi said earnestly, failing to take the bait, or avoiding it; Brunetti was not sure.

'I've heard it's very expensive,' Brunetti said, using the voice of one citizen to another.

'We had a little put by,' Morandi said.

Brunetti leaned forward and took the key from Morandi's hand. 'Is this where they are?' he asked, holding it up. When the old man did not answer, Brunetti slipped the key into the watch pocket of his trousers.

Morandi placed his right hand on his thigh, as if to cover the place where the key had been. Then he put the left on the other thigh. He looked at Brunetti, his face paler than it had been. 'Did she tell you?'

Brunetti did not know if he meant Signora Sartori or Signora Altavilla, and so he answered, 'It doesn't matter who told me, does it, Signore? Just that I have the key and know what's there.'

'They don't belong to anyone, you know,' the old man insisted. 'They're all dead, all the people who wanted them.'

'How did you get them?'

'The old French woman had them in the house. Inside a hamper for the washing.' He must have read the flash of concern on Brunetti's face for he said, 'No, they were in a plastic case on the bottom. They were safe.'

'I see,' Brunetti said. 'But how did you get them?' He used the plural form of 'you'.

Morandi reacted to the word this time. 'Maria didn't know anything about them. She wouldn't have liked it. Not at all. She wouldn't have let me take them.'

'Oh, I see, I see,' Brunetti said, wondering how many more times he would have to say this same thing when, as now, what he heard was unlikely to be true? Morandi had had them in his possession for decades, and she had not known?

'Cuccetti gave them to me. The same night we witnessed the paper.' Brunetti noticed the man could not bring himself to call it a will. Then Morandi added, sounding angry, 'I made him do it.'

'Why?'

'Because I didn't trust him,' Morandi said with great force.

'And the apartment?' Brunetti asked, in lieu of pursuing the subject of Cuccetti's honesty.

'That was what he promised me at the beginning, when he asked me if we'd sign something. I didn't trust him then, and I didn't trust him later. I knew what he was like. He'd give me the apartment, then he'd find a way to take it back. Some legal way. After all, he was a lawyer,' Morandi said in much the same way he would say that a bird was a vulture.

Brunetti, wise in the way of lawyers, nodded.

'So I told him what I wanted.'

'How did you know about them and what they were?'

'The old woman used to talk to Maria, and she told her about them, about how much they were worth, and Maria told me.' Then, before Brunetti could get the wrong opinion, he quickly added, 'No, it's not what you think. It was just something she told me, when she talked about work and the patients and the sort of things they told her.' He looked away for a moment, as if embarrassed to find himself in the company of a man capable of thinking such a thing of Signora Sartori. 'It was my idea, not hers. She didn't know about it. And she's never known I have them.'

Then, Brunetti found himself thinking unkindly, how did she know about the key?

'What did Cuccetti say?'

'What could he say?' Morandi asked harshly. 'The old woman wasn't going to last very long.' Then to explain things further, he said, 'Anyone could see that, so I knew he had to hurry.' Brunetti remained silent in the face of Morandi's failure to realize what this said about himself.

'I told him I wouldn't sign anything until he gave them to me.' As the old man told his story, Brunetti was reminded of why he had thought him a thug. His voice hardened, as did his eyes; his mouth grew tighter in the telling of the tale. Brunetti's face was impassivity itself.

'And then the old woman had some sort of crisis – I forget what it was. Breathing, something like that. And he panicked, Cuccetti, and he must have gone to her place and got them, and he brought them to the hospital and put them in her closet.'

'Why would he do that?' Brunetti asked.

Morandi answered immediately. 'If anyone asked, he could say she asked him to bring them to her so she could look at them again.' His nod showed how clever he judged this move on Cuccetti's part to have been. 'But she didn't see them. She was gaga by then.'

Brunetti thought again of Dante's lizards and of the way

they repeatedly changed shape, returning ineluctably to the form of what they had once been.

'So you signed it?'

'Yes,' Morandi said.

'And was that really Signora Sartori's signature?'

Morandi blushed again, far more strongly than at any time in the past. The fight went out of him; he actually seemed to deflate again. 'Yes,' he said and bowed his head to await the blow of Brunetti's next question.

'What did you tell her?'

Morandi started to speak but then burst into nervous coughing. He bowed his head over his knees and kept it there until the coughing fit ended, then pushed himself up and against the back of the sofa and closed his eyes. Brunetti would not let him go to sleep again, would poke him in the side before he'd allow that. The old man opened his eyes and said, 'I told her that I'd watched the old woman write it. That Cuccetti and I had been there and she'd written it by herself.'

'Who really wrote it?' Brunetti asked.

Morandi shrugged. 'I don't know. It was on the table when I went into the room.' He looked at Brunetti and said, making no attempt to disguise his eagerness, 'So she could have written it, couldn't she?'

Brunetti ignored this. 'It could have been anyone who signed it?' Brunetti demanded levelly. 'But you and Signora Sartori witnessed her signature?'

Morandi nodded, then covered his eyes with his right hand, as if the sight of Brunetti's knowledge was too much for him to bear. Brunetti glanced away for a moment, and when he looked back he saw that tears were seeping from beneath his fingers.

For some time the old man sat like that, then heaved himself to one side and pulled an enormous white handkerchief from his pocket. He wiped his eyes and blew his nose, folded the handkerchief carefully, and put it back in his pocket.

As if he had not heard Brunetti's question, Morandi said, 'The old woman died a few days later. Three. Four. Then Cuccetti submitted the will, and we were asked about it. I had to explain to Maria that she had to say we saw her sign it, or we'd all get in trouble.'

'And she did?'

'Yes. Then.'

'But later?'

'But later she began not to believe me.'

'Was it because of the apartment?'

'No, I told her my aunt left it to me. She lived in Torino and she died about then, so I told Maria that's what happened.'

'She believed you?'

'Yes. Of course.' Seeing Brunetti's face, he said, voice almost pleading, 'Please. You have to understand that Maria is an honest person. She couldn't lie, even if she wanted to. And she doesn't think other people can.' He paused, considering, and then added, 'And I never had. Not to her. Not until then. Because I wanted us to have a home we could be proud of and be together there.'

How convenient that desire made things for him, Brunetti found himself thinking.

'What did you do with the drawings?' Brunetti asked. He was tired of this, tired of having to consider everything Morandi said to determine which of the two men he had seen in him was speaking.

As if he had been expecting the question, Morandi said, with a vague gesture towards Brunetti's pocket, as if they were there, 'I put them in the bank.'

Brunetti stopped himself from smacking his palm against his forehead and shouting out, 'Of course, of course.' People like Morandi didn't live in large apartments near San Marco, and no one expected poor people to have safe deposit boxes.

But what else was that key if not the key to a safe deposit box?

'When did she take the key?'

Morandi pulled his lips together in the manner of a schoolboy being reproved for some minor offence. 'A week ago. Remember, that warm day?' Brunetti did indeed remember: they'd had dinner on the terrace, but the warm spell had ended suddenly.

'I went out into the *campo* to have a cigarette. I left my overcoat lying on the bed. She must have taken the key when I was outside. I didn't notice it until I got home and opened the door, but it was too late to go back to the *casa di cura* then, and when I asked her about it the next day, she said she didn't know what I was talking about.'

'Did she know what the key was?' Brunetti said.

Morandi shook his head. 'I don't know, I don't know. I never thought she knew anything or understood what had happened. About the apartment. Or about the drawings.' He gave Brunetti a long look and said, his confusion to be heard in every word, 'But she must have, don't you think?' Brunetti did not answer, and Morandi asked, 'To take the key? She must have known? All these years?' There was a hint of desperation in his voice at the need to consider what this possibility did to his vision of and belief in the sainted Maria.

Brunetti found no words. People knew things they said and thought they did not know. Wives and husbands learned far more about the other person than they were ever meant to learn.

'I have to have the key,' Morandi blurted out. 'I have to have it.'

'Why?' Brunetti asked, though he knew.

'To pay the bills.' The old man looked around the room, ran his palm across the velvet of the sofa. 'You know what the public places are like: you've seen them. I can't let her go there.' At the thought, the tears began again, but this time

Morandi was unconscious of them. 'You wouldn't put a dog there,' he insisted.

Brunetti, who had not put his mother there, said nothing.

'I have to pay them. I can't move her now, not from this into one of those places.' He choked on a sob, as surprised by it as was Brunetti. Morandi struggled to his feet and walked to the door. 'I can't be inside,' he said and headed for the elevator.

28

Brunetti had no choice but to follow him, though this time he took the stairs and arrived sooner than the elevator. Morandi's face softened when he saw him there, and together they walked out into the early evening sun. The old man went back to the same bench, and within minutes the birds had altered their flight paths and were landing not far from his feet. They taxied up to him, but he had nothing to give them, nor did he appear to notice them.

Brunetti sat on the bench, leaving a space between them.

The old man reached into his pocket and pulled out cigarette papers and tobacco. Sloppily, spilling tobacco on to his trousers and shoes, he managed to roll a cigarette and get it lit. He took three deep puffs and sat back, ignoring the birds who, in their turn, ignored the tobacco that fell around them. They looked up at him, their indignant peeps making no impression on Morandi. He puffed again and again, until his head was encircled in a cloud and he went off into another fit of coughing. At the end of it, he tossed the cigarette from him in disgust and turned to Brunetti.

'Maria doesn't let me smoke in the house,' he said, sounding almost proud of the fact.

'For your health?' Brunetti asked.

The old man turned to him, face washed clean of emotion at the idea. 'Oh, I wish,' he whispered and looked quickly away.

Morandi glanced around the entire *campo*, as if seeking someone who would care about whether he smoked or not. Turning his attention to Brunetti, he said, 'You have to give me the key, Signore.' He tried his best to sound reasonable but managed only to sound desperate. He looked earnest, tried a friendly smile, then let it fade away.

'How many are left?' Brunetti asked.

Morandi's eyes narrowed, and he started to ask, 'What do you . . .' but gave up the attempt and stopped. He folded his hands, rammed them between his thighs, and leaned forward. He noticed the birds then; showing no fear, hopping closer, they began to peep up at the familiar face. He reached into his jacket and pulled out a few pinches of grain, which he let fall between his feet. The birds picked at them avidly.

Head still bent, attention apparently on the birds, he said, 'Seven.'

'Do you know what they are?'

'No,' the old man said, shaking the idea away. 'I've tried to go into galleries to look at other ones, or into the museums. I get in for free now, because of my age. But I can't remember what I see, and the names don't mean anything to me.' He unfolded his hands and raised them apart as an indication of his ignorance and confusion. 'So I just have to trust the man who tells me what they are.'

'And what they're worth,' Brunetti added.

Morandi nodded. 'Yes. He was a patient when Maria still worked in the hospital; she told me about him then. I remembered him when . . . when I had to sell them.'

'Do you trust him?'

Morandi looked at him, and Brunetti saw a flash of intelligence as the old man said, 'I don't have any choice, do I?'

'You could go to someone else, I suppose,' Brunetti suggested.

'They're a mafia,' Morandi said with absolute certainty. 'Go to one, go to another: it's all the same thing. They'll all cheat you.'

'But maybe someone else would cheat you less,' Brunetti suggested.

Morandi shrugged away this possibility. 'By now they all know who I am and who I belong to.' He spoke as though he was sure that this was true.

'What happens when they're gone?' Brunetti asked.

Morandi lowered his head to consider the birds that still crowded round his feet, looking up and demanding food. 'Then they're gone.' He sounded resigned. Brunetti waited and finally the old man said, 'I might get enough to make the difference for two years.'

'And then?' Brunetti asked with bulldog tenacity.

The old man's shoulders rose as he gave an enormous sigh. 'Who knows what will happen in two years?'

'What did the doctor tell you?' Brunetti asked, nodding in the direction of the *casa di cura*.

'Why do you ask?' Morandi asked with a return to his former sharpness.

'Because you seemed so worried. Before, when you talked about it.'

'And that's enough to make you want to know?' Morandi asked, as though he were an anthropologist being exposed to an entirely new form of behaviour.

'She seemed like a woman who has had enough trouble in her life,' Brunetti risked saying. 'I hoped she wouldn't have any more.'

Morandi's eyes drifted towards the windows of the second

floor of the *casa di cura*, windows which Brunetti thought might be those of the dining room where he had first seen Signora Sartori. 'Oh, there's always more,' Morandi said. 'There's more and more, and then it's over and there's no more.' He turned to Brunetti and asked, 'Isn't that right?'

'I don't know,' was the best thing Brunetti could think of, though it took him some time to bring himself to speak. 'I hoped she would have some peace.'

Morandi smiled at the last word, but it wasn't a pleasant thing to see. 'We haven't had any of that since we moved.'

'To San Marco?' Brunetti asked.

He nodded, loosening one of the strands of hair, which shifted over to lean against its neighbour. 'Things were all right before then. We worked, and we talked, and I think she was happy.'

'Weren't you?'

'Oh,' he said, and this time it was a real smile, 'I've never been so happy in my life.'

'But then?'

'But then Cuccetti offered me the house. We were renting a place, down in Castello. Forty-one square metres; ground floor. We were like sardines in there,' he said, his mind obviously wandering back to that tiny place. Then, with another smile, he said, 'But we were happy sardines.'

He took another deep breath, pulling the air through his nostrils and pushing himself up again. 'And then he talked about the house we could have. More than a hundred metres. Top floor, two baths. It could have been a castle, it sounded so wonderful.'

He looked at Brunetti as if willing this man who had no idea what it meant to live in a forty-one-metre apartment to imagine what this would represent for people like them. Brunetti nodded. 'So I said I'd do it. And get Maria to do it because Cuccetti said he needed two witnesses. And then I thought about the drawings that the old woman had. She'd told Maria about them.' He tilted his chin to one side and asked, a real question, 'Do you think that's what made it go wrong? That I got greedy and told him I wanted the drawings?'

'I don't know, Signor Morandi,' Brunetti said. 'I can't make a judgement like that.'

'Maria knows that's when it all went wrong. But she doesn't know why,' the old man said, his despair audible. 'So it doesn't matter what I think about it, or what you do. She knows something bad happened.' Morandi shook his head and then continued to shake it, as if each motion renewed his guilt at what he had done.

'What happened when you went to Signora Altavilla's?' Brunetti asked.

His head stopped moving. He stared at Brunetti and suddenly crossed his arms over his chest, as if to show he had had enough of this and would say no more. But then he surprised Brunetti by saying, 'I went to talk to her, to try to make her understand that I needed the key. I couldn't tell her about the drawings. She might have told Maria, and then she'd know what I did.'

'She didn't know?'

'Oh no, nothing,' he said very quickly. 'She never saw them. They were never in the house. When Cuccetti gave them to me, I took them right to the bank, and I paid them in cash once a year for the box. There was no way Maria could know about them.' The very possibility infused his voice with fear.

'But she knew you had the key?' Brunetti said, thinking that, over the years, she would surely have figured out what the key was for.

'Maria's not stupid,' Morandi said.

'I'm sure she's not.'

'She knew the key was important, even if she didn't know what it was. So she took it and gave it to her.'

'You know that?'

Morandi nodded.

'Did she tell you?'

'Yes.'

'When? Why?'

'At first she wouldn't tell me anything. But – I told you she couldn't lie – after a while she told me she'd taken it. But she wouldn't tell me what she did with it.'

'How did you find out?'

Morandi looked across at the front of the building, like a sailor seeking a lighthouse. His mouth pulled back and he made an animal noise of pain, then he leaned forward again and put his face in his hands. This time he started to sob the way a child sobs, suddenly and brokenly, all hope of future happiness gone.

Brunetti could not endure it. He got to his feet and walked over to the church, stood in front of the stone announcing that it was the baptismal church of Vivaldi. Minutes passed. He thought he could still hear the sobs, but could not bring himself to turn and look.

After reading the inscription again, Brunetti went back to the bench and resumed his seat.

Morandi reached out suddenly and grabbed Brunetti's wrist. 'I hit her.' His face was blotched and red, and two strands of hair had fallen down on either side of his nose. He hiccuped with residual grief, then said it again, as if confession would purge him, 'I hit her. I never did that, not in all the years we were together.' Brunetti looked away but heard the old man say, 'And then she told me she'd given her the key.'

He pulled at Brunetti's wrist until he was turned round and facing him. 'You have to understand. I had to have the key. They won't let you into the box unless you have it, and I had to pay for the *casa di cura*. Or else she'd go to the public place. But I couldn't tell her that because then I'd have to tell her everything.' His grip intensified to add significance to what he had to say. He started to speak, coughed, and then said in a whisper, 'And then she wouldn't respect me any more.'

Brunetti's mind flashed to Signora Orsoni's account of her brother-in-law's justification for his every act of violence. And here he was listening to the same story. But what a gulf between them. Or was there? With his right hand he prised Morandi's fingers, one by one, from his wrist. To enforce the action, he took the old man's hand and placed it on Morandi's thigh.

'What happened when you went to see Signora Altavilla?' Brunetti asked.

The old man seemed taken aback. 'I told you. I asked her for the key.' As if aware of his disarray, he ran his hands up over his face, pulling his hair free to hang across his collar.

'Asked?'

Morandi showed no surprise at either the word or the tone in which Brunetti repeated it. 'All right,' he said reluctantly. 'I told her to give me the key.'

'Or else?'

This startled him. 'There was no or else. She had the key and I wanted her to give it to me. If she didn't want to, there wasn't anything I could do about it.'

'You could have threatened her,' Brunetti suggested.

Morandi's face showed bafflement as well as confusion, and Brunetti thought it was genuine. 'But she's a woman.'

Brunetti refrained from saying that Signora Sartori was a woman, too, and that had not prevented him from hitting her. Instead, voice calm, he asked again, 'What happened?'

Morandi looked at the ground again, and Brunetti watched his head flush with embarrassment. 'Did you hit her?' asked Brunetti, stopping himself from adding, 'too.'

Keeping his eyes on the ground, like a child attempting to escape a reprimand, Morandi shook his head a few times. Brunetti refused to allow himself to be manipulated by the other man's silence and asked again, 'Did you hit her?'

Morandi spoke so softly as to be almost inaudible. 'Not really.'

'What does that mean?'

'I grabbed her,' he said, shot a look at Brunetti and went back to staring at the pavement. Again, Brunetti decided on silence. 'She told me to leave, that there was nothing I could say that would make her give me the key. And then she moved towards the door.'

'What was she going to do with the key?' Brunetti asked.

Morandi raised a blank face to Brunetti. 'I don't know. She didn't say.' Brunetti's imagination vied with his knowledge of the law. The only person who had the right to open the box was the keyholder, accompanied by a representative of the bank with the second key. For anyone else to use it, a court order was necessary, and to get that, evidence of a crime was necessary. But after so many years, there was no longer a crime.

Morandi could have told the bank he had lost it. It would have taken time, but eventually he would have been given access to the box and its contents. Possession of the key was meaningless: it conveyed no power and no authority to the person who had it; only the authorized person could open the box. Signora Altavilla did not know this, and apparently neither did Morandi. Empty threats. Empty menaces.

Relentless, Brunetti asked, 'What happened?'

It took a long time, and Morandi had no obligation to answer, but he didn't know that, either, and so he said, 'She walked over to the door, and I tried to stop her.' As he spoke, Morandi raised his hands in front of him and cupped his fingers. 'I said her name, and when she turned around, I put my hands on her shoulders, but when I saw her face, I remembered my promise.' He looked at Brunetti. 'I started to move my hands away, but she pulled herself free and went to the door and opened it.'

'And you?'

Voice even smaller, softer, Morandi said, 'I felt so ashamed of myself. First I hit Maria, and then I put my hands on this other woman. I didn't even know her, and there I was, holding her by the shoulders.'

'That's all you did?' Brunetti insisted.

Morandi covered his eyes with one hand. 'I was so ashamed I couldn't even apologize. She opened the door for me and told me to get out, so there was nothing else I could do.' He reached a hand towards Brunetti but then, remembering what had happened when he touched him before, he pulled it back. 'May I tell you something?'

'Yes.'

'I started to cry on the staircase, on the way down. I hit Maria and then I frightened that poor woman. I had to stand inside the door until I stopped crying. That time, when I hit Maria, I made a promise that I'd never do a bad thing again, never in my life, but there I was, doing a bad thing again.

'So I told myself that, if I loved Maria the way I said I did, I'd never do another thing like that again in my life.' He stopped at the sound of his words, looked at Brunetti with an embarrassed grin and added, 'Not that there's much of *that* left.' The smile faded and he went on. 'And I told myself I'd never lie again and never do a single thing that Maria wouldn't like.'

'Why?'

'I told you why. Because I was so ashamed of what I'd done.'

'But what did you think would happen if you did what you promised?' Brunetti asked.

Morandi put the tip of his right forefinger on the centre of his thigh and pushed it in a few times, each time waiting for the small impression to disappear before pushing it down again.

'What would happen, Signor Morandi?'

Pushing, waiting, pushing, waiting, the right moment

would come. Finally Morandi said, 'Because maybe, if she knew, she'd love me.'

'You mean go back to loving you?' Brunetti asked.

Morandi's astonishment was total: Brunetti read it in the wide blankness of his eyes as he turned to look at him. 'No. Love me. She never has. Not really. But I came along when she was almost forty, and so she took me and lived with me. But she never loved me, not really.' The tears were back, falling on to his shirt, but Morandi was unaware of them. 'Not the way I love her.'

Again, he gave that doglike shake. 'We're the only people who know that,' he said to Brunetti, placing his hand fleetingly on his arm, touching it and quickly off, as if afraid for his hand. 'Maria doesn't know it, or she doesn't know that I know. But I do. And now you do.'

Brunetti didn't know what to say in the face of these awful truths and their even more awful consequences. There was no answer to be had, neither from the façade of the church nor from the *casa di cura*.

Brunetti got to his feet. He reached a hand down for the old man to take and helped him to stand. 'Why don't you let me walk you home?'

29

The old man had to be helped up the stairs. Brunetti disguised this fact by saying he was curious about the view a top floor apartment in this area would have of the Campanile and the Basilica and asked Signor Morandi if he would show it to him. Brunetti, his grip under the old man's arm secure, paused on every landing, inventing an old knee injury that slowed him down. They arrived at the top, Morandi pleased to have had less trouble than a much younger man, and Brunetti pleased that the old man had been protected from acknowledging his own infirmities.

Morandi opened the door and stepped back to let his guest enter first. Knowing that this old man had been living alone in the apartment for three years, Brunetti had prepared himself to find disorder, if not worse, but nothing could have prepared him for what he found. The late afternoon sun flowed down the corridor from a room at the end. The light glistened up from the high-polished *cotto Veneziano*. It looked like the original surface, rarely seen in the higher floors of *palazzi* and today all but impossible to imitate and difficult to repair. Though the ceiling was not particularly high, the entrance hall was large, and the corridor was unusually broad.

'You can see the Basilica from this room,' Morandi said, starting down the corridor and leaving Brunetti to follow. There was no furniture against the walls, and there were no doors to the rooms on either side. Brunetti glanced into one room and saw that it was entirely empty, though the windows glistened and the floor gleamed up at him. After a moment, Brunetti realized how very cold it was, how the cold seeped up from the floor and through the walls.

In the last room, the view was, indeed, splendid, but there was so little furniture – a table and two chairs – that it had the feel of a house that was no longer lived in and was open only for inspection by prospective buyers. Off in the distance the domes bubbled up, their crosses poking the tiny balls that topped them at the sky, and beyond them Brunetti saw the back of the wings of the angel that looked out over the *bacino*. Behind him, Morandi said, 'Maria used to stand there for hours, looking at it. It made her happy to see this. In the beginning.' He came and stood next to Brunetti, and together they looked at the signs of the power of God and the power of the state, and Brunetti was struck by the majesty those things had once had, and had no longer.

'Signor Morandi,' he said, speaking in the formal '*Lei*' and making no grammatical concession to the things the old man had told him, 'were you telling me the truth when you said that, about wanting to lead a better life?'

'Oh, yes,' he answered instantly, sounding just like Brunetti's children, years ago, doing their drills for catechism class.

'No more lies?' Brunetti asked.

'No.'

Brunetti thought of those mind-twisters they had been given when they were in school. There was one about getting a hen and a fox and a cabbage across a river, and one about nine pearls on a scale, and one about the man who always lied. He had vague memories of the puzzles, but the answers had all fled. If Morandi always lied, then he would have to lie about not lying, wouldn't he?

'Would you swear on the heart of Maria Sartori that all you did was put your hands on Signora Altavilla's shoulders and that you did not hurt her in any way?'

Beside him, the old man stood quietly. Then, like someone beginning their t'ai chi exercise, he let his arms go limp beside him, then raised his hands slowly, hands cupped towards the earth, to shoulder height. But instead of pulling them back to prepare to push against an invisible force, Morandi rested them on some invisibility in front of him. And then Brunetti watched his fingers tighten, and Morandi saw that Brunetti saw the motion.

The old man lowered his hands and said, 'That's all I did. But I didn't hurt her.'

'What was she wearing? And where were you?'

Morandi closed his eyes, this time putting his memory through the same routine. 'We were in the hallway. Just in front of the door. I told you that. She never let me into the apartment, well, not more than a few steps from the door.' He paused and lowered his head. 'I don't know what she was wearing: a shirt, I think. It was yellow, whatever it was.'

Brunetti cast his own memory back to the dead woman on the floor of the living room of the house. Heavy blue sweater and the bright yellow shirt below. 'Only that?' he asked.

'Yes. I remember thinking that she should have been wearing something warmer. It was a cool night.'

As if seeing the emptiness for the first time, Brunetti looked around the room and asked, 'Where is the rest of the furniture?'

'Oh, I've had to sell that, too. There's a *badante* who goes in to Maria every afternoon for three hours: to wash her and brush her hair and see that her clothes are clean.' Before Brunetti could ask, he said, 'And that's expensive because the *casa di cura* won't let them help unless they're legal, and that makes it twice as expensive, with the taxes.'

The wind had started to whip things up in the Piazza, and the tips of the flags on the other side of the Basilica flashed into sight now and again, waving at them. 'What will you do, Signor Morandi?'

'Oh, I'll sell everything here, little by little, and just hope it lasts long enough to pay them for as long as she lasts.'

'Have her doctors given you a time?'

Morandi shrugged, no anger now at the 'doctors'. He limited himself to saying 'pancreas', as if that would clarify things for Brunetti. It did.

'And then?'

'Oh, I haven't thought about that,' he said, and Brunetti believed him. 'I just have to be here as long as she is, don't I?'

Unable to answer that question, Brunetti asked, 'What about this?' waving his hand to take in the apartment that had belonged to Cuccetti's wife and had passed to Morandi, after which both Cuccetti and his wife had died. 'You could sell it.'

Morandi could not hide his surprise. 'But if Maria could come home, even for a few days, before . . . ?' The old man glanced at Brunetti, smiling. He pointed with his chin towards the windswept panorama beyond the window. 'She'd want to see that, so . . .'

'It must be worth a great deal,' Brunetti said.

'Oh, I don't care about that,' Morandi said, speaking of it as though it were an old pair of shoes or a stack of newspapers neatly tied up for the garbage man. 'Maria has no relatives, and all I have is a nephew, but he went to Argentina fifty years ago and I never heard from him.' He paused, thinking; Brunetti said nothing. 'So I suppose the state will take it. Or the city. I don't care. It doesn't matter.' He looked around the room, up at the beamed ceiling, then returned to his study of the view: the flags had grown more agitated, and Brunetti thought he could hear the rising wind.

Finally the old man said, 'I never liked this place, you know. I never felt it was mine. I worked like a dog to pay the rent on the old place, the one in Castello, so it was really mine. Ours. But this one came too easily; it's like I found it, or I stole it from someone. All it ever brought me was bad luck, so it will be a good thing if someone else takes it.'

'Where do you live?' Brunetti asked, well aware of how silly a question that was to ask while standing in a person's home.

But Morandi had no difficulty in understanding him. 'I spend most of my time in the kitchen. It's the only room I heat. And my bedroom, but all I do is sleep there.' He turned away, as if to lead Brunetti to that part of the house. Brunetti let him take a few steps, and while the old man's back was turned, he took the key out of his pocket and set it on the table beneath the window.

Brunetti called him, and when Morandi came slowly back to the window, Brunetti extended his hand. 'Thank you for letting me see the view, Signore,' he said. 'It's wonderful.'

'It is, isn't it?' the old man said, ignoring Brunetti's hand because his eyes had moved to the domes, the flags, the clouds that were now busy scuttling towards the west. 'Isn't it sad,' Morandi continued, 'that we spend so much time worrying about houses and having them and making them beautiful inside, when the most beautiful part is out there, and there's nothing we can do to change that?' This time it was Morandi who waved in the direction of the Basilica, his hand taking in the church and the past and the glory that was no more.

Donna Leon's
next novel is now available
from Grove/Atlantic in hardcover

Read on for the first chapter of

THE *NEW YORK TIMES* BESTSELLING AUTHOR

DONNA LEON

Beastly Things

A COMMISSARIO GUIDO BRUNETTI MYSTERY

1

The man lay still, as still as a piece of meat on a slab, as still as death itself. Though the room was cold, his only covering was a thin cotton sheet that left his head and neck free. From a distance, his chest rose inordinately high, as though some sort of support had been wedged under his back, running the length of it. If this white form were a snow-covered mountain ridge and the viewer a tired hiker at the end of a long day, faced with the task of crossing it, the hiker would surely choose to walk along the entire length of the man to cross at the ankles and not the chest. The ascent was too high and too steep, and who knew what difficulties there would be descending the other side?

From the side, the unnatural height of the chest was obvious; from above – if the hiker were now placed on a peak and could gaze down at the man – it was the neck that was conspicuous. The neck – or perhaps more accurately the lack of one. In fact, his neck was a broad column running down straight from beneath his ears to his shoulders. There was no narrowing, no indentation; the neck was as wide as the head.

Also conspicuous was the nose, now barely evident in profile. It had been crushed and pushed to one side; scratches and tiny indentations patterned the skin. The right cheek, as well, was scratched and bruised. His entire face was swollen, the skin white and flaccid. From above, his flesh sank in a concave arc below his cheek-bones. His face was pale with more than the pallor of death. This was a man who had lived indoors.

The man had dark hair and a short beard, grown perhaps in an attempt to disguise the neck, but there was no disguising such a thing for more than a second. The beard provided a visual distraction, but almost instantly it would be seen as camouflage, nothing more, for it ran along the jaw line and down that column of a neck, as if it did not know where to stop. From this height, it looked almost as though it had flowed down across the neck and off to the sides, an effect exaggerated by the way the beard grew increasingly white at the sides.

His ears were surprisingly delicate, almost feminine. Earrings would not have looked out of place there, were it not for the beard. Below the left ear, just beyond the end of the beard and set at a thirty-degree angle, was a pink scar. About three centimetres long, it was as wide as a pencil; the skin was rough, as though whoever had sewn the skin shut had been in a hurry or careless because he was a man, and a scar was nothing for a man to worry about.

It was cold in the room, the only sound the heavy wheeze of the air conditioning. The man's thick chest did not move up and down, nor did he stir uncomfortably in the cold. He lay there, naked under his sheet, eyes closed.

He did not wait, for he was beyond waiting, just as he was beyond being late or being on time. One might be tempted to say that the man simply was. But that would be untrue, for he was no more.

Two other forms lay, similarly covered, in the room, though they were closer to the walls: the bearded man was in the centre. If a man who always lies tells someone he is a liar, is he telling the truth? If no one is alive in a room, is the room empty?

A door was opened on the far side and held open by a tall, thin man in a white lab jacket. He stood there long enough for another man to pass in front of him and enter the room. The first man released the door; it closed slowly, giving a quiet, almost liquid click that sounded loud in the cold room.

'He's over there, Guido,' Dottor Rizzardi said, coming up behind Guido Brunetti, Commissario di Polizia of the city of Venice. Brunetti stopped, in the manner of the hiker, and looked across at the white-covered ridge of the man. Rizzardi walked past him to the slab on which the dead man lay.

'He was stabbed in the lower back three times with a very thin blade. Less than two centimetres wide, I'd say, and whoever did it was very good or very lucky. There are two small bruises on the front of his left arm,' Rizzardi said, stopping beside the body. 'And water in his lungs,' he added. 'So he was alive when he went into the water. But the killer got a major vein: he didn't have a chance. He bled to death in minutes.' Then, grimly, Rizzardi added, 'Before he could drown.' Before Brunetti could ask, the pathologist said, 'It happened last night, some time after midnight, I'd say. Because he's been in the water, that's as close as I can come.'

Brunetti remained halfway to the table, his eyes going

back and forth between the dead man and the pathologist. 'What happened to his face?' Brunetti asked, aware of how difficult it would be to recognize a photo of him; indeed, how difficult it would be even to look at a photo of that broken, swollen face.

'My guess is that he fell forward when he was stabbed. He was probably too stunned to put out his hands to break his fall.'

'Could you take a photo?' Brunetti asked, wondering if Rizzardi could disguise some of the damage.

'You want to ask people to look at it?' It was not an answer Brunetti liked, but it was an answer. Then, after a moment, the pathologist said, 'I'll do what I can.'

Brunetti asked, 'What else?'

'I'd say he's in his late forties, in reasonably good health, isn't someone who works with his hands, but I can't say more than that.'

'Why is he such an odd shape?' Brunetti asked as he approached the table.

'You mean his chest?' Rizzardi asked.

'And the neck,' Brunetti added, his eyes drawn to its thickness.

'It's something called Madelung's disease,' Rizzardi said. 'I've read about it, and I remember it from med school, but I've never seen it before. Only the photos.'

'What causes it?' Brunetti asked, coming to stand beside the dead man.

Rizzardi shrugged. 'Who knows?' As if he'd himself just heard a doctor saying such a thing, he quickly added, 'There's a common link to alcoholism, sometimes drug use, though not in his case. He wasn't a drinker, not at all, and I didn't see signs of drug use.' He paused, then went on, 'Most alcoholics don't get it, thank God, but most of the men who get it – and it's almost always men

4

– are alcoholics. No one seems to understand why it happens.'

Stepping closer to the corpse, Rizzardi pointed to the neck, which was especially thick at the back, where Brunetti could see what appeared to be a small hump. Before he could ask about it, Rizzardi continued, 'It's fat. It accumulates here,' he said, pointing to the hump. 'And here.' He indicated what looked like breasts under the white cloth, in the place where they would be on the body of a woman.

'It starts when they're in their thirties or forties, concentrates on the top part of the body.'

'You mean it just grows?' Brunetti asked, trying to imagine such a thing.

'Yes. Sometimes on the top part of the legs, too. But in his case it's only the neck and chest.' He paused in thought for a moment and then added, 'It turns them into barrels, poor devils.'

'Is it common?' Brunetti asked.

'No, not at all. I think there's only a few hundred cases in the literature.' He shrugged. 'We really don't know very much.'

'Anything else?'

'He was dragged along a rough surface,' the pathologist said, leading Brunetti to the bottom of the table and lifting the sheet. He pointed to the back of the dead man's heel, where the skin was scratched and broken. 'There's evidence on his lower back, as well.'

'Of what?' Brunetti asked.

'Someone grabbed him under the shoulders and dragged him across a floor, I'd say. There's no gravel in the wound,' he said, 'so it was probably a stone floor.' To clarify things, Rizzardi added, 'He was wearing only one shoe, a loafer. That suggests the other one was pulled off.'

Brunetti took a few steps back to the man's head and looked down at the bearded face. 'Does he have light eyes?' he asked

Rizzardi glanced at him, his surprise evident. 'Blue. How did you know?'

'I didn't,' Brunetti answered.

'Then why did you ask?'

'I think I've seen him somewhere,' Brunetti answered. He stared at the man, his face, the beard, the broad column of his neck. But memory failed him, beyond his certainty about the eyes.

'If you did see him, you'd be likely to remember him, wouldn't you?' The man's body was sufficient answer to Rizzardi's question.

Brunetti nodded. 'I know, but if I think about him, nothing's there.' His failure to remember something as exceptional as this man's appearance bothered Brunetti more than he wanted to admit. Had he seen a photo, a mug shot, or had it been a print in something he'd read? He'd leafed through Lombroso's vile book a few years ago: did this man do nothing more than remind him of one of those carriers of 'hereditary criminality'?

But the Lombroso prints had been in black and white; would eyes have shown up as light or dark? Brunetti searched for the image his memory must have held, stared at the opposite wall to try to aid it. But nothing came, no clear image of a blue-eyed man, neither this one nor any other.

Instead, his memory filled almost to suffocation with the unsummoned picture of his mother, slumped in her chair, staring at him with vacant eyes that failed to know him.

'Guido?' he heard someone say and turned to see the familiar face of Rizzardi.

'You all right?'

Brunetti forced a smile and said, 'Yes. I was just trying to remember where I might have seen him.'

'Leave it alone for a while and it might come back,' Rizzardi suggested. 'Happens to me all the time. I can't remember someone's name, and I start through the alphabet – A, B, C – and often when I get to the first letter of their name, it comes back to me.'

'Is it age?' Brunetti asked with studied lack of interest.

'I certainly hope so,' Rizzardi answered lightly. 'I had a wonderful memory in medical school: you can't get through without it: all those bones, those nerves, the muscles . . .'

'The diseases,' volunteered Brunetti.

'Yes, those too. But just remembering all the parts of this,' the pathologist said, flipping the backs of his hands down the front of his own body, 'that's a triumph.' Then, more reflectively, 'But what's inside, that's a miracle.'

'Miracle?' Brunetti asked.

'In a manner of speaking,' Rizzardi said. 'Something wonderful.' Rizzardi looked at his friend and must have seen something he liked, or trusted, for he went on, 'If you think about it, the most ordinary things we do – picking up a glass, tying our shoes, whistling . . . they're all tiny miracles.'

'Then why do you do what you do?' Brunetti asked, surprising himself with the question.

'What?' Rizzardi asked. 'I don't understand.'

'Work with people after the miracles are over,' Brunetti said for want of a better way to say it.

There was a long pause before Rizzardi answered. At last he said, 'I never thought of it that way.' He looked down at his own hands, turned them over and studied the palms for a moment. 'Maybe it's because what I do lets me see more clearly the way things work, the things that make the miracles possible.'

As if suddenly embarrassed, Rizzardi clasped his hands together and said, 'The men who brought him in said there were no papers. No identification. Nothing.'

'Clothing?'

Rizzardi shrugged. 'They bring them in here naked. Your men must have taken everything back to the lab.'

Brunetti made a noise of agreement or understanding or perhaps of thanks. 'I'll go over there and have a look. The report I read said they found him at about six.'

Rizzardi shook his head. 'I don't know anything about that, only that he was the first one today.'

Surprised – this was Venice, after all – Brunetti asked, 'How many more were there?'

Rizzardi nodded towards the two fully draped figures on the other side of the room. 'Those old people over there.'

'How old?'

'The son says his father was ninety-three, his mother ninety.'

'What happened?' Brunetti asked. He had read the papers that morning, but no mention had been made of their deaths.

'One of them made coffee last night. The pot was in the sink. The flame went out, but the gas was still on.' Rizzardi added, 'It was an old stove, the kind you need a match for.'

Then, before Brunetti could speak, the doctor went on, 'The neighbour upstairs smelled gas and called the firemen, and when they went in they found the place full of gas, the two of them dead on top of the bed. The cups and saucers were beside them.'

In the face of Brunetti's silence, Rizzardi added, 'It's a good thing the place didn't blow up.'

'It's a strange place for people to drink coffee,' Brunetti said.

Rizzardi gave his friend a sharp look. 'She had Alzheimer's and he didn't have the money to put her anywhere,' then added, 'The son has three kids and lives in a two-bedroom apartment in Mogliano.'

Brunetti said nothing.

'The son told me,' Rizzardi continued, 'that his father said he couldn't take care of her any more, not the way he wanted to.'

'Said?'

'He left a note. Said he didn't want people to think he was losing his memory and had forgotten to turn the gas off.' Rizzardi turned away from the dead and moved towards the door. 'He had a pension of five hundred and twelve Euros, and she had five hundred and eight.' Then, like doom itself, he added, 'Their rent was seven hundred and fifty a month.'

'I see,' Brunetti said.

Rizzardi opened the door and let them into the corridor of the hospital.

AVAILABLE FROM PENGUIN

BY DONNA LEON

PENGUIN
BOOKS